TOMORROW
I'LL BE TWENTY

ALAIN MABANCKOU

Translated by Helen Stevenson

Culture

This project has been funded with support from the European
Commission. This publication reflects the views only of the author, and
the Commission cannot be held responsible for any use which may be
made of the information contained therein.

A complete catalogue record for this book can be obtained from the
British Library on request

First published as *Demains J'aurai Vingt Ans* in 2010 by Editions Gallimard

First published in this translation in 2013 by Serpent's Tail,
an imprint of Profile Books Ltd
3A Exmouth House
Pine Street
London EC1R 0JH
website: www.serpentstail.com

ISBN 978 1 84668 584 2
eISBN 978 1 84765 789 3

Designed and typeset by sue@lambledesign.demon.co.uk
Printed by CPI Group (UK) Ltd, Croydon CR0 4YY

10 9 8 7 6 5 4 3 2 1

For my mother Pauline Kengué – died 1995
For my father Roger Kimangou – died 2004

To Dany Laferrière

The sweetest thought
In the child's warm heart:
Soiled sheets and white lilac

Tomorrow I'll be twenty

TCHICAYA U TAM' SI
Wrong Blood
Edited by P.J. Oswald, 1955

In this country, a boss should always be bald and have a big belly. My uncle isn't bald, he hasn't got a big belly, and you don't realise, the first time you see him, that he's the actual boss of a big office in the centre of town. He's an 'administrative and financial director'. Maman Pauline says an administrative and financial director is someone who keeps all the company's money for himself and says: 'I'll hire you, I won't hire you, and I'm sending you back to where you came from.'

Uncle René works at the CFAO, the only company in Pointe-Noire that sells cars. He has a telephone and a television in his house. Maman Pauline thinks things like that cost too much for what they are, there's no point having them because people lived better lives without. Why put a telephone in your own home when you can go and make a call from the post office in the Grand Marché? Why have television when you can listen to the news on the radio? And anyway, the Lebanese down at the Grand Marché sell radios, you can beat them down on the price. You can also pay in instalments if you're a civil servant or an administrative and financial director, like my uncle.

I often think to myself that Uncle René is more powerful than the God people praise and worship every Sunday at the church of Saint-Jean-Bosco. No one's ever seen Him, but people are afraid of His mighty power, as though He might tell us off or give us a smack, when in fact He lives far far away, further than any Boeing can fly. If you want to speak to Him, you have to go to church and the priest will pass on a message to Him, which He'll read if he has a spare moment, because up there He's run off his feet, morning, noon and night.

Uncle René is anti-church and is always saying to my mother: 'Religion is the opium of the people!'

Maman Pauline told me, if anyone calls you 'opium of the people' you should punch him straight off, because it's a serious insult, and Uncle René wouldn't go using a complicated word like 'opium' just for the fun of it. Since then, whenever I do something silly, Maman Pauline calls me 'opium of the people'. And in the playground, if my friends really annoy me I call them 'opium of the people!' and then we get into a fight over that.

My uncle says he's a communist. Usually communists are simple people, they don't have television, telephone, or electricity, hot water or air conditioning, and they don't change cars every six months like Uncle René. So now I know you can also be communist and rich.

I think the reason my uncle is tough with us is because the communists are strict about how things should be done, because of the capitalists stealing all the goods of the poor wretched of the Earth, including their means of production. How are the poor wretched of the Earth going to live off their labours if the capitalists own the means of production and refuse to share, eating up the profits, instead of splitting them fifty-fifty with the workers?

The thing that gets my Uncle René really angry is the capitalists, not the communists, who must unite because apparently the final struggle won't be long now. At least, that's what they teach us at the école populaire in Moral studies. They tell us, for instance, that we are the future of the Congo, that it's up to us to make sure that capitalism doesn't win the final struggle. We are the National Pioneer Movement. To start with we children belong to the National Pioneer Movement and later we'll belong to the Congolese Workers' Party – the CPT – and maybe one day one of us will even become President of the Republic, who also runs the CPT.

Hearing me – Michel – use the words my uncle uses, you might think I was a true communist, but in fact I'm not. It's just that he uses these strange, complicated words so often – 'capital', 'profit', 'means of production', 'marxism', 'leninism', 'materialism', 'infrastructure', 'superstructure', 'bourgeoisie', 'class struggle', 'proletariat', etc., I've ended up knowing them all, even if I do sometimes mix them up without meaning to and don't always understand them. For instance, when he talks about the wretched of the Earth, what he really means is the starving masses. The capitalists starve them, so they'll turn up to work the next day, even though they're being exploited and they didn't eat yesterday. So before the hungry can win their struggle against the capitalists, they must do a tabula radar of the past and take their problems in hand, instead of waiting for someone else to come and liberate them. Otherwise they're truly stuffed, they'll be forever hungry and eternally exploited.

When we sit down to eat at Uncle René's house, I always get put in the worst seat, bang opposite the photo of an old white guy called Lenin, who won't take his eyes off me, even though I don't even know him, and he doesn't know me either. I don't like having an old white guy who doesn't even know me giving me nasty looks, so I look him straight back in the eye. I know it's rude to look grown up people in the eye, that's why I do it in secret, or my uncle will get cross and tell me I'm being disrespectful to Lenin who is admired the world over.

Then there's the photo of Karl Marx and Engels. It seems you're not meant to split these two old guys up, they're like twins. They've both got big beards, they both think the same thing at the same time, and sometimes they write down both their thoughts in a big book together. It's thanks to them people now know what communism is. My uncle says it was Marx and Engels who showed that the history of the world was actually just the history of people in their different classes, for example, slaves and masters, landowners and landless peasants and so on. So, some people are on top in this world, and some are on the bottom and suffer because the ones on top exploit the ones at the bottom. But because things have changed a lot and the ones on top try to hide the fact that they're exploiting the ones at the bottom, Karl Marx and Engels think we should all be quite clear that the differences still exist, and that nowadays there are two big classes at odds with each other, engaged in a ruthless struggle: the bourgeoisie and the proletariats. It's easy to tell them apart in the street: the bourgeois have big bellies because they eat what the proletarians produce and the proletarians or the starving masses are all skinny because the bourgeois only leave them crumbs to eat, just enough so they can come to work the next day. And Uncle René says this is what you call the exploitation of man by his fellow man.

My uncle has also hung on the wall a photo of our Immortal, comrade president Marien Ngouabi, and one of Victor Hugo, who wrote lots of poems that we recite at school.

Generally speaking, an Immortal is someone like Spiderman, Blek le Roc, Tintin or Superman, who never dies. I don't understand why we have to say that comrade president

Marien Ngouabi is immortal when everyone knows he's dead, that he's buried in the cemetery at Etatolo, in the north of the country, a cemetery which is guarded seven days a week, twenty-four hours a day, all because there are people who want to go and make their *gris-gris* on his grave so they can become immortal too.

Anyway, there you go, we have to call our ex-president 'The Immortal', even though he's no longer alive. If anyone's got a problem with that, the government will deal with them, they'll be thrown in prison and given a trial once the Revolution has got rid of the capitalists and the means of production at last belong to the wretched of the Earth, to the starving masses who struggle night and day, all because of this business with the classes of Karl Marx and Engels.

Maman Pauline knows I'm very frightened of Uncle René, and she exploits it. If I don't want to go to bed at night without her coming in to kiss me goodnight she reminds me that if I don't go to bed her brother will think that I'm just a little capitalist who won't sleep because he wants a kiss from his mummy first, like those capitalists' children who live in the centre of town or in Europe, especially in France. He'll forget I'm his nephew and give me a good hiding. That shuts me up pretty quickly, and Maman Pauline leans over and just touches me on the head, but she doesn't give me a kiss like in the books we read in class that take place in Europe, especially in France. That's when I tell myself that not everything you read in books is true, and you shouldn't always believe what you read.

Sometimes I can't get to sleep, though not always because I'm waiting for my mother's goodnight kiss, sometimes just because the mosquito net bothers me. Once I'm inside it I feel as though I'm breathing in the same air as the evening before, and then I start sweating so much you'd think I'd wet the bed, which I haven't.

The mosquitoes in our *quartier* are strange, they just love sweat, it means they can really stick to your skin and take their time about sucking your blood till five in the morning. Also, when I'm inside the mosquito net, I look like a corpse, the mosquitoes buzzing round me are like people weeping because I've just died.

I told Papa Roger this. I did, I told him I'm like a little corpse when I'm inside my mosquito net, and one day, if they're not careful, I'll really die in there, and I'll never be seen on this earth again, because I'll have gone up on high to join my two big sisters, who I've never known because they were in too much of a hurry to go straight up to heaven. I was in tears myself as I told him that, imagining myself as a tiny little corpse in a tiny little white coffin surrounded by people crying pointlessly, since if you're dead you're not coming back, except Jesus who can work miracles, and resuscitate, as though death, for him, was just a little afternoon siesta.

It worried Papa Roger that I was starting to talk about death like that at my age. He told me children never die, God watches over them at night while they're sleeping and He gives them lots of air to breathe so they don't suffocate in their sleep. So I asked him why God hadn't put lots of air in the lungs of my two big sisters. He looked at me kindly. 'I'll see to it, I'll take off the mosquito net.'

But it was weeks and weeks before he did anything about it. He finally took my mosquito net off yesterday, when he got home from work. He'd been to buy some Flytox from someone in the Avenue of Independence. Usually any self-respecting mosquito who hears the word Flytox buzzes off quickly, rather than die a slow, stupid death.

Papa Roger put this stuff all over my room, so the smell would last longer. Now the mosquitoes in our *quartier* are no fools, you can't trick them that easily, particularly since you can see the picture of a dying mosquito on the Flytox packet. Is it likely they'll commit suicide instead of fighting for your last drop of blood? They wait till the smell wears off, then they come right back and bite you all over because they're angry with you now for waging war on them. When in fact they're just like you, they want to live as long as they can.

So, even if you pump your house full of Flytox, you should never claim victory too soon. The mosquitoes will always win in the end, and then they'll go and tell all the other mosquitoes in town that in fact you can get round the product after all. Mosquitoes aren't like us, they never keep secrets, they spend the whole night chatting, as though they'd nothing else to do. And since they're the same ones as in the Trois-Cents *quartier*, and they've seen you spraying Flytox in your house, first of all they go to the neighbours' houses, where they don't have it and then when they've finished there they come back to your room to see if it still smells of Flytox. Some mosquitoes are even used to it, and explain to their mates how to protect themselves against it. They say, 'Watch out for those guys, it stinks of Flytox in their house; if you don't want to die, take cover for now in a wardrobe or a cooking pot or a pair of shoes or some clothes'. And they'll wait till you turn down the light on the storm lantern. They're pleased because they can see you're scared of them. If you're really scared, it means you've got lots of nice warm blood to feed them on over the winter, and you didn't want them to find out. If one of them comes looking for a fight and you try to squash it with your hands or a bit of wood, the others then turn up with their sisters and their cousins and their aunts and bite you all over. One little group makes the noise, the others attack. They take turns. The ones making the noise aren't always the ones that attack, and the ones attacking wait behind them in a circle. There you are, all on your own, you've only got two hands, you can't see what's happening behind you, you can't protect yourself, they're a well-trained army out for revenge because you've tried to wipe them out with your Flytox. You're itching all over, you've got mosquitoes up your nose, mosquitoes in your ears, and they're all biting away and laughing their heads off.

And that's why I woke up this morning covered in red spots. If I sniff my arms, they still smell of Flytox. A really angry mosquito – the leader, perhaps – bit me just above my eye, it's so swollen, you'd think the devil had thrown me an invisible punch. Maman Pauline put some boa grease on it and said, to cheer me up, 'Never mind, Michel, your eye will be better by sunset. Boa grease, that's what they used on me when I was little. Tonight we'll put back the mosquito net your father took off. That Flytox the Lebanese sell is rubbish. And he knows it.'

When Caroline looks at me, I feel like the best-looking guy in the world. We're the same age, but she knows all there is to know about us boys. Maman Pauline says she's very *advanced*. I don't know what that means. Maybe it's because Caroline acts like a real lady. Even at her age she wears lipstick and she braids almost every woman's hair in our neighbourhood, including my mother's. Caroline listens to what the fine ladies say about men, and she can't wait to be like the women she goes shopping with in the Grand Marché. Maman Pauline says Caroline knows how to make a dish of beans and manioc leaves, which a lot of grown-up people still can't do. She is really very *advanced*.

Caroline's parents and mine are friends. They live at the far end of the Avenue of Independence, just before the road that leads to the Savon *quartier*, where Uncle René lives. It's a short walk from their house to ours, ours is the one painted green and white halfway down the same avenue, opposite Yeza, the joiner, who makes loads of coffins and lines them up in front of his lot, so people can come and choose.

Caroline and I used to go to school together, at Trois-Martyrs, but now she's at a different place, in the Chic *quartier*. The reason she's not at the same school as me now is because her father had a row with the headmaster.

I really miss those days when she'd come strolling down the Avenue of Independence, and meet me outside our house.

We avoided the tarmacked roads because our parents said it was too dangerous, because none of the cars had brakes and the drivers drank corn spirit before they set off. We specially avoided the crossroads at Block 55, where someone got knocked down by a car at least once a month. In our *quartier* people blamed Ousmane, a shopkeeper from Senegal, just opposite the crossroads. Apparently he had this magic mirror that fooled the poor pedestrians, so they thought the cars were a long way off, like a kilometre away, when in fact it was more like a few metres, and bam! they ran them over, just as they started crossing. It looked like Ousmane had loads of customers, more than the other shops, because people died right outside his shop. We'd go round behind his shop, without even looking at it. Because we were scared of Ousmane's magic mirror. Sometimes I'd be behind Caroline and she'd turn round and take my hand and give me a shake and tell me to get a move on because the devils in the magic mirror always caught children who lagged behind.

'Michel, don't look in Ousmane's shop! Close your eyes!'

I walked fast. I didn't want to vanish while she wasn't looking. Our school was an old building painted green, yellow and red. When we finally got to the playground we had to separate. Caroline went into Madame Diamoneka's class, and I went into Monsieur Malonga's. My hand was damp because Caroline had been holding it tight all the way.

Around five in the evening we'd come home together. She'd drop me outside our house, then carry on home. I'd stay outside, watching her go. Soon she'd be just a little shape way off in the crowd. And in I'd go, happy.

My best friend, Lounès – who's Caroline's brother – liked walking to school alone. Was that because he didn't want to walk alongside his sister? I think it was to show he was older than us. That he was in class with the big kids. Now he's at middle school where you learn even harder things than you do at primary. And since he's at Trois-Glorieuses, that's where I want to go after primary school. If I went anywhere else I'd have to make new friends. I like Lounès, and I think he likes me too.

Caroline and Lounès's father limps with his left leg, and people snigger when he walks by. It's not nice to laugh at Monsieur Mutombo, it's not like he said to God: I'd like to have a limp all my life please. He was born like that, and when he was a little boy and he tried to walk, his left leg was shorter than his right, or maybe his right leg was longer than his left.

In a way, Monsieur Mutombo could get rid of his limp if he wanted, all he has to do is wear Salamander shoes, they have these heels that are so high, a pygmy could wear them and look like an American sky-scraper. But I don't think that's a solution, since the right leg would still go on up higher and the left leg, the sick one, couldn't match it. Unless if he cut off a bit of the sole of the right shoe, but then everyone would laugh at him because his shoes wouldn't be the same height. The only thing to do is to ask God on his dying day to send him back with normal legs, because once God's made a human being and sends him down to our world, that's it, he won't go back on his decision, otherwise people would stop respecting him. Besides, that would mean God could get it wrong, like the rest of us. Which has never been known to happen.

Monsieur Mutombo's a very honest man. Papa Roger says so, and he's his friend. He looks after Lounès and Caroline really well. He takes them to the Rex, where they've already seen films like *Demolition Man*, *The Good, the Bad and the Ugly*, *Ten*

Commandments, Samson and Delilah, Jaws, Star Wars and lots of Indian films.

When Monsieur Mutombo comes to visit my father on Sundays, they go out to a bar in the Avenue of Independence. They drink palm wine, they talk in our ethnic language, bembé. If they stay too long at the bar Maman Pauline says to me: 'Michel, look at you, sitting around like an idiot while your father and Monsieur Mutombo are out at a bar! You get up now, and go and see if they're buying drinks for the local girls, and kissing them on the lips!'

I set off like a rocket, and arrive, panting, at the bar. I find Monsieur Mutombo and my father drinking, and playing draughts.

Papa Roger's surprised to see me. 'What are you doing here, Michel? Children aren't allowed in bars!'

'Maman told me to come and see if you were buying drinks for the local girls and putting your lips on theirs…'

And the two men part, laughing. I go home with my father, who's a bit drunk. I hold his hand and he tells me things I don't understand. Maybe when you've had a few drinks you can talk to invisible people who've been trapped inside the bottle by the people who brew it, that people who never drink can't see.

Another Sunday, my father goes to see Monsieur Mutombo, and again they go off to drink in one of the local bars, to talk in bembé, and chat with the invisible people in the bottles, and this time it's Lounès who goes to tell them that Madame Mutombo has asked her to come and check if they're buying drinks for girls, and kissing them on the mouth.

Monsieur Mutombo is the best tailor in the whole town. He makes school uniforms for almost all the children round here.

Some parents from other *quartiers* bring material for him to make up into uniforms for their children. He's not short of customers in his workshop, particularly after the summer holidays, when he's always behind because people wait till the last minute – often just three days before school starts – then come with their fabric and tell him to do it fast.

I like going to his workshop, with some fabric for my father over my shoulder, and watching him work with it, because he knows my father's not just anybody, that he's someone you can sit down and have a glass of palm wine or red wine with in a bar in the Avenue of Independence.

And you'd be amazed, if you saw the suit Monsieur Mutombo made, you'd think it was straight off the peg from Europe, except it's not cut from a single piece and there isn't that nice smell you get from Europe, and the Whites are so clever, they won't tell us their secret so that we'll carry on liking their clothes and wanting to wear them here, even though they're more expensive.

The day I said to my mother that Madame Mutombo was a great fat woman, like a pregnant female hippopotamus, she boxed my ears and told me that if a woman's big it means she has a big heart, and that the heart of someone who loves other people is always big. That made me think of Jeremy's mother, he's in my class, and I don't like him because he's too clever, he always comes second, after Adriano, the Angolan. Jeremy's mother is very fat and very horrid, and she's rude about all the other mothers in the neighbourhood.

My mother knew what I was thinking. She said, 'True, not all big women have a heart as big as Madame Mutombo's. I know you're thinking of Jeremy's mother, but that's different.'

When Madame Mutombo comes to see Maman Pauline, she brings us doughnuts and ginger root juice. I don't like her doughnuts, they're too oily. I don't like her ginger root juice because it burns the back of your throat and you end up in the toilet, pushing for an hour, with nothing coming out.

But Maman Pauline scolds me. 'Michel, you just eat those doughnuts, now, and drink your ginger root juice. If someone gives you a goat, you don't complain that it's got a hole in its tooth!'

Madame Mutombo and my mother go shopping together. They buy peanuts in bulk and sell them on at the Grand Marché. I see them at our house, or at the Mutombos', counting the money they've earned and splitting the profits fifty/fifty. You won't find a capitalist doing that.

I often think about the day Caroline and I decided we were married. It was a Sunday afternoon, my parents were out. Caroline arrived when I wasn't expecting her, with a little blue plastic bag with lots of things in. 'Michel, I'm sick of waiting till we're grown up, let's get married today.'

We went round the back of our house and built a little tent with mango tree branches and cloths my mother had washed and left out to dry in the sun. It was our house, just for the two of us.

Monsieur Mutombo always makes pretty dolls for his daughter, so she had two of them with her that day. She said the dolls were our children. And we put them on a plank, to play together. Caroline started to get the food ready, with pretend plates and spoons: empty margarine tubs and little sticks.

After a few minutes, she announced that the food was ready. 'Come, husband, let's sit down to eat.'

Then she said that first of all we had to feed our babies because they were very hungry and were crying all the time. But first they had to have a bath. I washed the boy. Caroline washed the girl because when a boy's naked he looks like me, and when a girl's naked she looks like Caroline, so it was right that she should wash the girl and I should wash the boy. After their bath we put their bibs on so the food wouldn't get on their clothes and then we fed them.

A few minutes later Caroline turned to me and said, 'There now, they've had a good meal, they even burped!'

We rocked them, put them into bed, then we pretended to eat too. We had a conversation, trying to do it like grown ups. I touched Caroline's hair and she touched my chin. She was the one who talked most. I listened, and nodded. We laughed a lot, and if I didn't laugh she got cross. So I laughed, anyway, even when I wasn't meant to.

I noticed she was sad, all of a sudden.

'What's the matter?' I asked.

'Michel, I'm worried.'

'What about?'

'Our children. We must put some money in the bank for when they're older, or they'll be unhappy.'

'You're right, we should.'

'You know, if they're unhappy, the state will take them away and put them in a place for orphans, and they'll end up like the thugs at the Grand Marché.'

'Well, they mustn't do that. We don't want them ending up thugs at the Grand Marché. They'll get sent to prison and we'll be unhappy all our lives.'

'And we must buy a nice red, five-seater car, and get even richer than the President of the Republic.'

'You can count on me. We'll buy our red five-seater from my uncle's company, he'll give us a family discount. I'm his nephew!'

'And how much d'you think a red car like that costs, with five seats?'

'I'll ask my uncle.'

She passed me a stick, and a little empty glass: 'Here, smoke your pipe, and drink up your glass of corn spirit.'

I pretended to smoke the pipe and drink my glass of corn spirit.

She took my hand. 'Michel, you know I love you, don't you?'

I didn't answer. It was the first time I'd heard someone tell me 'I love you'. And her voice was different, and she was looking at me, waiting for me to say something to her. What could I say? In the end I said nothing, I felt so light I thought I might just float up into the sky. My ears were hot. And my heart was beating so loud I thought Caroline must be able to hear it.

She was disappointed and let go of my hand: 'Honestly, you're hopeless! When a woman says "I love you", you have to say "I love you too", that's what grown-ups do.'

So, like a grown up, I said, 'I love you too.'

'Really?'

'Yes, really.'

'Swear!'

'I swear!'

'How do you love me, then?'

'I have to tell you *how* I love you?'

'Yes, Michel, if you don't tell me *how* you love me, what am I supposed to think? I'm going to think you don't love me at all, and I'm going to be sad the whole time. And I don't want to be sad because my mother says it makes women look old, that's why my mother looks old because my father's never told her *how* he loves her. I really don't want to grow old. If I grow old then one day you're going to tell me I'm not beautiful, and you'll go and find another wife…'

Suddenly a plane flew over head. So then I said: 'I love you like the plane that just went overhead.'

'No, no, you're not meant to say that! I want you to love me more than the plane because the plane's everybody's; it's for people going to France, who never come back.'

I thought we were just playing, but then she started really

crying. I felt like crying too, then. But Lounès had already told me men mustn't cry in front of women, or they'll think you're weak. So I cried inside.

'You still don't get it, Michel! I want you to love me like the red car with five seats, our very own car, and our children's and our little white dog's.'

'Yes, I love you like a red five-seater car.'

At last, she was happy, she touched my chin again, and I touched her hair, and dried her tears. When she tried to kiss me on the lips, I shrank back as though I'd been bitten by a snake.

'Are you afraid of me?'

'No.'

'You are!'

'No...'

'Well why do you back off when I tried to kiss you on the mouth like in white people's films?'

'Mouths, that's for when we're really married, with witnesses, chosen by our parents.'

'Who'll be your witness?'

'Your brother.'

'Mine'll be Léontine, she's my best friend.'

She was so pleased, she poured me another glass of corn spirit. I said nothing, so she added: 'I understand why you're not talking, you're tired, like men are when they come home from work. I'll just wash the plates, then we'll go to sleep.'

She turned her back to me, and pretended to wash the plates, by rubbing the margarine pots. She told me to carry on drinking my glass of corn spirit and smoking my pipe.

She counted up to twenty. 'There, that's done, I've washed everything! I'm going to shut the door, and put out the light, come to bed with me, don't be afraid.'

To switch out the light, she pressed an imaginary button.

'There you are, the light's off!'

She lay down in the middle of the tent on her back, and closed her eyes. I said to myself, 'She's going to go to sleep for real, I don't want to go to sleep in broad daylight. Besides, if my parents find us sleeping, I don't know what they'll think. I'd better get going, yeah, I'd better get out of here.'

Just as I was about to get up and leave the tent, she caught my hand. 'Come on, lie down on top of me, close your eyes. That's what grown-ups do.'

Maman Pauline goes into the bedroom. I follow her. She comes back into the living room, I come back too. She's in front of the mirror, I'm just behind her. She puts on lipstick and powder, I make the same gestures, though I don't put anything on because that kind of thing's only for women, and apparently if boys put on makeup it means they're done for, there's something not right in their brain.

She's wound a *pagne* round her head, for a scarf. I'm wearing a hat in the colours of our football team: green, yellow and red. She picks up her handbag, looks everywhere for the house keys. I can see them from here, but she just goes on and on looking, and finds them in the end behind the wardrobe.

I don't like this at all. I don't want Maman Pauline to go out when Papa Roger's not here. It's true my father didn't come home last night. He sleeps at our house one night, at Maman Martine's the next. On Monday he's with us, on Tuesday at Maman Martine's, she lives in the Savon *quartier*, quite near my uncle's. Papa Roger goes back and forth between the two women all week long, he's like the postman you see in the streets of Trois-Cents. Now, there are only seven days in a week, not eight, so Papa Roger can't divide the week in two, however good he is at arithmetic. He's found a solution: one Sunday he sleeps at our house, the next at Maman Martine's. That's why he's not at home today.

. . . . .

I'm never in a good mood when Maman Pauline's making herself pretty. I glance again at her hair, which Caroline's braided. She's put on her orange high-heels, a camisole wrap the same colour as her headscarf, and a pair of orange trousers. I don't like it when she puts on the shiny orange trousers that are too tight round her legs and butt. Whenever she wears them, men stare at her walking, and whistle as she goes by. It makes me wonder what goes on in their heads, why they only have eyes for Maman Pauline, when there are other women walking around in shiny orange pants that are too tight round the legs and butt. Sometimes I even pick up a stone and aim it at one of the guys whistling at my mother. She stops walking, turns round and shouts: 'Are you crazy? If that's the way it's gonna be, you're not coming out walking with me again! I don't like wild boys! Opium of the masses!'

But why didn't she tell me she was going out before lunch? I don't know where she's going. The people out there might trap her at the end of the Avenue of Independence, for all I know, or in a bar. Lounès says some of the men in our *quartier* are really bad, they hang around at the corner of the Avenue of Independence and when a woman goes by they shout rude things at her or force her to drink a beer in a bar where it's all dark inside, and then dance the rumba of Tabu Ley or Franco Luamb-Makiadi, and then end up in a room where they have to do all this stuff. I can't imagine Maman Pauline dancing with anyone but Papa Roger. I can't imagine Maman Pauline going to a room and doing stuff with any man except Papa Roger. I'm not having that. No. Besides, once, I remember, I gave a man who was talking too much with my mother what he deserved. Lounès told me about this secret way he had of protecting Madame Mutombo from bad men who look at women like that and whistle when they've gone by, like someone hailing a bush taxi in the street.

He said: 'Michel, I promise you, if you put sugar in the tank of a moped, it'll break down and won't start. Sugar's nice, we all like sugar, and mopeds like it too. And the moped will like it so much it'll take off suddenly at two hundred kilometres an hour.'

I couldn't think of anything better, so I said to myself: 'I might as well try Lounès's secret. What have I got to lose?' So I did, because it made me really angry to see the man talking with Maman Pauline, and the way she listened to him, laughing, instead of shooing him away like I shoo away mosquitoes that come and bite me till all hours of the morning, Flytox or no Flytox. I'd never seen her laugh like that with Papa Roger. What did this guy have that my father didn't? What could he be saying to make Maman Pauline laugh like that? And anyway, are you meant to make women laugh like that? Did I ever make Caroline laugh like that? I don't like making Caroline laugh, whenever a woman laughs I feel embarrassed for her, I avert my eyes, so she won't be embarrassed too. A woman looks awful when she laughs, you can see her teeth, and her tongue. Now you shouldn't show your teeth or your tongue to just anyone in the street. Perhaps that's why since the beginning of time, people have always hidden in the shower to brush their teeth.

So, I took a sachet of sugar and I went round the back of our house where the nasty man had parked his old moped, emptied the sachet into the petrol tank and came back and sat down by the front door, like a good boy. Maman Pauline and the nasty man were still laughing, showing each other their tongue and teeth. It felt like the whole thing lasted about a hundred years and ten days.

At last the nasty man said goodbye to Maman Pauline and put his arm round her waist. I thought: He's suffocating my mother! But Maman Pauline just laughed again, while he was suffocating her. She showed him her teeth again, and her tongue was hanging out. I was embarrassed for her, she's always so beautiful when her mouth is closed. I spat angrily on the ground because my mother hadn't moved her body away from the rude man's arm. She even seemed pleased he was squeezing her, she put her arm round the bad man's waist, and the two of them carried on suffocating each other and laughing.

The man went off round the back of our house, he was pleased with himself, singing as he went.

A few minutes later he came rushing back, just as though he'd seen the devil himself.

And he was shouting, 'My motor! My motor! My motor's not working!'

At first I didn't realise he was talking about his moped.

'Where are the kids round here? Get them to come and push my bike!'

But there were no children around. They were all at mass that Sunday, and mass at Saint-Jean-Bosco lasts so long, even God starts yawning after a bit, the prayers go on forever, and they all say the same thing over and over in the hundreds of different languages of our country. I think God has a pretty heavy workload round here, even on public holidays.

Maman Pauline and I pushed the moped. It was no good, it still wouldn't start. We went on pushing like slaves or the cart-pullers from Zaire you see at the Grand Marché. We got as far as where the Avenue of Independence gets so steep that cars always break down. This man saw us and took pity on us. I thought he was going to help us push the bike, but he said he was a Solex repair man, and though he was only really supposed to mend Solexes, he would take a look at this moped for no charge. That really annoyed me, I didn't want him to fix the bike. He leaned over the moped, concentrating hard, like a watch mender. He opened the tank, tilted the moped so all the petrol ran out on the ground and discovered there was something white in there. He tasted it, and his eyes grew big and green as limes.

'It's sugar! Whoever did that's a cunning rascal! Oooh, this is serious, really serious. I know this problem, believe me, this bike's not going to start, not even if you push from here to the border with Cameroon!'

He looked about him, as though in search of whoever could have played this trick on him. I was sitting pretty in my corner, no one could accuse me since I'd been pushing the bike myself. You can't accuse someone who's been helping you. So he thought it was some jealous guy in the Trois-Cents who'd sabotaged his bike.

Anyway, the Solex repair man accepted a note for five hundred CFA francs. He advised our man to go and fill up at a petrol station, and off he pedalled towards the Savon *quartier*.

Maman Pauline and I walked back home in silence. I was happy I'd just saved her from the bad man, but she was sad.

The next morning, when I was getting my bags ready for school, she came and said, 'Michel, I'm not stupid! I don't like what you did yesterday! And since there's no sugar left in the house, you'll just have to go to school without breakfast!'

Now Maman Pauline wants to go out this Sunday. I want to protect her because Papa Roger sometimes says 'people don't like people'. Another thing he says is: 'another man's wife is always sweeter'. And the bad men down the Avenue of Independence are going to think my mother's really sweet because her clothes and her hair are really nice. I'm going to wipe out those bad guys, one by one. I'm really strong. Oh yeah, I'm like Superman, the Incredible Hulk, Asterix and Obelix, like Spiderman, Zembla or the Great Blek. I've read about the deeds of these true immortals, Lounès gave me all that to read. I've got big muscles, too, like them, that swell up when I'm angry.

But my mother asks me to stay home because on Sundays schoolchildren do their homework for Monday. I'm not ok with that: 'I've already done my homework, I knew we were going to go out this Sunday and…'

'Well, you'll just have to check it and see if there are any mistakes!'

I had no answer for that, so I said: 'Maman, did you know bad men always go out on Sundays? They don't have public holidays like Papa Roger, they don't go to church, they'll catch you and hurt you and take you to a bar where it's all dark inside and then to a bedroom, to do nasty things to you.'

She laughs, tells me no one's going to attack her. I don't agree, and I keep on saying so because the people out there are the ones stopping Maman Pauline from giving me my good night kiss each evening. She can see I'm not going to calm down, that I'm going to follow her.

'Michel, think carefully: you really want to come with me?'

'Yes', I say, in a small voice, like I'm about to cry.

'Ok, ok, come with me then!'

It always worries me when she says 'ok', in that voice that seems to be hiding something really bad that's going to happen to me. I worry when I see that little smile at the corner of her mouth, as though she's thinking: 'You come with me and see what happens, if that's what you want.' But I don't care today,

I'm happy, nothing's going to happen to me. I'm already smiling, I'll go along with her. We'll walk out together. I'll protect her.

I put my hat back on straight again and button up my shirt to the neck, and she comes up behind me and takes me by the shoulders. 'My, you're well dressed today! But do you know where we're going?'

'No…'

'To Uncle René's.'

I take a few steps backwards.

'D'you still want to come?'

I shake my head. No I do not want to go to Uncle René's house. I can just picture old bald Lenin. Marx's beard, too, and Engel's, and the sideburns of that well-known immortal, Marien Ngouabi. And I picture Uncle René, his wife and my cousins, eating with their eyes on their plates.

No, I don't want to go to Uncle René's.

Maman Pauline can see I've decided not to come, and off she goes on her own. I stand outside the house, watching her go. I can smell her perfume in the air. I breathe in deeply, with my eyes closed. Then when I open them, I see my mother, walking along the Avenue of Independence. Every now and then she turns around to check I'm not behind her. I want to see which direction my mother goes in. Usually, to go to my uncle's house, you turn right at the end of the avenue, then carry on straight towards the Savon *quartier*.

There she is, getting into a taxi further on down. The car sets off but doesn't turn right, it turns left, in completely the opposite direction to Uncle René's, and disappears, heading for the Rex *quartier*. I'm standing in the middle of the road, a car could just come and knock me over because I'm busy thinking.

I guess the taxi's going to turn round and come back, that he's set off the wrong way.

The cars drive round me, hooting their horns at me. One driver yells at me, says I'm mad, a street child, a son of a proletariat.

Me, son of a proletariat? Sounds like my uncle talking. But coming from Uncle René, proletariat's a compliment. The proletariat's someone who's exploited by a capitalist, a bourgeois. I shouted back at the driver, 'Opium of the people!'

He didn't hear. If he had he'd have stopped to punch me in the face.

There's still no taxi turning round in the street to bring my mother back, but I'm still standing there. I know Maman Pauline didn't tell me the truth. Sometimes she tells me that the truth is a light and that you can't hide a light in your pocket. That's why the sun's always stronger than the night. Yes, it was her that told me God created the sun so that men would know the truth. But men prefer the night, because it's easier to cheat people in the dark. I have eyes that can see in the dark. My eyes are torches that never go out. Why did Maman Pauline hide the light and pretend day was night? Has she gone to meet the man with the old moped? Is there another guy, apart from this bad one with the gorilla arms?

I can almost feel myself starting to hate her. I want to destroy everything, like a caterpillar, or a bulldozer, or one of the National People's Army tanks. I'm deaf to the noise of the street. I'm surrounded by immortals. I'm Superman, I dream that I'm flying over the city of Pointe-Noire to where my mother is. You can't hide the light from Superman. Superman can light up the sun at midnight, and put it out on the stroke of midday. So I decide I'm going to put the sun out now, to punish Maman Pauline. I close my eyes and spread my arms wide. But nothing happens. I can't take off like Superman. I close my eyes again and imagine I'm pressing a big red button to put out the sun, which has stolen my mother. I open my eyes, the sun's still there. It's shining even brighter now. And it's very hot.

I know Maman Pauline isn't going to Uncle René's house. I know it's often Uncle René who comes here to shout at her about the inheritance of my Grandma Henriette Nsoko, the fields and animals she's left to us in the village of Louboulou. Or sometimes he just comes by the house to give me a little plastic truck, a spade and a rake, so I can play at being a farmer. My uncle has told his white bosses that I'm one of his sons, that way the white people give him lots of money at the end of each year. Apparently the more children you have, the more toys and money the white people give you. I've even heard that some fathers in this country have children on purpose so the white people will give them lots of presents. And if they haven't got any children they go and fetch their nephews from the villages and bring them back to town and alter their birth certificates. The white man never checks it, he just hands over the present, without even trying to work out why the faces of the father and child are as different as night and day. It was easy for me because I have the same name as Uncle René. He comes to our house before Christmas, leaves the toys – always the same ones – and a 1000 CFA franc note which Maman Pauline refuses to accept. Uncle René throws the note on the ground, my mother takes it as soon as he starts the car. When they're arguing, I hear Maman Pauline threatening her brother: 'If you keep our mother's inheritance all for yourself I'm going to tell those white bosses of yours that Michel's not your son, he's your nephew, and you'll be kicked out of your job! If you're lucky they might let you stay on at the CFAO, but you'll have a tiny little office like the kiosks down the Trois-Cents!'

My uncle replies, 'What are the Whites going to do to me, eh? Michel's got my name, I gave it to him! I delivered you from shame, Pauline! You should shut up and be grateful! And while we're on the subject, why did Michel's real father run off when he was born, huh? Why doesn't the child have his father's name? Simple: he has no father!'

'Michel does have a father, it's Roger!'

'Oh yeah! Roger's just his foster father! Besides, he's already got a wife, her name's Martine! And they've got children, real children!'

And they go on arguing like that. They only stop when they hear me cough. Uncle René starts up his car, winds down the window and throws a 1000 CFA note, without even looking at us. It's me that runs to pick it up.

We're sitting at the table, eating beef and beans. Maman Pauline and Papa Roger are opposite me. From where they're sitting they can see everything going on in our lot, because the door's often left open, but not me, because I've got my back to the door. I pass the salt and hot pepper when they want it.

Maman says: 'Michel, salt!'

Papa says: 'Michel, pepper!'

Maman says: 'Michel, top up your father's wine!'

Papa says: 'Michel, look, your mother's glass is empty. Pour her some beer!'

I feel like a referee, all I need is a whistle and some cards.

I eat fast because I'm hoping Papa Roger will give me his big piece of meat, which I've had my eye on for a few minutes. I'm already dreaming of the moment he puts it on my plate, how I'll swallow it. First I'll eat the beans, then I'll start on the meat. I'll scrape off all the flesh, than I'll dig inside the bone with my fork to get the marrow out. When I've finished I must belch to please my mother, because she knows it's my favourite meal. If I don't belch she'll think I didn't like it, she'll give me a cold look and say I'm the opium of the people in this house, which isn't true. That's why I've invented my own technique for belching after a meal I don't like: first of all I drink lots of lemonade, then I hold my breath for a while, and press the base of my stomach.

And the belch that comes out is so loud that they both look at me astonished. Maman Pauline can tell it's not natural, that I've forced it, and she scolds me, saying: 'Michel, are you trying to get funny with me or what? You don't usually like spinach with salted fish! Anyway, that's not the way you belch after beef and beans!'

So Papa Roger often gives me his big bit of meat. That's why this evening I'm giving him my hangdog look across the table, but he's not looking at me very much. If he goes on not looking at me I'm done for because he won't realise I really want the big piece of meat glistening on his plate. I've never seen a piece of meat glisten like that one. Maybe because today I can tell I'm not going to get it the way I usually do. Maybe, also, because the thing you're worried you won't get is always better than the thing you've already got on your plate or in your mouth. Maybe because in my head I'm telling myself I'm already eating my father's meat.

Suddenly I feel my heart drop into my boots: my father's started clearing his beans to one side before starting on the piece of meat in question. Oh no, don't let him do that, he mustn't eat it himself, it's mine, it's mine! My head follows his hand as it moves, I close my eyes as the piece of meat finally disappears into his big wide mouth. For several minutes he can't speak, that meat is so tender, so good, that if you talk too much you can't appreciate it as you should.

The moment he placed it in his mouth, I closed my eyes, imagining it was me, Michel, that had picked up the piece of meat, that was chewing it, me that had the aroma of tomato sauce and Maggi-cube in my nostrils, that the slab of meat had gone straight down into my little stomach, which is only too happy to continue the work begun in my mouth.

I open my eyes and see that my dream has not come true. The meat did not go into my stomach, but into Papa Roger's. I'm sad to have lost out, though I don't let my father see. But I can see from the way he's looking at me that he knew I wanted that piece and is pretending he didn't. I hear him belch, picking the remains of the meat from between his teeth.

To cheer myself up I think: 'It doesn't matter, maybe Papa Roger didn't give me the big piece this evening to stop me getting greedy like my cousins, Kevin and Sebastien.'

I've cleared the table. Maman Pauline will wash the plates before we go to bed. Maybe she won't even wash them till tomorrow morning, before she goes to the Grand Marché, sometimes she leaves them when she's tired.

Now Papa Roger announces he's got something very important to show us, something it seems we've never seen in our lives before. I'm still a bit cross with him because I didn't get the piece of meat. He's not going to wipe out my disappointment just by showing me something important.

He raises his wine glass above his head, as if he'd beaten Brazil in the World Cup.

'Let's celebrate! You'll see, it's wonderful!'

So my mother and I wait. We don't know what he wants us to celebrate with him. We've checked there's nothing on the table, nothing hidden underneath it, or anywhere else in the room.

'Come on, raise your glasses!'

I think of all the wonderful things there are in the world and I wonder what Papa Roger can be about to show us that will stop me thinking about the bit of meat in his belly right now.

Perhaps he's going to say he's had a pay rise. Or that he's found a better job than the one at the Victory Palace Hotel. Or that now he's got a big office, bigger than Uncle René's, with a beautiful secretary and bodyguards as big as black American soldiers, and the bodyguards will stop just anyone coming into his office without an appointment. Or that he's bought a fantastic car. It'd be great if he'd bought a car, but I'm worried he's going to tell me the car in question is red with five seats. He's not allowed to buy a car like that. I'm going to buy one, so my wife, Caroline, will be happy, with our two children and our little white dog.

Papa Roger's so happy, he's going to finish the bottle of wine all on his own. If he goes on like that he'll end up drunk and start talking to the invisible people that the alcohol producers put in the bottles. If he's drunk he won't be able to show us anything amazing. That's why Maman Pauline quickly removes the bottle, but he just has time to fill his glass, and he raises it to his lips with a little smile at the corner of his mouth. It's almost as though he enjoys the fact that we're waiting, that we can't drink as we're supposed to unless he tells us what it is that's so amazing.

He talks about all sorts of things, about what's been happening at work, but not about the amazing thing. It seems his boss, Madame Ginette, has come back from Paris. They've repainted the walls in the hotel, and redone the garden behind because she called to tell them she was coming back from France with two men whose job it is to check all the things that aren't right in hotels and then blame people for being lazy, or have them sent home.

My father has the hiccups, but he still manages to say: 'These two people... hic... these two people came over from France... hic... they were just trying to find fault. That's their job. One of them… hic… went looking everywhere, even behind the pan of the WC. Meanwhile the other one was looking at every single bill with a magnifying glass… hic… and in the end he saw there wasn't a single CFA franc missing from the till… hic…'

Maman Pauline's had enough: 'You promised you were going to show us something very important and amazing! What is it?'

At last, my father empties his glass, pushes back his chair, gets up and goes into the bedroom. He's not walking quite straight like a normal person. We hear him saying his boss's name. We look at each other and wonder what he's gone looking for.

Maman Pauline whispers: 'I think your father's had one or two glasses too many.'

Papa Roger comes back into the living room with a black briefcase, which he puts down on the table.

'It's in there, inside this case, hic… hic!'

My mother's still sulking. 'What are you waiting for then?'

Papa Roger presses a button, the briefcase opens. Maman Pauline and I almost bang our heads, because without realising it, we both decided at exactly the same moment to look what was in side the case. There's only a little black box. Papa Roger sees we're wondering what it can be for, and he tells us it's a radio cassette player, a new brand that's just come out over in Europe and that not many people in our country have, not even some of the capitalists. And you can also listen to the radio on it.

It's the first time I've seen a machine like this. Maman Pauline's looking at it fearfully as if it was a bomb that was going to blow up in a few minutes and kill all three of us.

Papa Roger explains that you can record lots of things in it, you just have to press once on the button marked 'Play' and on another red one that says 'Record'. But for the moment he wants to play us something because he can't record anything, since he doesn't have a blank cassette.

Maman Pauline wants to leave the table.

'Here we are, with not much money, and you go buying things like that!'

'Hic… listen, Pauline…'

'How much did it cost, anyway?'

Papa Roger smiles as though he'd been waiting for this question. He takes his time before telling us it was a present, that he's already had the radio cassette player for several days, he'd hidden it at the Victory Palace Hotel. He didn't take it home to Maman Martine's because there are too many children there, they might damage it while he was out. And he tells us how he was given it by a white man, Monsieur Montoir, as a thank you because he is always so nice to him when he comes to spend his holidays at the hotel. He's so happy talking about this white man, that suddenly his hiccups disappear.

'Monsieur Montoir is a regular at the hotel, a White. When he arrives from France, I look after him personally. I post his letters, I tell him where all the best bars are.'

He adds quietly, 'It's thanks to me he has such a nice time here. I bring him back very beautiful, very young girls, to his room.'

I think, 'Next time Uncle René comes round to our house there's going to be serious trouble. He's going to think we're gradually turning into capitalists, and soon we'll have television, hot water and air conditioning. Well, he has television too, after all, and hot water, and air conditioning, perhaps he'll be a bit jealous because he hasn't got a radio cassette player, it's a new model, but he can't be cross with us for that, he can go out and buy one anytime.'

My father warns us, 'Listen carefully: we must be very discreet and not go round telling everyone in the *quartier* we've got a radio cassette player.'

Will I tell Lounès the secret? I think I will. I don't hide anything from him, and he tells me loads of things. So why shouldn't I tell him?

My father's rummaging in the case again, and brings out a cassette. He presses the button of the cassette player and a little window opens. He puts the cassette in, closes the little window and presses again on 'Play'. My mother and I almost bang heads trying to see how it works inside the machine. There's a tape that turns in the cassette and our eyes follow the rhythm of the brown coloured tape. We can't hear anything, but the tape is turning.

Suddenly a loud voice makes us leap backwards. Papa Roger keeps very calm, he's not afraid like us.

Someone starts singing. My father turns up the volume slightly. I look at my mother's face. It is completely still. Her mouth is half open, her hands are crossed, resting on the table. She looks exactly like a statue in Saint-Jean-Bosco church.

Now we hear a chorus that makes me start wiggling my shoulders, though this isn't the kind of music we normally dance to round here.

At the foot of my tree
I lived happily
I never should
Leave the foot of my tree.
At the foot of my tree
I lived happily
I never should
Take my eyes off my tree.

Maman Pauline's starting to move about now, but not to dance with me, I sense she's just getting annoyed. For the moment she says nothing, but she looks at my father, who's moving his head to the rhythm of the song. I think, 'It's your head you have to move, not your shoulders. So I stop dancing with my shoulders and I start moving my head, like my father. I also tap my fingers on the table because Papa Roger needs to know that at least there's one person in this house who's happy about this music he's brought home, the kind you don't hear in the bars around here.

The man is still singing. You must be able to hear his booming voice out in the street. And all he's talking about is a tree that he wishes he hadn't taken his eye off. I think: 'What's he crying like that for over a tree? We've got millions of trees in the forest, people cut them down all the time and they never cry, not a bit, they make it into firewood for cooking with. Even we've got three trees on our land! And if our mango trees ever disappear, am I going to start crying like the man singing in the radio cassette player? The singer must just be someone who's always sad. Something bad must be happening in his life for him to be crying over a tree, when you should really cry about human beings when they leave this earth. Maybe the singer lives in a place where there are no trees left. And since he's gone away from the only tree he had, well, that's why he's crying the whole day. Besides, his voice is like someone who sings at burials around here, and makes all the women and children start crying.' The voices of the people who sing at burials are so sad, and so warm, that even when it isn't a member of your own family who's died you'll stop for a few minutes in the street and weep too. And if you weep in the street, the family of the dead person will see and get even sadder and cry even more.

While the singer's going on about his tree, I pick up the box that the cassette came in. I turn it over and at last I see the photo of the singer. It's a white man, with lots of hair and shining eyes. He has a moustache and a sad expression, but his face is kind. I think: 'He's never hurt anyone, you can see that. Other people bother him, but he just goes on thinking about his tree. Like all kind people, the singer must have lots of white globules, even whiter than teeth when you've just cleaned them with Colgate or Landry Enamel. He'll go to paradise and he'll leave his white globules to all the children who've been good. So I should listen to what he says because perhaps he's secretly talking about something else, not the tree. I must go on nodding my head like Papa Roger and pretend to sing, as though I know the words.'

There's another thing that attracts me, something between the singers' lips: a pipe. It's not like the pipe Caroline asked me to smoke when we got married, it's a real pipe, not a little stick.

But the thing that really interests me is his moustache. I really like his moustache. Papa Roger doesn't keep his, he shaves it almost every day. When I'm big I hope I'll have a moustache like the one the singer has, and from now on I'm going to call him 'the singer with the moustache' even if his real name, on the cassette, is Georges Brassens.

'm sitting with Lounès at the foot of their mango tree. It's the only tree they have. We've got a mango, a papaya and an orange tree. But the Mutombo family's mango tree has more branches and leaves than ours. When I come round to see Lounès we always sit under this tree, in a corner, by the entrance to their house. We only collect the mangoes that have fallen because Monsieur Mutombo gets cross if we pick them. He says you have to wait for a fruit to fall off the tree in the wind because then it's God Himself who's decided. So we've never picked a single fruit from that mango tree. We often sit waiting for God to hand them to us Himself.

Lounès is older than me. I'm growing fast, so I hope we'll soon be the same height, but he needs to stop growing first. He's muscular, I'm thin. If he hasn't seen me for three or four days he drops by to see if I'm at home. Sometimes he even goes looking for me at Maman Martine's, and whistles three times from the street to tell me to come out. I do the same when I'm looking for him: first I walk past their house, and whistle three times. If he's not there I go to Monsieur Mutombo's sewing workshop, sometimes I find him there helping his father to stack the materials they've brought in town, or putting coal in the steam iron.

Today we're sitting underneath the mango tree because we haven't seen each other for a while. I've been sleeping at

Maman Martine's the last two nights, while my mother was at the wake for Monsieur Moundzika, who's died 'after a long illness' as they put it in the announcement on the radio. As Maman Pauline's a friend of Madame Moundzika, she had to be with her in her grief.

Before she left she said to me: 'You're going to Martine's for a few days, I'll come and collect you after the wake. Be good, and behave as you do with me. If I hear you got up to any tricks I'll make sure you feel it.'

A wake lasts at least two or three days, sometimes as long as a week, even two if the dead person's not happy with his family and is sulking in his coffin. Then you have to wait for the traditional chiefs to arrive from their village with their tam-tams and fetishers, to make *gris-gris*. The fetishers will ask the dead person to move on to heaven for good, and not come back haunting people round midnight. Some dead people are really tricky, they start bothering people on the day they're to go to the cemetery: they jam the wheels of the hearse, so it can't move forward, they throw thunderbolts around the *quartier*, make rain, and their ghost comes to the funeral ceremony to check no one's making fun of the corpse, or that the men aren't flirting with the women when they should be weeping. If the corpse's ghost sees he hasn't been washed properly, or that the sheets on the body are bargain sheets, the ones the Senegalese sell down at the Grand Marché, and that no one's crying much, they'll start pestering folk at night.

When Maman Pauline went to the wake, I said to myself: 'Let's hope the ghost of this corpse isn't too tricky.' She came back two days later, the ghost in question had behaved properly, he was happy with the wake and was prepared to depart at the same time as the body, and leave people in peace.

. . . . .

As soon as a mango falls off the tree, Lounès and I eat it. Since he's bigger than I am, he gets first bite. He gets two bites, I just get one. That's only right, his stomach's bigger than mine.

Sometimes we just sit there in silence, with our eyes shut, so we can hear the butterflies flying up above us. Most of all we like watching the planes flying overhead, guessing which country they'll land in. If one of us says the name of a country, he has to say the name of its capital too. That's how I know that the capital of Belgium is Brussels, the capital of England is London and Germany's is Berlin. But Lounès does world history at Trois-Glorieuses secondary school and he explained that with Germany it was a bit complicated because it's a country that's divided in two, with a big wall to keep the people apart, though they're all Germans. One part's capitalist, the other's communist. I didn't know the name of the capital of the communist bit, though it's a country that likes us because we're all struggling against the capitalists. It was Lounès who explained to me that the capital of the other Germany which is communist like us is called Bonn.

I watch him munching his mango, it takes me back to Monsieur Mutombo's workshop, when Monsieur Mutombo's saying, 'My son's name is Lounès, it's a promise I made to my Algerian friend.'

Then he explains that he lived in Algeria for a year and a half, in a *quartier* of the town of Algiers called Kouba. At that time he wanted to be a tradesman like the Arabs in our country, who are now the richest people in Pointe-Noire.

I listen to him tell his story, waving his hands around: 'I only went to Algeria because I believed we could be businessmen too. We could make lots of money like the other tradesmen, or else one day they'd be selling us cassava, even though we've been producing it ourselves since the dawn of time.'

If you go into Monsieur Mutombo's workshop he'll tell you his Algeria story at least ten times. The one thing you mustn't say is, 'You told me that last year.' If you do that he'll just down tools straight away and you won't get your shirt or your trousers for at least another two weeks. You just have to hear him out, and he'll start by telling you it was in the *quartier* called Kouba that he first learned the trade of cobbler, before giving it up to become a tailor. He'll also tell you it was there he first met the man who's like a brother to him: an Algerian called Arezki.

The longer I look at Lounès, the more he reminds me of his father talking about his friend Arezki. 'Meetings like that are meant to happen! Every morning, from the window of his house, Arezki would see me getting off the bus. Every time he met a black man he'd tell the story of his journey to Senegal, where he and his family had lived for many years. He'd wave at me from a distance and I'd wonder if he was someone I'd known in the Congo, or if he'd confused me with someone else. Then one day he invited me to drink tea at his house, and he told me: "No, we've never met, but my door is always open to you, brother."'

Monsieur Mutombo will then explain that in Algeria there are lots of black people like us, and that these black people are Algerians. He'll add quietly that people with our colour skin suffer almost as much as Blacks in South Africa, where Whites and Blacks can't sit next to each other on the bus, even though buses are there for everybody. Some people get on with animals that have fleas, so why can't black people go in the bus too? And Monsieur Mutombo will suddenly get angry, but you mustn't think it's against you, just because you're listening.

'People don't talk much about the suffering of the Blacks in Arab countries! What's that about then? You don't find many pale skinned Arabs there marrying Arabs with dark skin. Racism and slavery don't just exist between White and Blacks, you know! Arabs had black slaves too, they whipped them like the Whites whipped us back then, and when I see the way the pale skinned ones treat the Blacks over there I think nothing's changed since slavery. Now my Algerian brother, Arezki, he didn't care if his neighbours thought the Black who came to drink tea with him was his servant. That's right, in Kouba they took me for a "boy". Arezki's wife was called Saliha, and they had two sons: Yacine, the older brother, who was studying in Europe, and then the little one, Lounès, who was very clever, with bright blue eyes. There was a daughter between the two boys, Sara. Sometimes I'd walk in the streets of Algiers with the two children. And people would turn round and wonder if they could be my children. If so why weren't they as dark as me? Then they'd think I must just be the servant who was looking after the children of an Algerian capitalist family. Does that seem right to you?'

Once he'd finished being angry he'd talk about Algeria in a sad voice, while continuing to stitch your suit.

'I gave up cobbling to learn tailoring in a little workshop in an old quarter of Algeria called the Casbah. It made more sense for me to learn tailoring because back home the school children change uniforms every year, but many of them go to school barefoot. You can see, my workshop's doing well. I've bought my own plot, I've built a big house, and I'm not one to go round moaning. But, oh, I did love the Casbah! In that part of town the houses are all squeezed together and look out across the sea. It's like living in ancient times. You see people threading their way through the zigzag alleyways. There are steps everywhere, everything's up and down. If you don't know your way round you can get lost. During the war with Algeria the French wouldn't go into the Casbah, they were afraid they'd get lost and be attacked by the Algerians, even the children know where the steps lead and which little passage goes where. Before I left Algeria I made a promise to Arezki and his wife. I told them that if God gave me a son he too would be called Lounès. That's how things were with our ancestors, they named their children after people who were dear to them, not just after their own relatives.'

In his workshop there's a big black-and-white photo of him surrounded by his family in Algeria. Monsieur Arezki and his wife are on either side of him. The children are squatting down in front and the little Algerian boy called Lounès is the one with very dark hair, like his father's, looking down at the ground. Monsieur Mutombo explains proudly that the little Algerian Lounès was looking at the ground in the photo because he was trying to hide his tears at the return of his father's friend to the Congo.

The wind blows and too many mangoes fall. We can't eat them all. He'll give me some and keep the others for his parents and Caroline.

I look at the sky and wonder if it will rain. When it rains it's like a river running through the *quartier*. But I don't think it will rain, the sky's still clear.

Lounès tells me he's got hairs growing down there.

'Where down there?'

'Down in my pants, inside.'

I don't believe him, so he opens the zip of his pants and

shows me. Little shiny black hairs like on a baby's head. He says I'll get them too. You have to have hair down there for girls to respect you. Otherwise they think you're just a child and you can't yell at them. Hairs are the sign you're a man now, not your normal beard, even goats have that.

'But I don't want hairs down there!' I tell him.

'You'll still get them.'

'I want to stay the way I am!'

He changes the subject, and asks me if I've seen Caroline. So he's picked up that something's not right between me and his sister. I can't hide it.

'Don't talk to me about Caroline!'

'What is it? Has she upset you?'

'Did you know it was her that did my mother's braids, and that's why Maman Pauline went out without me?'

'Is that all?'

'What d'you mean, is that all? Do you like it, then, when your mother goes out? If Caroline hadn't done braids in her hair, she'd never have gone out without me that Sunday!'

We hear someone coming up behind us. It's Madame Mutombo coming out of the house. Maybe she heard us talking.

'What are you two whispering about?'

'Nothing. Just chatting,' Lounès says.

She moves slowly forward, carrying her big heart inside, and passes just in front of us. She's got a sack of peanuts on her head, she must be going to the Grand Marché. We watch her go, then I put my lips close to Lounès's ear.

'I'll tell you a secret, but you mustn't tell, not even your sister...'

'She's not here, she went to braid our aunt's hair this morning.'

'Yes, but even when she comes back, you mustn't tell her, or I'm done for!'

'I won't tell her.'

'Ok, you're not going to believe it. We're capitalists now, in our house...'

'Really? Proper capitalists?'

'Yes, we've got a brand new machine, no one else has got one here yet, it's a radio and a recorder at the same time. It's a radio cassette player.'

I tell him about the singer with the moustache.

'His name's Georges Brassens. He's a nice man with a moustache. He keeps talking about this tree he liked but that he can't see now. And all day long he sings this song, all about his tree! I feel sorry for him, we have to help him. It's not right that a man gets so sad about a tree he starts crying.'

'Is he white?'

'What d'you think, who else would cry about a tree?'

Before I leave him I promise him one day when he comes round to our house, we'll listen to the singer with the moustache. One day when my mother and father are out.

I t's good being a boss. When I say 'boss', I don't mean like my uncle, he's not such a big boss as the President of our Republic, who's President, Prime Minister, Minister of Defence, and President of the Congolese Workers' Party, the CPT, all at the same time. You might get the impression he's a bit greedy, holding all these positions himself. People do say whenever there's a meeting of the President of the Republic, the Prime Minister, the Minister of Defence and the President of the CPT, our President sits on his own in a room, talking things over with himself, first as President of the Republic, then as Prime Minister, then as Minister of Defence, and last as President of the CPT. Which is why the meeting goes on longer than when he's with his ministers.

You have to remember that he's taken on all these posts to protect himself, which I can understand. If he accepts a Prime Minister who isn't himself, the Prime Minister's going to want to be President of the Republic too, and overthrow the Minister of Defence in a *coup d'état*, because he's a dangerous member of the armed forces who has already carried out one plot to kill the immortal Marien Ngouabi, and succeeded. As a military man he knows all the other military men, and they all respect him because it's not something everyone can claim, that he's killed one of the immortals.

Papa Roger doesn't like military men and he thinks ours are

always hungry. You'd think the last time they'd eaten was a century and ten days ago. They're not going to be much use if Zaire attacks us at five in the morning to take over our petrol and our Atlantic waters, with all the big fish, which are meant to belong to us as well. Our military men are too thin, they don't do any keep-fit, not like the Americans and the Russians, who train all the time because they know that world wars come along all of a sudden, and when that happens you don't have time to say, 'Wait for me, I'm just going off to have a pee before I start fighting.'

Papa Roger also thinks our military men don't do any sport because if we do have a war it won't be tomorrow, and in any case if there is a war, a little country like the Congo's never going to win. So their stripes are worth nothing. They've never fought a real war. Even though it's not allowed, they'll mount a *coup d'état* and bump off immortals with anyone who's prepared to offer them new uniforms, ranks, crates of foreign beer and a fat salary.

Our President knows all this, which is why he's decided to make himself Prime Minister, Minister of Defence and President of the Congolese Workers' Party. The reason he's decided to make himself President of the CPT is because, as Uncle René is fond of saying, it's not rocket science to be president, first of all you have to be the boss of the CPT. The CPT chooses the president because we don't like wasting time with elections, not like in Europe, where they even ask the people to choose who they'd like to be president! What kind of a joke is that? You don't ask the people themselves who they'd like for president! What if they get it wrong, what then? It would ruin the country! Now, the members of the CPT have never got it wrong. So it's right that they should be the ones who choose the

President of the Republic for us. Besides, the President's always reminding us in his speeches that the elections the Whites go in for, and tell us we have to have too, are a bad thing – they slow down the Revolution. Our country's running late, we're in a hurry, we need to catch up with Europe, and we can't catch up with Europe if we're constantly asking people to choose a President of the Republic. Besides, not everyone would be able to vote. Some people won't even be there on the day, they'll have toothache and have to go to the dentist. Others will go off to work on their plantations, and die of malaria or sleeping sickness. And it's not nice, telling old people they've got to go and vote when they're tired and have a right to a rest.

Lounès thinks our President's a dictator because he's a military man, but I don't agree. I'm sure that in a lot of countries around the world there are dictators who aren't in the army. So I don't care if our President's a dictator, it just annoys me that he says he's been sent personally by God. Now if God wanted to send someone to be president of our country He would have sent his son Jesus because He's already done that once to save men on earth. At least, that's what the priest says on Sundays in the church of Saint-Jean-Bosco.

When the President tells us he's been personally sent by God, people believe him, without stopping to check if it's true or not. And we learn his speeches at school, like the sheep down at the Grand Marché, because what he says is supposedly for our good, and comes directly from God. We learn about his glorious life story. How he defeated the enemies of the Revolution in the north of the country, how he single-handedly massacred his enemies who had stolen our army's tank and were preparing to bombard the north of the country, and then go back down south and bombard the little villages down there, including animals and poor peasants. They had to find the tank again fast, it was the only one the French left behind for us after Independence. The French really liked us, and we liked them too. They still like us, in fact, because they go on looking after our oil for us, which is in the sea near Pointe-Noire, because if they don't we'll only go and waste it or sell it to the Americans, who need it to run their enormous cars.

And apparently, because he was born invincible, our President's the one who went into battle back when he was just a soldier and didn't know it was written on the lines of his right hand that he would become president after a battle against the enemies of the Revolution. So he just turned up in the north of the country on an old Vespa, so well disguised that no one could tell if he was a soldier or a bit of grass waving in the wind. He crawled, he swam, he climbed trees. He attacked hundreds of enemies of the revolution who'd gathered by a river to work out how they could wipe us out in less than twenty-four hours. The future president let out a great war cry and began machine gunning them with his eyes closed. He was faster with a bullet than Lucky Luke himself. And when he'd run out of ammunition the spirits of our ancestors gave him heaps more. At one point even the spirits of our ancestors ran out of bullets too. The future president went and hid in a maize field, and there he met an old man of the Bembé tribe, who only had one tooth left in his head, and who told him to put maize kernels in his weapon. He was lying, and he didn't believe him, but he had no choice because the enemies were coming up behind him en masse. So he loaded his gun with maize kernels anyway. When he fired, the kernels exploded, like grenades in the first world war. He fired and he fired and he kept on firing while the enemies of the Nation fell, one after the other and died like rats. The future president finally discovered where they had hidden our lovely French tank. The tank still worked, the opponents of the Revolution hadn't used it. Then our future president came back with the tank, driving it himself, and the people cheered him and gave him flowers as he entered the national stadium with the tank.

As soon as he became President of the Republic, since he was by now a national hero, thanks to the tank, he wrote a big fat book that you have to read at middle school, high school and university. They only read us a few little bits because our brains are still too small, but when we get to middle school we'll read it all, from start to finish.

It's Saturday, and everyone out in the street is all dressed up, you'd think it was Independence Day. Some people always get dressed up like that on Saturdays. The minute I see all those suits and new wraps I know it must be Saturday. They all do it: come Saturday, they're out there in their fine clothes from morning to the late afternoon, then in the evening they're off to cruise the bars in the Avenue of Independence. They go dancing all night, and some of them sleep from Sunday to Monday midday and forget to go to work. The priest at Saint-Jean-Bosco complains his church is empty these days. How can you expect people to get up for church on a Sunday morning if they've been out partying from six in the evening till six in the morning and only found their way back home again by some small miracle?

It's not too hot. The sky above me is calm and blue. When a plane goes by, I think of Caroline, even though I'm still cross with her. Now every time I think of my wife I have to think of a red car with five seats. And our two children, a girl and a boy. Not forgetting the little white dog.

While I'm busy imagining my life with Caroline, someone comes up behind me and touches my shoulder. It's Lounès.

He laughs and asks if he frightened me.

'Not at all,' I say.

He likes creeping up on me. He's brought some boiled sweets, two for himself and one for me. He gives me mine as soon as he creeps in. My father's sleeping at Maman Martine's today and my mother's still at the Grand Marché selling peanuts with Madame Mutombo, so there's no need to worry.

Lounès sits where I sit when I eat with my parents. I sit in my father's place. I've left the door open. From where I'm sitting I can watch what's happening outside.

Lounès looks at a new photo my mother's put on the dresser. It was taken only a few days ago when we went to buy me some new Spring Court shoes at Printania, where they sell apples, grapes, and lots of fruit brought over from Europe. On the way home we stopped in a bar on the Avenue of Independence. A photographer came in with his camera, and forced my parents to have a picture taken.

'Look at you all! All so handsome, the three of you, it'll be a marvellous photo! I promise you, if you don't look good, I won't charge you.'

My mother said no because it's wrong to waste money. But my father listened to the photographer's pitch, about how he fed his ten children with his camera, and he hadn't had a single client in the last month. He showed us a great gash on his tibia.

'See that? I haven't even got the money to buy drink, or Mercurochrome. And I've got two cousins and two uncles just turned up from the village and it's up to me to feed them. There's another problem too, I rent the house where we live, and the owner...'

'All right, all right, take the photo!' my father said. My mother frowned and gave my father a dirty look. He added: 'I'm paying. Michel, come and stand between your mother and me.'

So now the photo's there on the dresser. Sometimes I look at it for a few minutes and I'm happy I'm standing there between my parents. I know my mouth's hanging open, that's the photographer's fault. He told us to smile at the little bird that popped out of his camera. I wasn't going to smile till I'd seen what kind of bird it was: what colour, where it came out, if it flew, if it could sing like real birds that don't hide inside cameras. I was standing there waiting for the bird with my mouth hanging open, but it wasn't a bird came out, it was a light, which startled me. And another thing: I had no time to button up my shirt. You can see my chest, it's a bit flat still, I'm too small to have muscles like Blek le Roc. My mother's got a scarf wrapped round her head and a glass of beer at her lips. My father's leaning slightly towards me, as though he'd like to protect me from the enemies of the Revolution who might wipe us out and win the final struggle. Out of the three of us, Maman Pauline is the tallest. I've got a glass of beer in front of me, but not to drink, just for the photo, because my mother told me if I didn't have a drink in front of me the photo wouldn't work out because the neighbours would think we'd only gone into the bar for the photo. So there's a glass of beer in front of me, And so no one could say I was just pretending to drink, Maman Pauline took a sip from my glass. So if you look carefully at our photo, you'll see my glass isn't quite full, and you'll think I was drinking beer that day, but it's not true.

While Lounès is looking at the photo, I go into my parents' bedroom, fetch my father's briefcase and come back into the living room.

I have to do it like Papa Roger. I open the briefcase carefully and take out the tape recorder. I press a button, the little window opens. I pick up the only cassette we have and put it in the little window, then I close it, still being very careful. I press 'Play' and the singer with the moustache starts singing.

So there we are, listening to Georges Brassens and looking at his photo on the cassette box. Each time, Lounès tells me to be quiet, and replay the song once it gets to the end. On the cassette player there's a button with an arrow pointing left. On the button it says 'RWD', that's where you press to go back to the beginning of the song. I saw Papa Roger doing that before. I don't like arithmetic much, but by my reckoning I've pressed this button at least ten times to get back to the start of the song.

We've stopped talking, we're just listening now. We're beginning to know the words, but from time to time I have to ask Lounès what some of the difficult words mean. He knows more words than me because he's in fifth grade at secondary school. For example, I don't understand it right at the beginning of the song when the singer with the moustache says:

I left my old oak
My saligaud
My friend the oak
My alter ego

What's a *saligaud*? I don't know. Lounès doesn't know. We give up, it doesn't matter.

But then, what's *alter ego*? We won't want to give up on that one, *alter ego* may be what the song's actually about.

'"*Alter ego*"'s not French,' says Lounès.

'What language is it then, if it's not French?'

'It must be a kind of dialect, of some European tribe.'

'A tribe?'

'Yeah, some really small European tribe that still speaks real French, because that's where French started.'

That's what he says, but I can tell he's not sure. It can't be that, and we go on trying to work it out, and Lounès tells me that *alter ego* means someone really egotistical, like Monsieur Loubaki, who owns a bar called Relax, and makes the clients pay up the same day as they drink, whereas in the other bars you only pay at the end of the month.

'Yeah, Monsieur Loubaki, he's *alter ego*!'

I say the singer with the moustache can't be saying the tree is his *alter ego,* his selfish person. Because why would you be weeping for a selfish person and missing him? You wouldn't, you'd be being rude to him, the way people are to Loubaki in his bar.

Lounès promises to ask his teacher at school, I mustn't ask mine, because if by any chance he doesn't know what *alter ego* and *saligaud* mean I'll get into trouble. The teacher will be embarrassed in front of the pupils and think I'm trying to make fun of him, and whip me with a bicycle chain. At Trois-Glorieuses they don't hit the pupils, they're too big, some as big as the teachers, sometimes a lot bigger. So Lounès is safe.

I don't know why, I feel like going up to Loubaki and saying 'saligaud' and calling Lounès my 'alter ego'. A little voice in my head says that *saligaud* is bad, and *alter ego* is ok. Better to be an *alter ego* than a *saligaud*. I'm quite sure the singer with the moustache wishes his tree, his *alter ego*, all the very best, and that's why he weeps for it, the whole day long.

In the evenings Papa Roger tunes in to Voice of America, a radio station that broadcasts the news in French, from America. I do wonder how the news makes it as far as a little country like ours and why our President doesn't interrupt the signal because they do put out a lot of serious stuff on that station, stuff Radio Congo can't say, or there'd be no more radio in our country.

My father only listens to Radio Congo to hear the death notices for the towns and villages in our country. They never say why these people have died, they say 'after a long illness', like when Monsieur Moundzika died and Maman Pauline went to the wake for two days. What *are* these long illnesses that they can't explain over the radio? Another thing, they always say they 'regret' to announce the death of so and so. Papa Roger says a lot of people 'regretting' the death of these people are actually in a hurry for them to depart this life, so they can go and take over the land and animals they've left behind: 'Never trust anyone who makes an announcement on the radio, in the end they're the ones who drive the widow and her children from the home of the deceased and seize their inheritance.'

When it's time for the announcements to come on, they play this sad music first of all, then the person reading them out puts on this sad voice as though the deaths he's about to announce had occurred in his own family. I go to my room because I don't like that music, and I hate the voice of the announcer. I know she's pretending to be upset, that she gets paid to be sad. It's just then that Maman Pauline sits up attentively. She asks us to turn the sound up, brings her chair up to the table and practically glues her right ear to the radio. And if she hears the names of the villages in the Bousenza region, like Moussanda, Nounga, Ntséké-Pemb Batalébé, Kimandou or Kiniangui, she turns round and says to us: 'I know the people who've just lost their relative. They live near the river Moukoukoulou, behind where the Kibonzi family plant their crops.'

And she cries, as though it was our relative who had just died.

There's a journalist on Voice of America that Papa Roger really likes, his name is Roger Guy Folly. During meals that's all he ever talks about now. Is it because the journalist in question has the same name as him, Roger? When my father says his name you'd think he was talking about his own brother: Roger Guy Folly this, Roger Guy Folly that.

It's this American who tells us the time every evening:

It's twenty-one hundred hours, universal time, and you're listening to Voice of America. Coming straight up, the evening news from Washington, with your faithful servant, Roger Guy Folly.

Now, when Roger Guy Folly says 'twenty-one hundred hours' and I look at the alarm-clock on our dresser, I can see it's not the same time in our country. So, when it's night here, in other countries it's still bright daylight, with children out playing. When we're up and about here, in other places people are sleeping, and when we're sleeping here, people elsewhere are up. It's pretty weird.

Papa Roger always agrees with what Roger Guy Folly says. Sometimes he shouts, turns to us, tells us to be quiet, and promises he'll explain what's being said in a few minutes because Maman Pauline gets sick of listening to things she doesn't understand and countries she's never heard of before. Papa Roger writes down the names of the people, towns and countries on a piece of paper for me.

For example, this evening Roger Guy Folly is telling us about a town called Phnom Penh, the capital of Cambodia. Phnom Penh is too complicated to pronounce. It's complicated to write down too, but once you've done it, it's as easy as swallowing. Otherwise how would the Cambodians manage to write it and say it every time, when they're only human, like us?

Maman Pauline can't say 'Phnom Penh'.

Papa Roger says: 'Pauline, it's very simple. To say Phnom Penh you make your mouth really small, you breathe out through a little hole, like when you're whistling, then you suddenly open you mouth wide, like when you're surprised by something really bad that's happened, which it usually has in Cambodia!'

Roger Guy Folly tells us that the Vietnamese army has just taken the town of Phnom Penh and driven out the wicked people called the Khmer Rouge even though they are Cambodian too. The wicked people were treating their own people very badly, though they're communist like we are. So the Vietnamese – their country is just next to Cambodia – said: Since these Khmer Rouge are threatening our borders, let's get on over to Cambodia and take Phnom Penh out of the hands of the Khmer Rouge, that will give the Cambodian people a bit of a break after all that torturing, killing and liquidating by the Khmer Rouge. When the Cambodians went into Phnom Penh there was practically no one left in the city because of the Khmer Rouge, who'd driven everyone out. The Khmer Rouge had been really looking for a fight for ages. They pushed their Vietnamese neighbours over the edge, after years and years of fighting, like most countries with a common border. And then what happens is, one country says: This is my territory, the territory of my ancestors, I want to get it back, by fair means or foul. The other country says: Oh no, it's not your territory, it's mine, and I won't let you take it back by fair means or foul. I'm going to protect it by fair means or foul. And they start fighting by fair means or foul for years on end. That's why when the Vietnamese went into Cambodia, the Cambodians were frightened to begin with and said to themselves: What are these Vietnamese guys going to do to us? Have they come to take our country from us by fair means or foul? As soon as the Cambodians realised that the Vietnamese were actually after the Khmer Rouge, many of them helped the Vietnamese army, because they'd had enough of being tortured, killed and liquidated. The government of the Khmer Rouge fled, and went to hide in the bush. Their boss is called Pol Pot and he's so wicked he wiped out over a million and a half people, then fled when the Vietnamese invaded his country.

If I, Michel, was Cambodian, I would have supported Vietnam, no question. Not everyone likes the fact that Vietnam went into Cambodia to drive out the wicked Khmer Rouge. The Russians are ok with it, but countries like China or America and lots of others that secretly support the Khmer Rouge say: It's wrong for Vietnam to go into Cambodia like that, we don't agree, we're going to carry on supporting the Khmer Rouge who are hiding in the bush. The Chinese even declared: We're going to punish the Vietnamese too, we're going to attack them good and proper, we're going into their country like they went into Cambodia and we'll see what happens then. Fortunately the Chinese plan failed.

The result is, it's a mess down there: now there's a new government in Cambodia and from now on their country's called the Popular Republic of Kampuchea. So in a way they're like our brothers, but I don't know if our country is against Vietnam or for it, because Roger Guy Folly doesn't mention us in all this. Why would he talk about us? Who wants our opinion? Our country is so small, it's never mentioned in the news. If we have a conflict here one day, like what's happening in Cambodia, then they'll talk about us all the time, as if we were a big country. On the other hand, I prefer it if they don't talk about us on the radio. Yes, I prefer being a little country, at least that way they leave us in peace; we can take it easy, which means no war, no grabbing another country's cities, no Khmer Rouge here; no Pol Pot either, giving the Popular Republic of Kampuchea grief from where he's hiding out in the bush.

I feel really sick when Uncle René tells my mother that Papa Roger isn't my real father, that he's just a 'foster father'. I don't care for Papa Roger because he 'fosters' me, and he didn't decide to be my father so he could do some 'fostering'. Even 'adoptive' father's better than that, at least that means he chose me and chose me after careful reflection. Papa Roger did actually see me before he decided to make me his child. Normally you don't get to choose what your children look like, you don't even see them before they come into the world. You wait for the doctor to say it will be a girl, or a boy. If Papa Roger really hadn't wanted me when he first set eyes on me, he'd have left me alone with my mother. But I smiled at him that day – and according to Maman Pauline I was very happy, apparently that's the moment when I came alive, and said to myself: 'I, Michel, will be someone in life.'

Papa Roger is my father, that's all there is too it. I don't want to know if I've got a *real* father somewhere. I've no wish to see the face of some man I don't know, who's supposedly my *real* father. He's a coward, who left Maman Pauline all alone in hospital when he had married her back in Louboulou, my mother's village. He was a policeman there, before he brought my mother to live in the district of Mouyondzi where he'd been transferred to. Maman Pauline was a little girl to him. And only two years after they married, this policeman said to her: now I'm going to do what I like, I'm sending you back to your bush, if you don't agree. If you dare open your mouth, I will take more wives if I feel like it, Miss village girl from Louboulou, I'll have your family put in prison till the end of time.

Whenever Maman Pauline tried to speak, the policeman waved his pistol at her, like in a cowboy film and shouted: 'What use to me are you, eh, Pauline? You've been pregnant twice. And twice the child was born dead, straight from your womb! So what use are you, eh? Your family are all sorcerers. They've put a *gris-gris* in your belly! You'll never have children!'

The policeman had stopped sleeping at home. He turned up for a few minutes in the morning to change his clothes, then he'd rush off again, as though our house was occupied by demons. Maman Pauline kept her mouth shut. What could she say to the guy? She knew very well that he lived with other women he loved more than her, other women he could have children with, who wouldn't die as they came out of their mother's womb. Maman Pauline left the door open all night because the policeman got angry with her if she shut it. He wanted to come and go whenever he pleased, whatever time of day. But he only came every other day, then every third day, then once a week, then once a month. Then Maman Pauline saw him no more. She didn't even try asking at the police station where he worked. By the time the policeman had been gone three months, she had another problem which made her very sad: her belly was getting bigger. And she stopped leaving the house – she didn't want the neighbours to see. She waited till nightfall to go out and do her shopping, from the women who sold soup in the streets. She wore several pagnes, to hide her belly.

Maman Pauline often tells me how, on the night when I started kicking like a little bandit to be let out of her womb, she walked all the way to the central hospital in Mouyondzi. I nearly didn't make it into this world because I was afraid of the men and women sitting round chatting in the delivery room. I thought that when I arrived on this earth there'd be silence, that I'd be all alone with her, like I was inside her, when I swam around holding on to the tube that sent me my food every day. But there you go, I didn't want my mother to be unhappy, I didn't want to go to heaven like my sisters. If people were sitting around talking, then there must be something wrong, and I wanted to know what, because no one was going to explain to me up in heaven why people like sitting around talking on earth, even when they're in a hospital room. I wanted to see these people's faces with my own eyes, hear their voices with my own ears. In fact, the people sitting round talking in the delivery room thought I was going to be silly enough to go the same way as my two sisters. But I wanted to live, I wanted to follow my mother wherever she went, I wanted to protect her against all the policemen on earth who threaten their wives with pistols when they're meant to be threatening criminals. So the nurses watched me round the clock. I watched them too, with one eye, and on their sad faces I read that they were expecting the worst, because they'd already seen my mother in this hospital, in this same room, seen her leave in tears with a stone-cold baby in her arms, heading for the morgue, where she leaves the baby in the fridge. Some of the nurses were checking to see if I was breathing still. I said to myself: 'I'm going to have a game with these adults, I'm going to show them I know their language, I know what they're thinking.' I had this little game, where I held my breath, closed my eyes, squeezed my lips and my buttocks, and sometimes went so pale I looked like the corpse of a white baby, since black babies, when they come into this world, are generally all white. And only turn black afterwards. Otherwise their parents will argue and think the real father's a white man from up town. Thinking I was truly dead, the nurses rushed towards me. They started whimpering with my mother. Suddenly I opened my eyes. I felt like shouting: leave me alone, can't you see I'm breathing? Can't you see I've been alive for three days now, and my sisters were not even here for one day? If I really wanted to go to heaven would I be hanging around here all this time like an idiot who doesn't know what he has to do to die? I may be a baby, I still know how to die, but I don't want to stop breathing! I want to live! Let me rest now, I've come a long way! And let's have a bit of quiet please. We're in a hospital here!

Maman Pauline came home with me a week after I arrived in this world. Her policeman's never shown up, though he must have heard of me. My mother heard he was already going round saying he wasn't my father, that she'd made this child with some local guy, the postman, maybe, or the palm-wine tapper, who, like the postman, passed by our house each morning. That's what they were saying, all over Mouyondzi, and people came to spy on us. But they never found a man living in our house, or who came round at midnight and left in secret at five in the morning. In the market some of the women said that my mother had had a child with a devil who came to our house at night. I don't think anyone there ever saw my face. When we went out, my mother covered my body from head to foot, leaving just two little holes so I could at least see the colour of the sky, because up there no one's wicked.

Maman Pauline left the district two months after my arrival. No way was she going to spend her time arguing with women who said untrue things about herself and me. Not that she was afraid of them, she knows how to scratch the face of a wicked woman. When she scratches a wicked woman it looks like she's written a whole book on her face, in Arabic or Chinese. But she didn't want any of that.

I don't actually know what Mouyondzi district looks like, out in the region of Bouenza, in the southern bush. Since all I've seen there is the sky, I imagine the earth must be red, like everywhere in Bouenza. That's what our teacher says in geography, anyway. I also imagine that people's animals down there – particularly pigs – go wandering wherever they like. I mention pigs because according to my mother the inhabitants of Mouyondzi love pig and eat it with plantain bananas whenever there's a party, or someone's just died. I imagine, too, that if the fathers in this district are all like Maman Pauline's policeman, there must be lots of other children without a father and lots of other mothers living alone with their children. I have no wish to go there, not now or ever, I'll only hate the people and want to wage global war on them, especially the policemen.

I feel like a real child of Pointe-Noire. Here's where I learned to walk, to talk. Here's where I first saw rain fall, and wherever you see your first rain fall, that's where you come from. Papa Roger told me that once, and I think he was right.

When she left Mouyondzi district, Maman Pauline didn't want to go back to the village where she'd been born – she knew the people of Louboulou would laugh at her. She chose the town of Pointe-Noire because Uncle René already lived there and had just finished his studies in France. With our people it is common for the children to be given the names of the uncles, and my mother gave me Uncle René's name, even though he's not my father. My uncle was very pleased my mother chose him rather than their big brother, Uncle Albert Moukila, who worked for the electricity company.

The good thing was that Uncle René was quite happy for Maman Pauline to come and live at his house, with me too, and he gave her a bit of money so she could set up her peanut business at the Grand Marché. She got up in the morning and went straight down to Mtoba, where she bought sacks of peanuts from the farmers. After that she shelled the peanuts and put them into bowls. At the Grand Marché she sat behind her table and waited for customers. Sometimes business was good, sometimes not. But even when it wasn't, she'd say it didn't matter, tomorrow would be better than today. She was never going to get rich with this business. At least she could buy me milk and nappies instead of having to ask Uncle René all the time. Now what she didn't know was, there in the Grand Marché, her life was about to change. Mine too.

. . . . .

It was one very hot Sunday afternoon. The Grand Marché was pretty empty. She looked up and saw a man in front of her table, not very tall, well-combed hair, a well-ironed shirt and a briefcase in his left hand. At first she thought it was one of those bad men who sometimes come round asking the stall-holders to pay a fee to the town hall, or else there'll be no table for them the next day at the market. When you come across a bad man, you always feel a bit afraid, but in this case she felt her legs trembling, as though her heart was about to fall into her stomach – she says that's what happens when she's in love. The man with the briefcase bought lots of peanuts and my mother guessed straightaway that anyone who buys peanuts like there's no tomorrow must have a large family to feed. No one can eat all that themselves. So she added lots of extra peanuts, and even reduced the price.

After that, the man with the briefcase turned up regularly at my mother's table. He stopped buying peanuts from anyone else, and if she wasn't there he left and came back the next day, which really annoyed the other stallholders, who now spread a rumour that Maman Pauline hid Bembé *gris-gris* under the table to snare clients, and that her peanuts were prepared overnight by the spirits, who put a bit of salt on them. They said the moment you tasted one of my mother's peanuts you were done for, you'd be condemned to return forever to her table, like it was the Congolese National Lottery, which you can never win unless you're part of the President's family.

When Maman Pauline got to her table she found the ground all around it was wet, and there was a strong smell of fish. In fact, it was the other stallholders who threw seawater on the ground so customers wouldn't stop at my mother's stand. I couldn't understand why anyone would be afraid of seawater, and Maman Pauline explained that there are lots of spirits in the sea, including the spirits of our ancestors, who are angry because they were captured and taken into slavery on the white men's plantations, and whipped from dawn till dusk. So that's why seawater is salty, from the sweat of our ancestors and their anger, which makes the waves.

My mother found it quite funny that people threw seawater under her table, as though the spirits were going to waste their precious time on a little peanut stall when there are more important things in this world. The customers still came, including the man with the briefcase. But Maman Pauline could tell this man didn't just come to buy peanuts. He had something else in mind, he had his eye on that place where men like looking at women and imagining things I'll like imagining too, when I'm twenty. Now it wasn't the man with the brief-case's fault because Maman Pauline did wear bright orange, shiny trousers stretched tight across her behind. Men just couldn't take their eyes off it, it was too good to miss. When she walked in the streets of Pointe-Noire men would turn round and whistle, but she pretended not to notice and just went on her way to the Grand Marché.

When my mother had finished serving him, the man with the briefcase would linger by her table, talking and talking. And little by little his banter did the trick, because my mother enjoyed listening to him. He finally saw me in the flesh one day when Maman Pauline put me in a big aluminium basin with bedding in, because prams were too expensive and I hated being carried on her back in a sling, the way women in our country carry their children in the street. The man with the briefcase leaned over the basin, pulled aside the bedding hiding my face and asked how old I was. Maman Pauline told him I was only five and a half months. He looked at me in silence for a few minutes, then began pulling faces, to make me laugh. He remarked how like my mother I looked, and that I wasn't crying, even though the Grand Marché was full of noise and people shouting. Maman Pauline swears at that moment I smiled at the man. And, again according to her, what my smile meant was: Maman, this is your man, you stick with him, I want this man as my father, my true father, a man who smiles like that isn't going to abandon us; besides, he's not a policeman, he's not going to threaten you with a gun, like in the films.

My mother and the man with the briefcase would go and drink in the bars at the Grand Marché. They hid away like that for months and months. Sometimes they took me with them, when there was no one to look after me. I went on smiling at the nice kind man, whenever he leaned over to look at me, and pull faces. After a year and a half they'd had enough of playing hide-and-seek as we call it in the playground at Trois-Martyrs. The man with the briefcase came to introduce himself to Uncle René one afternoon. He said his name was Roger Kimangou and he worked in the town centre at the Hotel Victory Palace. He explained that he was a responsible man and would do whatever was necessary for Maman Pauline to become his wife.

My uncle said in a quiet aside to Maman Pauline, 'I don't like this man, he's too short, it doesn't feel right.'

Maman Pauline replied, 'The President of the Republic is short, but he defeated an army of wicked men, single-handedly! And people love him, including you, you belong to his party.'

They couldn't get into much of an argument in front of the

man with the briefcase, particularly as he had a demi-john of palm wine and a white cockerel with him. The custom of our people is, if you want a woman, you have to give presents to her big brother. After that, even if you don't go to the Mairie with the woman to sign papers, it doesn't matter. Our ancestors are stronger than any papers, you can't tear the ancestors up when you fall out of love and stand round fighting in the street like deadly enemies.

Uncle René accepted the demi-john of palm wine and the white cockerel. He asked the man with the briefcase why he wanted to take a second wife, when he already had one, who he'd had lots of children with. Maman Pauline flared up at this and said she was leaving my uncle's house and not coming back. The man with the briefcase stopped her, he spoke calmly and told my uncle again that he loved my mother, he loved me too, that Maman Pauline was a good woman and he would treat her exactly equal with his first wife. He would split his salary in two: some for his first wife and some for Maman Pauline. His first wife knew all about it. He raised his right hand and swore on the name of his father and mother, both deceased.

At this my uncle said, 'Brother-in-law, let us drink! All this discussion has parched our throats!'

Before drinking the palm wine they poured a little of it on the ground so our ancestors could have a drop too, otherwise there'd be hell to pay because you mustn't do anything behind your protectors' back. And they spent the afternoon discussing Karl Marx, Engels, Lenin and the immortal Marien Ngouabi and drinking palm wine.

When the man with the briefcase was about to leave, my uncle went round back of the house with him. 'I don't want my little sister going to live in the same house as your first wife. If that happens, I will never set foot there.'

The man with the briefcase found us a house on the Avenue of Independence, not far from the house of his first wife. He bought the house for us. So it belongs to us, he always said he'd bought it with me in mind. That's why, if you read what's written on the papers for our house, you'll see my name.

As soon as I see Papa Roger coming, I'm like a different boy. I want to feel his arms around me, stay with him and hear him speak to me, feel his hands on my head. Sometimes I go and wait for him at the bus stop for Vicky's Photo Studio. When I see a little man in a brown suit getting off the bus, walking very quickly, with a briefcase in his left hand, looking straight ahead, I run towards him, like the world 100 metres champion. He lets me carry his briefcase, I take it in my left hand and I lift my chin up, walking like a grown up. I want everyone who sees us to know he's my real father. We stop at a bar, he buys a bottle of red wine, beer and lemonade. And we continue happily on our way home. I put his briefcase in the bedroom while he takes off his shoes and suit and changes his clothes, then comes and sits down in the living room. He tells my mother a few funny stories before we sit down to eat. He tells us what's happened at the Victory Palace Hotel. He tells us lots of Whites arrived this morning. One of them is a Monsieur Montoir, who's very nice to him. He talked a lot with this Monsieur Montoir, who's come from Paris, with his wife and their only child, Zachary. And little Zachary talks like a big boy, even though he's only my age. He can see I'm getting jealous of Zachary, so he tries to make me feel better. 'Michel, you talk like a big boy too. I'm sure if you meet Zachary you'll be great friends.'

While he's talking to us, I watch his face carefully, his black eyes shining with the light from the storm lamp, and I say to myself, he's got a lot of white globules, he'll go straight to Paradise, somewhere close to God. Papa Roger's a handsome man, perhaps the most handsome of all the papas in our town – and when I'm big I want to be handsome like him and take off my shoes and my suit and change my clothes and come and sit down in the living room and tell Caroline some funny stories before we sit down at the table with our two children.

I look at Papa Roger again, and I think, 'Why does he love my mother and me? He must work so hard, for our house and Maman Martine's. I say Maman Martine because I don't like saying 'stepmother', like they do round here when they talk about your father's other wife. A stepmother is a kind of witch you get in stories of the bush and the forest. A stepmother is forever cursing the child of the other woman, and her husband. Maman Martine's not a stepmother. She's my mother too.

Papa Roger always gets up at five in the morning to go and catch the bus at the Vicky's Photo Studio stop. The bus takes him to the town centre and drops him outside the Hotel Victory Palace, the big white building behind Printania, the shop where white people buy their apples. That's why when my father brings me home a nice green apple I eat it really slowly, thinking about all those people in our *quartier* who never get to eat apples. Before I take a bite, I hold it up to my nostrils. I think how far it's travelled, and how, when I eat it, I'm transported far from our little country, to other, bigger countries, where they speak languages I don't understand yet, but will do one day soon. And then I feel suddenly calm, I feel as though I'm going to live to over a hundred, like my maternal grandfather, Grégoire Moukila, that there will be an end to all the problems in this little country of ours, because the smaller a country, the bigger its problems and everyday life's impossible. I don't want all the problems of the big countries coming here and making life even more impossible than it is now because we're already too small. Sometimes when Papa Roger brings me some apples, I suddenly find myself in the middle of a great wood, in Europe, full of apple trees, and I can feel snow falling and see little snowmen grinning at me because they know my name's Michel. I lie down under one of these apple trees, on the banks of a river, it's not cold, though, not like in a European country, and I dream that I'm growing bigger.

The Victory Palace Hotel belongs to some French people. Papa Roger writes down the names of the people who arrive, and the people who leave. He's been the receptionist there for over twenty-five years; he knows his job, otherwise he wouldn't still be there. He has a telephone in front of him, the keys of all the rooms of the hotel behind him. You can't get into a room in this hotel unless Papa Roger gives you the key. To work at the reception desk you have to be able to speak French because most people who come for their holidays are French. And not only that: you have to be able to make the clients laugh. Papa Roger always thinks of something to make the Whites laugh because, he says, it's so cold over there in Europe, people don't laugh much. Their face muscles are frozen. And if they've had a good laugh they give my father some money the day they leave. The more generous ones, like Monsieur Montoir, give things like the tape recorder and a cassette of the singer with the moustache.

Before he tells his jokes to the Whites, my father tries them out at home. He tells us to sit down and listen to him. He promises we'll be doubled-up laughing because the jokes in question are extremely funny, he himself finds them very funny. He takes out a piece of paper from his pocket and reads out loud.

'Listen to this one: one dry season, a workman's told to dig a hole by the river bank. He says, "I can't work between a croc and a hard place!"'

No one laughs, but he's doubled up.

He goes on, 'When President Georges Pompidou was annoyed, he'd shout, "That's the least of my woollies!"'

No one laughs, but he's doubled up.

He goes on, 'A man goes to the dentist for a bridge, but it's too expensive. He gets up and walks out, saying "Oh no, that's a bridge too far!"'

No one laughs, but he's doubled up.

He adds, a little disappointed by our reaction, 'If you want to find out about your family tree, consult a gynaecologist!'

Still no one laughs. We watch him wipe away his tears, he looks back at us, and we start laughing for the very reason that he couldn't make us laugh. He puts his piece of paper back in his pocket. Maybe the Whites will laugh when he tells them his jokes, but we couldn't work out when we were supposed to.

Uncle René's always criticising my father's work. He thinks Papa Roger's office isn't a real office, just a place where the hotel guests come to pick up their room key. He also thinks my father has no power, compared to him, since he's the administrative and financial director of the CFAO. He thinks when the bosses of the Hotel Victory Palace talk to my father he looks at the floor and says 'yes boss, yes boss!' He thinks that's how black people used to reply to their white bosses before our countries got independence. My uncle says a receptionist in a hotel is just like a Boy working for the Whites, that it's shameful.

So what? As far as I see, everyone's someone's boy. Even Uncle René's someone's boy because there's always someone higher up who says, 'Do this, don't do that.' The only person who's not someone's boy is the President of our Republic. And even then I'm not sure because our President isn't as powerful as the presidents of countries like the United States of America, the USSR or France. Put him in front of presidents like that, and our President curls up small, like he's their boy, suddenly he's the receptionist and they call all the shots. When the Americans, the Russians and the French speak, our President looks down at the floor, too, and answers 'at your service, boss!' And if our President refuses, if he's stubborn and disrespectful towards the Americans, the Russians and the French, they can bombard our country in a single day, blast us off the map of the world or give our land, our oil, our river, our Atlantic ocean to Zaire, who would be only too happy to accept.

So Uncle René's the receptionist at the Hotel Victory Palace. What's wrong with that? Jobs are like hoops. You have to jump through them. I don't know where I heard that – I think it's what Monsieur Mutombo says when parents come and shout at him in his workshop because he's late with the school uniforms because he's always going on about Algeria. They insult him, tell him he's rubbish, and that's when he says jobs are like hoops. You have to jump through them. Everyone laughs then, because he's talking about people jumping through hoops when he's got a limp.

In fact my uncle doesn't realise that Papa Roger is a very intelligent man, who knows what's going on all over the world. He stayed at school right up to his Certificate of Primary Studies, which is like having a diploma that lets you go to a

French university and study with the Whites. Also, Papa Roger always reads the newspapers he finds at work. The Whites leave them at reception when they've finished reading them over their coffee. They also leave books. My father takes them and brings them home and says to us, 'Don't you touch my books, now, I'll read them when I'm retired.'

Caroline walks past our house. My heart starts pounding. I'm happy, I leave the house, I run towards her. I'm out of breath, as though I'd been running for an hour and she doesn't wait for me to get my breath back.

'Why are you running like that? I haven't come to see you!'

'But you're here, outside our house, and I thought...'

'You thought what? Am I not allowed to walk past your house then? The Avenue of Independence is open to everyone, you know!'

She makes out she's going to the market, but I don't believe her. You don't set out to market like that. She hasn't got a basket with her. What's she going to put her shopping in?

I tell her to come on inside with me.

'Come on, my parents are out. We'll be alone in the house and...'

'No, I don't want to!'

I look her up and down. She's got nice new red shoes on. I like her white dress with yellow flowers.

'That's a lovely dress...'

'Don't you try smooth talking me! You leave my dress out of this, I'm not wearing it for you! You think I'd put on a dress for you?'

'Listen, stop talking like that and come inside with me.'

'What for? It's all over between you and me!'

'I want to show you something. You'll see, it's really amazing and…'

'No. There's nothing amazing in your house!'

She looks at me as though she doesn't know me, as if I was her enemy.

'So you're still cross with me?'

'Yes I am. We're not married any more, we're divorced! I'm never having two children, a white dog and a red five-seater car with you!'

'Why not?'

''Cause I'm marrying someone else.'

'Oh, right, I see. And would it by any chance be a boy called Mabélé you're thinking of marrying?'

She's astonished. 'You're not meant to know that! Anyway, who told you his name?'

'Lounès…'

'He's not meant to tell you his name! I was meant to tell you myself, today, not him!'

'So you did come to see me…'

'No, I'm going to the market!'

Deep down inside, I think: 'I have to calm her down and calm myself down too. If we both get angry we'll end up getting divorced for real. And she's angrier than I am, so I'd better stay calm.'

'I don't want us to get divorced, Caroline…'

'Well you're just a horrible little boy, so that's too bad!'

'I know, but I was a bit cross because you did my mother's braids and that's why she went out that Sunday, but it's over now, I'm not angry now…'

'It's too late! I've already promised Mabélé he can be my husband and buy me the red five-seater car.'

Now that really got me. That damn Mabélé really annoys me. I go on the attack.

'I'm going to tell my uncle not to sell you that car! He won't let you have it, he's my uncle and he's the only person who sells cars in this town!'

'If you tell your uncle that I won't braid your mother's hair, and she'll be ugly then, like Jérémie's mother!'

She looks me straight in the eye to see if I'm worried about her not doing Maman Pauline's hair any more. But I'm actually quite pleased. Suits me fine, at least if my mother's hair isn't braided she'll stop going out and I can stay with her on Sundays.

But Caroline's realised what I'm thinking and she adds: 'And besides, if you tell your uncle not to sell us the red five-seater car, I'll never speak to you again, ever again, and we'll go and order our car somewhere else and you and I will be deadly enemies! And if I see you in the street I'll spit on the ground!'

She fumbles in the pocket of her dress and takes out a piece of paper, which she unfolds and passes to me. It's a page torn out of the *Redoute* catalogue. There's a photo of a girl and a boy in front of a red five-seater car. They're about our age, but white. The girl has a white dress and a red hat and shoes. The boys are all dressed in black with a white shirt and a bow tie. They look like they've just got married and the photographer's just said: stand over there and I'll take your picture.

I look at the picture again, close up. Caroline's guessed what I'm looking for. 'The white dog's not in the picture. He's at home with their two children.'

That makes me want to laugh because I've already looked through *La Redoute* at Monsieur Mutombo's workshop. He copies the European clothes out of it. The customers choose their style in the catalogue, then Monsieur Mutombo tells them if it's possible to make it, how much it will cost and how long it will take. Now I know they don't sell cars at *La Redoute*. But I don't want to annoy Caroline, I want to carry on talking to her because I love her. Because I want to have two children with her. So I need to find a good reason why she should leave this Mabélé.

'Lounès said Mabélé's ugly, he's not even as good looking as me! Your children are going to be ugly like Mabélé, if you had them with me they'd be attractive.'

'That's not true! Mabélé is intelligent and he's two years older than us!'

'Yeah, and what else has he got that I haven't?'

'He's read lots of books.'

'Oh yeah? Which books has he read then?'

'Marcel Pagnol.'

'Who's Marcel Pagnol?'

'See, you don't even know! He writes books about his mother and his father and their four castles. And Mabélé says he's going to buy me a beautiful castle like the one in the books by Marcel Pagnol.'

'Can't you tell he's lying? A book about castles, that's a book for capitalists who exploit the proletariat!'

'Well then, while you're busy slagging off Mabélé and Marcel Pagnol, what have you read?'

I don't answer. I try to think of the books we've read in class, but they're just little extracts in the primer we have, and in the book by the President of our Republic. If I mention the book by the President of the Republic, Caroline's going to laugh at me. So I think hard about the reading book we have in class, with its extracts, and I say: 'I've read the fables of La Fontaine!'

'Yes, but it's the animals that talk in those stories, I've recited those in class too. Marcel Pagnol has real people, who live in real castles!'

I think about Papa Roger's books in the bedroom. I've never looked inside them, they're still waiting for when my father retires. I don't even know a single title.

'And anyway, Mabélé writes me poems every day, in his poems I have bright blue eyes and really long blond hair like the dolls little girls have in Europe. You never wrote me any poems. You didn't love me! You're a bad husband, now stop answering back, I'm going now, yes I am, I'm off!'

And she walks away and I shout, 'Come back, come back Caroline!'

She can't hear me. She's already gone. She's not going to the market, she's going home. So she did come to see me. No other reason, I say to myself.

My father's shouting, 'No! It can't be true! It's unbelievable! They can't do this to me! What have I done to deserve it?'

Maman Pauline, who was outside, comes running back into the house. Her wrap's almost slipped off her waist and she snatches at it hastily.

'What is it, Roger?'

'They've overthrown the Shah of Iran!'

My mother shouts angrily, 'Is there really nothing else to listen to on the radio? Besides, he's not even one of ours! That radio's going to drive you nuts!'

My father fiddles with the aerial as though he's not sure the information he's just heard can be true. Sometimes the sound cuts out; Papa Roger moves about, stands by the window, as though the news comes into the house that way, and if we close the window there'll be no more radio. He tries each corner of the dining room and I follow him like a shadow.

Whenever the radio starts crackling, I realise how far America is from our little country. But then I realise Radio Congo crackles too, and it makes me want to say to my father, 'Let's sit down again, we'll hear better that way, if we sit at the table, like we do when we're eating our meat and beans.'

Papa Roger's standing by the window and I'm behind him. He turns round, and bends down, so the radio's just level with my ears. The American, Roger Guy Folly, is talking about Iran.

He explains where it is, what language they speak, a language we don't speak here. I hear names I can't pronounce, and places I've never heard of. Papa Roger tells us again that Iran is far far away, in Western Asia, and the capital's called Teheran. And when I ask him if the Iranians have the same money as us, he says no.

'So how do they buy food at the market if they don't have our money?' my mother asks.

'With their own money.'

I think there must be another reason why Iran doesn't want to use our money – because the Iranians don't want to have to look at our President's head on every one of our notes and coins. In Iran they have a revolutionary leader, like us, and it must be *his* head on the notes and coins. They are our brothers because we have a revolutionary leader, like them. All leaders are brothers, so we must help this brother of ours.

Looking at my mother, Papa Roger tells us that the shah who's been overthrown isn't an animal, he's a man, even if in our folk stories the animals are like kings, ruling the earth, and men must respect them, and tip their hats when they walk by.

'The shah's a man, ok, an important man, but the new top leader in Iran is another Iranian, the Ayatollah Khomeyni. There's ingratitude for you! He's been totally straight with Ayatollah Khomeyni, he even pardoned him when he was out to undermine the revolution which was there to give women the vote! What's going to happen there now, eh? Now Khomeyni's trying to get hold of the great man, and fling him in prison. What sort of a world do we live in?'

Papa Roger looks at us, and shrugs, because he knows our sadness is not the same as his sadness. It's the first time we've ever heard of the Shah and Ayatollah Khomeyni.

When Maman Pauline asks us to sit down at table, my father comes away from the window, looking disappointed. He goes outside, and takes the radio with him. My mother signals at me not to follow him.

'You sit down, let him get on with his Iranians, we'll eat.'

From where I am I can see my father sitting under the mango tree, his hands on his head and the radio cassette player on the ground. From a distance we hear the words of 'Sitting by my tree'. And when the singer gets to the bit about 'alter ego' and 'saligaud', I stop eating and think to myself, 'my father's thinking about his own *alter ego*'s problems with its *saligauds*'.

My parents are arguing on the other side of the wall between their room and mine.

I hear my mother say, 'It's not fair! If God wanted me only to have one child, why couldn't he at least give me a daughter instead of a son? Look at the Mutombos, they're lucky: they've got Lounès and Caroline, a boy and a girl!'

She starts to cry, and when she cries it's as though her tears were coming from my eyes, not hers. And I think too: It's not fair that Maman Pauline had a boy instead of a girl. And it makes me want to dress up as a girl, talk like a girl, walk like a girl, pee like a girl. Perhaps then my mother will only be half as unhappy. It's not easy to copy what girls do and hide the fact that you're a boy. People will just say, 'You're not a girl, you're a boy disguised as a girl.' And they'll throw stones at you in the street like a mangy dog. And they'll say, 'If you think you're a girl, what did you do about that thing between your legs, did you change that into a girl's thing too?'

No, better stop thinking like that, since it's not my fault I'm not a girl.

I go on listening to what they're saying behind the wall. Papa Roger's explaining that the reason children turn up in my mother's womb but don't make it out into the world is because they get lost somewhere along the way. So, instead of arriving here below they go directly to heaven, which is not the best way of making people on earth happy.

Maman Pauline reminds my father that before me she had two daughters in two and a half years, and both died the same way: they came out of her womb ok, they cried, then they just closed their eyes for ever. And by the time someone checked to see they were breathing, it was too late – they'd already gone.

When Maman Pauline reminds Papa Roger about this, I listen carefully. I want to know, after all this time, what those two sisters of mine were called. No, she doesn't say their names, she says 'my two daughters' or 'my two queens'. Am I like them? I think I must be, because I look very like Maman Pauline and I can't imagine my two sisters not looking like my mother but like some horrible policeman from Mouyondzi.

So what can my sisters have seen the day they arrived on earth, that made them want to turn round and go back to heaven quite so soon? Did the nurses who helped them out have red globules? I can understand one of the sisters leaving, but why, when the next one was due out, a year and a half later, did she do the same thing? What's going on up there in heaven, why do some children head straight on up there as fast as they can? One way I have of cheering myself up is to imagine my sisters are stars and perhaps they talk to me without my even knowing. Now, when night falls, I always look for two stars close to one another. And there always are, if you look hard enough. Since I don't know my sisters' names, I've decided to call my big sister 'Sister Star'. I haven't got a name for the other one. I keep looking, I keep trying, but I still can't think of one. Until I think of something pretty I'm going to call her 'Sister No-name'.

I'm hiding under my sheet, trying not to move around, because every time I move I feel like the mosquito net's going to fall down on top of me. I've got my ears open. I don't want to miss what's being said behind that wall. Papa Roger's talking now. He's speaking very quietly, and I can hardly hear him. So I come out from under my sheet and pull the mosquito net to one side and get out of bed and stand next to the wall.

Papa Roger's trying to comfort my mother.

'It'll be ok, we'll have more children, I promise…'

'Lots more?'

'Yes.'

'Roger, I want daughters, even just one, I don't want boys, I've already got one and—'

'That's not up to us, Pauline. Let's ask the Lord for a child, to start off with, let's not worry if it's a boy or a girl.'

My mother falls silent. Papa Roger goes on talking. He says that the children he had with Maman Martine are my mother's children too, and my brothers and sisters. He adds that he's never made any distinction between them and me. It's true, when I go to Maman Martine's, she treats me as though I'd come out of her own belly. Besides, my brothers and sisters are very fond of me. Papa Roger also says that I love little Maximilien, that's it's touching to see little Félicienne weeing all over me, and that Marius talks to me a lot, Mbombie respects me, Ginette looks out for me, Georgette is a true big sister to me, and Yaya Gaston, big brother to all of us, always wants me to sleep with him in his studio.

Whatever he says, Maman Pauline insists that she wants to have children from her own belly because if I fall out with my sisters and brothers from the other house they'll probably remind me that I'm not their blood brother, and they'll say it deliberately to upset me.

'Roger, are you blind and deaf? You know people round here

are saying you're not Michel's real father, that your children with Martine are not his real brothers and sisters, and that they're not my children! Now stop talking to me like I'm an idiot!'

At this my father starts to get angry. He talks so loud you'd think he was actually in my bedroom.

'That's just stupid talk, Pauline! Stupid! Are we going to spend our lives worrying about the local gossip? We don't give a damn about them, don't do their dirty washing for them! You mustn't listen to them, I love you and nobody's going to come between us, d'you hear?'

'Yes, but did you know, at the Grand Marché the other sellers say the only reason I have lots of customers is because I'm a witch and I can't have children?'

'Pauline, listen, we'll go to see a doctor, and you'll see, we'll sort it out!'

'We've already seen doctors, that's all we've been doing for the past few years, I'm sick of it! Is there a single doctor in this town we haven't seen since we've been together?'

'I've just been recommended a new doctor, he…'

'I don't want to go to another Congolese doctor! He'll only tell everyone our business and people will go on laughing at me!'

'It's a white doctor, everyone knows he's the best in town, and he's new…'

There's a silence. I think to myself, Maman Pauline's going to say yes.

My father continues, 'Anyway, those gossips down at the Grand Marché are idiots! People should mind their own business! I'm going to show them I'm not a nobody! Next month I'll give you some money, you can set up a business away from here. You can go into the bush, to Las Bandas, and buy bunches of bananas there. Then you can load them onto a train and take them to Brazzaville to sell. They say that's where business is best at the moment.'

This set my alarm bells ringing. Maman Pauline would be away at least one week a month. I feel like banging on the wall, to tell my parents I don't want this, they must ask my opinion too. There are three of us in this house, they shouldn't take decisions without consulting me. The people in Brazzaville will kill my mother. Brazzaville's too far away. That's where the President of the Republic lives, who runs this country. You have to sleep two whole days on the train, almost, to get there. What's Papa Roger thinking of?

They carry on halfway through the night. I think of Maman Pauline going once a month to Brazzaville. I turn this whole question of her wanting children at any price round and round in my head. What can a doctor do, even a white one, if the children inside a woman choose to go straight to heaven without stopping off on earth? Does any man, white, black, yellow or red, really have the power to change God's plan? Wouldn't it be better just to go and pray really hard at the church of Saint-Jean-Bosco even if the prayers there do go on too long?

My parents have switched the light out now, and are talking very quietly. My mother was crying earlier, but now she's laughing and my father says, 'Hush, don't laugh so loud. Michel can hear us.'

'No, he'll be fast asleep by now. I know him.'

One day when I'm older, I'll take you far away
To where the crabs walk on the sand of the Côte Sauvage.
Our little girl will wear red shoes
Shiny red shoes and a white dress
With yellow flowers
Like you
Our son will wear a hat
I want to wear a hat too
One day when I'm older.

I'll take our daughter by the hand,
Her right hand,
We'll call her Pauline like my mother
You'll take our son by the hand,
His left hand,
We'll call him Roger like my father.
Our little white dog will stay in the car,
A fine red car, with room for five,
We'll call him Miguel, like my uncle's dog
But he won't be fierce,
He'll be a nice dog,
And eat at table with us.
I promise you this, I'll read all the books
by Marcel Proust
One day when I'm older.

But I won't build a castle for you
It'll just be a little house, a pretty house of wood,
Like Maman Pauline's and Papa Roger's.
Castles are too big,
I might lose my dreams in a castle,
Then they'll call me a capitalist
And I don't want that, I don't want their red globules
If I do, my sisters might not know me
They might show me the door when I get to Heaven...

Michel

ounès says: 'You missed something yesterday, I
looked everywhere for you.'

It's about Jérémie's mother, a horrible woman, who goes
round insulting all the local mothers. This time it seems she's
had a row with her husband. It all started inside their house, in
front of their children, and ended up in the street with people all
round them, like a football match at the Tata Lubuko stadium.
Lounès tries to imitate Jérémie's mother's voice for me, talking
rudely to her husband and yelling in front of everyone, 'You
asshole, you idiot, you useless bugger! Call yourself a husband,
do you? You can't even do right by me in bed these days, not like
a real man! I've done everything, I have, I've tried everything,
and you never managed anything, just went on sleeping, snoring
your head off! Impotent bastard! What are you, a husband, or a
post, not even a post for electricity, like the ones in the Avenue
of Independence! No woman could put up with that! Just you
wait and see, things are going to change from now on! It's time
for a revolution, I'm going to find a good-looking young man
around here and that fine young man's going to give me such
a good seeing to of an evening, by the time you get round to
touching me I'll be snoring my head off like you! You think I'm
only good for having children, do you? Bastard!'

I laugh, but only to please him. I went and whistled three
times outside their house today, so we could go down to the
river together. I want to show him something, not listen to what

this woman I don't even like's been saying, when she's already been rude to Maman Pauline because her business is doing too well. So I let Lounès get to the end of his impression of her. I laugh again when he adds that Jérémie's mother was wearing a red pagne tight across her behind and lifted her pagne high up her thighs. She asked the crowd if anyone wanted to give her a seeing to till she was too tired to move. Some of the men whistled and shouted, 'Me! Me! I'll give you a seeing to!'

Lounès noticed I wasn't laughing as much now.

'You wanted to tell me something, Michel…'

At this I get my piece of paper out of my pocket and hold it out to him.

'Can you give that to Caroline?'

He takes the piece of paper and starts reading what I've written. My heart's all shaken up. I close my eyes for a few minutes. When I open them again I see his face, it's like a mask. He says nothing. He starts reading again. Can't he read my writing?

'Michel, this isn't a poem! It's fine, but it's not a poem. In a poem the end of every line has to sound the same. Listen, I'll recite you a real poem, you'll see, at the end of every line you hear the same sounds:'

> *My baby, sleeping close to me, all pink and fresh,*
> *So like a tiny drowsy Jesus in his crèche;*
> *Your sleep so free of care, so calm, so full of love*
> *You do not hear the bird who sings far from the light.*
> *But I breathed in the heavy sweetness of the night*
>
> *And the sombre mysteries of the world above.*

I take back my piece of paper and put it back in my pocket.

I haven't read the poem he's just recited in class. He says it's by Victor Hugo, for his daughter. When he says that it makes me think of the photo of Victor Hugo on the wall at my uncle's house.

We don't mention my poem, though I want to know if he thinks it's good or bad. We listen to the grass singing in the wind and it makes us sleepy.

Lounès stands up and says he has to go to karate club. It's just started, over in Savon, run by someone called Maître John.

'I have to be there on the dot of five o'clock.'

'Who's this Maître John?'

'He's this really strong man, he flies through the air, like in the Bruce Lee films. He's a black belt, sixth degree. As soon as I learn how to fly like that, I'll teach you.'

He can see I'm still feeling sad, so before we say goodbye, he touches my right shoulder and says, 'I really want to help you, but Caroline's gone to stay at my mother's sister's house, over in the Fouks *quartier*. I don't know when she's coming back. Anyway, it'll give you time to get your poem right.'

The American, Roger Guy Folly announces that the president of Uganda – called Idi Amin Dada – has just fled his own country because his neighbours in Tanzania have marched into the capital, called Kampala. The Tanzanians were angry because the Ugandan military had invaded Tanzania, supposedly to get rid of the Ugandans who were making trouble for Idi Amin Dada.

When I hear Papa Roger say that name, 'Idi Amin Dada', I howl with laughter. He looks at me very sternly, like I've committed a sin. 'Careful, Michel, it's no laughing matter! This is a serious business. Are you aware this president has killed over three hundred thousand people? And not just Ugandans, he's been killing foreigners too, for the past eight years he's been in power. He doesn't just kill, kill and kill again, he eats people too, he cuts their heads off, and their private parts too, like meat at the Grand Marché.'

That does make me stop laughing at the name of the Ugandan president, even though I still think it's funny to be called 'Dada', like the dog that lives near us, with a wiggly tail and one eye that waters all the time.

My father turned down the radio so he could explain to us that Idi Amin Dada was a monster, worse than a dragon, and ate people with spicy pepper and salt. I'm amazed to hear that in fact he couldn't read very well, when he was almost two metres high. Why didn't he take the time to go to school like everyone else? Ok, you're going to say Maman Pauline can't really read or write either, but she's never killed anyone and she speaks French well, you can still speak a language even if you don't know how to read or write it. Otherwise, how come we manage to speak all our languages – like lingala, munukutuba, bembé, lari, mbochi or vili – without learning to read or write? It's not my mother's fault she didn't go to school when she was little, like I do. Maman Pauline told me that when she was little, people were so stupid they said school wasn't good for women, it would make them argue with their husbands about everything, and make them refuse to obey when their husbands ordered them about. If a woman goes to school, they'd say, she's finished, she'll end up talking French like those big cheeses over in France, saying NO every five minutes, like white women, who manage to shout at their husbands without getting wallopped. Even if Maman Pauline never went to school, she's still more intelligent than Idi Amin Dada, who killed over three hundred thousand people and ate some of them with salt and spicy pepper. Why didn't they catch him, instead of letting him escape and hide away in a Muslim country? My father reels off the names of the countries in question: Libya (capital, Tripoli), Saudi Arabia (capital, Riyad). Saudi Arabia gave the criminal a quiet little house with people to prepare his food, when there are people who've never killed over three hundred thousand people dying of hunger on this continent. Is that normal? Do you have to go out and kill over three hundred thousand people to get free housing in a Muslim country or what? And they give him pocket money every month, like he's some good pupil who's done well at school, when he never even went to one.

Yes, Idi Amin really is a monster, worse than a dragon. I don't want to hear any more about him, though Papa Roger's determined to make us listen. Since Maman Pauline's listening carefully, even though politics isn't really her thing, I can't really leave the table, it would look rude, people would think that boy Michel isn't interested in what's going on in a country that's part of our continent.

Papa Roger explains again that Idi Amin Dada was a military man who came to power by a *coup d'état*. Well that doesn't surprise me one bit, what self-respecting country's going to say to someone who can't read and write, 'You can't read, you can't write, but don't worry, you can still go and speak on our behalf to the whole of the rest of the world'? And how is this illiterate going to manage to sign the papers that real presidents who've been to school sign when they all get together? How will he know when he's actually signing his permission for the capitalist countries to steal the wealth of the Ugandans, for example? The worst thing is, Papa Roger says Idi Amin Dada was also the president of the Organisation for African Unity, the OAU, which is like being the head of all the African countries. The African presidents made him that, and not just for a joke either. It suited the Europeans very well that Idi Amin Dada couldn't read or write. In this case that meant the English – it wasn't just the French that colonised our continent. They had to leave a few countries for other Europeans too, otherwise a war would break out among the Whites. And the English said: 'It's a good thing Idi Amin Dada can't read or write, it means we'll be able to control him at a distance even if colonisation is meant to be over in his country.'

This makes Papa Roger really angry. 'The man's a dictator, but even the United States and Israel supported his *coup d'état* to become president! And after the *coup d'état* he stuffed the army with his own people and threw out people from other ethnic groups, and had them killed, the monster. He was so crazy, he woke up one morning looking sad and solemn, saying "I had a dream, sent straight from heaven"! It's not like he's a black American, like Martin Luther King! Why should his dream be special?'

Everyone has dreams, I think to myself. The problem is, according to my father, Idi Amin Dada had a really big dream: God asked him to drive out all the Asians from his country, even though they were the ones who ran the shops, so that the Ugandans could eat three times a day. Could God really be that wicked, to make someone dream a dream like that? Idi Amin Dada did drive out the Asians, saying, 'We're going to run our country ourselves now, we'll manage our own shops and businesses. We're sick of you eating the Ugandans' bread. If you haven't left Uganda, my ancestors' land, in three months from now, be warned. Now get out, leave everything, just take your toothbrush, pants and sandals.'

So the poor Asian people ran round madly like headless chickens, even though they'd been in Uganda for a long long time. They'd forgotten they were Asian, and the people in Asia had forgotten they had brothers who'd become Ugandan blacks. The poor Ugandan Asians went and hid in a neighbouring country, where nobody knew them.

Idi Amin Dada got more and more crazy by the day, he killed off entire villages, and if you didn't agree with him he'd cut your head off, or your genitals. His supporters – the Americans and Israelis – started saying to themselves, 'We'd better get out of this country, the president's sick, he's really crazy, we'd better stop selling him arms or one day he's going to turn them on us. And all the English people who'd stayed in Uganda after independence thought: 'We'll get out now too, it looks like things are going to end badly around here, we've never seen anything like it on the Black continent, when this guy's finished eating all the black flesh around here he's going to start putting us Whites in his pot.' And Idi Amin, who didn't care, replied: 'Yeah, that's right, you feeble old ex-colonisers-you, get out of my country, I'm telling you now, I'm going to make friends with the Russians and the Libyans, they like a good deal too, and they'll sell me lots of lovely weapons so I can go on massacring the Ugandans and the neighbouring countries that make trouble for me.'

And to really annoy the Israelis, who used to be his friends and were now his sworn enemies, Idi Amin Dada started chatting up the people in a country called Palestine. He invited the Palestinians to Uganda and said to them, 'You can come here if you like, the Israelis are always against you Palestinians, but I, Idi Amin Dada, will give you a huge place where you can have your office, it's a really good building, in fact it'll be in the same building as the Israeli embassy! Which is good, because then you can take your revenge on them, and I'll support you, all the way.'

Papa Roger explained that the Israelis are Jewish, and the Palestinians are mostly Arabs, and these two peoples have been fighting for many many years. Maman Pauline asks why, and my father replies, 'It's too long to explain all that now, I get confused myself, it's all to do with politics and religion and one people killing another and lots of countries don't recognise that Palestine's a country, just like us.'

And I think to myself: 'If it's not a country just like us, then what is it? Does nobody live there? Are there no children like me, going to school? Are there no roads, no cars to hoot when there's a traffic jam? Do they not have houses, or a flag, or music, or schools or a president?' Well, at least Papa Roger agrees that Palestine is a country, like it or not, and that the Palestinians' president's name is Yasser Arafat, it's a sort of nickname.

I'm just thinking how Yasser Arafat is a nice name, it sounds nice, when my father adds that there is a serious problem with this Palestinian guy.

'I'm disappointed in Yasser Arafat: he agreed to be the witness at the wedding of Idi Amin Dada, killer of over three hundred thousand people, when he married a fifth wife.'

When I hear that, I start to hate his name too.

My head's going to burst, it's letting in things more complicated than the ones they teach Lounès at Trois-Glorieuses Secondary School. I can hear my brain beginning to boil as Papa Roger starts telling us the story of a plane that landed in the capital of Uganda, with gangsters in it, who supported the Palestinians. The Palestinian supporters had diverted the plane and were threatening to kill the poor passengers if some Palestinians in prison somewhere or other weren't released. Idi Amin Dada was delighted to act as referee in this affair, so the whole world would think he was a good guy, with lots of white globules. He calmed everyone down, made long speeches, went to see the passengers trapped in the plane. But because the Israelis get angry about anything to do with the Palestinians, they sent their famous special forces, the scary ones, zooming into Uganda, and they set the hostages free. Papa Roger says that when the Israelis carry out an operation like that, they are very efficient and always succeed, because they train people for special missions like that, and sometimes the agents are actually women, whereas in our army they think women can't be soldiers.

Before they left Uganda with the people they'd freed, the Israelis took the opportunity to bomb the Ugandans' war planes. This made Idi Amin Dada very angry and he killed all the Ugandans working at the airport because he thought it was because of their stupidity that the Israelis had been able to land in his country, free the hostages and bomb the war planes. If he had no war planes, how was he going to defend his own country or attack neighbouring countries like Tanzania? He was so angry he even drove all the foreigners out of his country, and killed even more Ugandans. And because he thought no one was prepared to recognise he was the most powerful man in the world, he decided: 'I'll make myself a Field Marshal, I want lots of war medals pinned to my front, from my neck to the zipper of my trousers, and I want the whole world to know that I am the warrior who banished the English, so you must call me The King of Scotland, period. I want all foreigners who come to do business in my country to crawl on their hands and knees before me, like animals. Especially the English.'

Uncle René's coming to see us today because it's Saint Michel's Day. I don't actually know who this Saint Michel is, and I always wonder why my uncle chose to call me Michel. If Michel's a saint, it must be a story in the Bible somewhere, that's where you find all the saints and other people connected to God. On the other hand, when I look on the calendar it says Saint Michel's Day is the twenty-ninth September, which is the day and month I was born. So Uncle René must have looked at the calendar before he said to my mother, 'Let's keep it simple, I'll look at the calendar and just give him the name of the saint's day he was born on.'

So this year on the twenty-ninth September, as usual, my uncle brought me a plastic lorry, a little spade and a little rake, so I can play at farming. He says if ever there's a real revolution in our country, it will come from the farming community, from the peasants, the people who love the land. That's who the communists are fighting for, not for the people sitting in offices exploiting their fellow men. You need to get children into good habits so they'll love farming, which man has been doing since the world began.

We listen to my uncle talking about farming and telling us what Karl Marx and Engels think about it. Afterwards, he looks over at Maman Pauline. 'Engels was right and I agree with him: until now philosophers have only interpreted the world, now it must be changed...'

I repeat what he's just said to myself, inside my head, because I like the sound of it and my uncle says it shaking his fist like he wants to get into a fight with the enemies of Revolution. He can tell my mother and I don't understand what he's saying, so he leaves the house, goes out to his car and comes back two minutes later with a little book which he hands to me, even though my mother was the one he was quoting communists at.

'Here, have this, Michel. Everything I've been telling you is in this book. There's more in this book than in the bible, these are scientific truths, not just opium for fooling the masses.'

I take the book, and read the title, which begins with a difficult word to pronounce: *Ludwig Feuerbach and the End of Classical German Philosophy*. The guy who wrote it is called Friedrich Engels. Yes, I've seen his photo, at my uncle's house. Now I know that Engels' first name is Friedrich. Uncle René has always said 'Engels', never 'Friedrich Engels'.

There's isn't a picture of Friedrich Engels on the back of this book. I would have liked to compare it with the one at my uncle's house. Perhaps when someone's famous they stop putting their photo on the back of the books they write, and if they do put someone's photo on the back of the book it's to get them known, because no one has heard of them yet. Is Engels more famous than our President? I think he must be, and that's why on the book our President wrote there's a big photo of him, smiling.

I open the book by Engels just to see if there are any photos in it. There aren't, there are only words, in really small type, as if they didn't want us children to be able to read what it says.

'Michel, don't read it! You're still too young to understand. Even my comrades on the People's Neighbourhood Committee find it hard. Engels was a true visionary! The world has to change, and the change can only come about through farming; the peasants must own their means of production, we must put an end to capitalist profit, and set up a true proletariat dictatorship! And how can this be done? I'll tell you: we must re-read history, as Marx tells us, in the light of historical materialism or more correctly, new materialism, because in fact, though the popular masses – supposedly the beneficiaries of Marxist thought – don't like to hear it, Marx never talked about historical materialism, but about new materialism! It's a crucial distinction, and I might even say, a fundamental one. Do you follow?'

We nod our heads, though we still don't understand. He takes this as encouragement, and he goes on, 'It's blindingly obvious: all social relationships are of necessity founded on confrontation, textually speaking you might almost say on the class struggle. Our relationships are based on our everyday experience and not on ideology, I mean, the superstructure, since we now know that ideology will never change the world for us in the sense that it changes our living conditions, or our social relationships, etc. Marx is quite clear about that, he set it down in black and white, and I quote: *The new materialism sees things from the perspective of human society, or social humanity*, unquote.'

Talking about Engels, Lenin and Karl Marx, and the immortal Marien Ngouabi makes him sweat heavily. He takes a handkerchief from his pocket and wipes his brow. He's just realised that in fact we haven't understood a word he's been saying and once more he turns to my mother. 'Well, I'll leave it there. I get the feeling I'm preaching in the Sahara desert. You come with me, we need to sort out a few things. But not in front of the boy.'

They leave the house and go and talk out in the yard. But

they talk too loud, and I hear everything. Yet again, it's about the inheritance of my grandmother Henrietta Ntsoko's land. She was married to my grandfather, Grégoire Moukila, the chief of Louboulou village. My grandfather had land, chickens, sheep, goats, pigs, cattle, manioc fields and maize. He left it all to my grandmother. Now she's dead, Uncle René claims everything's his, because he's the older brother and my mother will have to wait till he dies to recover my grandmother's inheritance, along with Uncle René's.

Maman Pauline disagrees.

'René, this is family, not your politics that come from books by Angèle.'

'Engels!'

'Whoever! This is about our family. Why are you telling me these lies? You've already taken our brother's house, when it should be his children who get it!'

'Are you kidding? Why should his children get the house?'

'Because children should be the ones who inherit!'

'Oh no, that's a typical capitalist point of view. You see – we're still all under the sway of imperialism! We need to get back to our own traditions, get back in touch with ourselves. This house belonged to my brother and it's my job to look after it because I was the one who paid for his medicines when he was in hospital. And don't forget, I bought Albert's coffin and fed the people who came to his wake! What did Albert's children actually do for him while he was ill at the Adolphe-Cissy Hospital?'

The deceased brother they're talking about was my grandfather's oldest child, and worked for the electricity company in Pointe-Noire. He died when I was very small. Now I realise the beautiful house where Uncle René and his wife and children live is in fact Uncle Albert Moukila's house. My mother sometimes talks to me about his children, who I've never met. Some of them, apart from the older sister, Albertine, have names that make me giggle. The cousin they call 'Abeille' comes after Albertine and has studied in the USSR. Then there's 'Pretty Boy' Firmin, who has a little amateur band in the Rex *quartier*. Then there's Gorgeous Djoudjou, who's finishing his studies in France. Finally, there are the twins, Gilbert 'the Magician' and Nzoussi 'Miss Picky', who call my mother 'Papa Pauline'. Uncle René threw them all out of their father's house and took the inheritance for himself, as if he'd earned all this wealth through hard work.

'This time I'm not going to let you take all our mother's things,' Maman Pauline continues.

'You only have to wait till I die, then you'll get everything that's mine, mother's things and the house I inherited from Albert.'

'And what if I die before you?'

'There's your son, Michel. He'll get everything!'

'Michel isn't our mother's son, he's my son! And don't forget, there are other people in the family too!'

Then I hear the names of my aunts and uncles, who I haven't met yet: Aunt Bouanga, who lives in Dolisie, over two hundred kilometres from Pointe-Noire. Aunt Dorothée, who's married and lives in the village of Moussanda. Uncle Joseph who lives in Louboulou and is the youngest in the family, just after my mother. They're just names to me. I haven't met them yet. Maman Pauline often tells me they're all very nice, that they think of me, and would like to see me too, one day.

Uncle René acts like he's the big brother in this family, when in fact Aunt Bouanga and Aunt Dorothée are older than him. These two aunts are afraid of him, they can't stand up to him and he's just waiting for the day someone in the family dies so he can dash to the wake and announce, 'Everything belonging to the deceased is mine.' And if Maman Pauline dies, will he come and take our house and throw me out like he threw out Uncle Albert's children? I can't believe he will because this house was bought for us by Papa Roger and my name is on the papers. How could Uncle René come and take it? Papa Roger would wage a world war on him first, because usually the inheritance should go to the children. I try to understand why Uncle René acts the way he does, and I tell myself, 'Perhaps if you're rich in this life, you always want to get richer, and you stop noticing that the people around you have nothing.'

Before he left, my uncle threw a 1000 CFA franc note on the ground. My mother refused to take it. As soon as his car had started up, I quickly picked up the note, before the wind blew it away and into the middle of the street in the Avenue of Independence and everyone started fighting for it and saying it was theirs and we'd have no proof it belonged to us.

Lounès has been to the Rex with his father to see *Mandala, daughter of India.* They said people were weeping in the cinema, including Monsieur Mutombo, and it's not every day you see him cry.

While we're walking over to the football pitch in Savon, for a match between the Tié-Tié Caids and the Voungou Dragons, Lounès tries to explain the film to me. He tells me about a prince called Samsher and his sister, princess Rajshree, who live a life of such luxury that compared to them even capitalists look like paupers. They have elephants, tigers, lions, a beautiful palace in all the colours of the rainbow, rivers full of flowers and beautiful women, bathing and dancing, swaying their Netherlands. I listen to him, envy him, I feel jealous of him. But I do rather wonder if Lounès isn't adding a bit of spice to his story, to get me to ask Papa Roger to take us to see it, because children aren't allowed to go to the cinema on their own.

He describes how the prince and princess are cruel to the villagers. They're like the capitalists are towards the Wretched of the Earth. And yet they're rich, the princess and prince, why can't they leave the poor people in peace? Fortunately there's a young man called Jai who decides to fight back. It's not easy for him to attack an entire kingdom. He's a very courageous young man, besides which, he wants princess Rajshree to be his wife, which is no easy fix. The princess is too proud and she refuses to listen to all Jai's fine words, though they're sweet as honey. Thank God there's a country girl who loves Jai and sacrifices herself to save him from death. This is the point where the people all clapped in the cinema and Jai gets his own back and shows that just because you're rich doesn't mean you can mess the poor people around.

When I hear Lounès telling the story, I feel as though he's actually been to India and visited the palace he's describing in such detail. Then it occurs to me that it's a bit like what's happened to me with Caroline, now she loves Mabélé, when she should love me. Because I've got lots of plastic lorries and spades and rakes, I'm a bit like the peasant boy in *Mandala, daughter of India*. I should go and chat up princess Caroline but I don't want some peasant girl loving me and sacrificing herself for me and saving me from death. Mabélé is very proud, and thinks he's the only one who reads the work of Marcel Pagnol, and can write poems for Caroline.

'Michel, you're talking to yourself!'

I hadn't even noticed I was speaking out loud.

'I don't like Mabélé, you know,' he says.

'D'you know him then?'

'No, but I often see him in the street with the boys from over on Block 55.'

'I want to see him too, I want to know if I'm better looking than him...'

'You are better looking than him, I've already told you.'

'Really?'

'Anyway, you'll see him later, for real.'

'Where?'

'On the pitch.'

'What? On the pitch?'

'He's the number 11 for the Tié-Tié Caids.'

'But Jonas, the one they call Little Pelé, always plays number 11.'

'Jonas is out, he got dropped for being rude to the coach. He plays for the Voungou Dragons now.'

'You mean, Little Pelé's going to be playing against his own old team?'

'He'll be playing against our Tié-Tié Caids.'

Lounès and I have always supported the Tié-Tié Caids because we like the way Jonas dribbles from the halfway line to right in front of the other team's goalkeeper. That's how he got the nickname Little Pelé. There's no stopping him when he's got the ball at his feet. He flies through the air, taking off like a rocket, and when he kicks the ball with his left foot you know for sure it's going to hit the back of the net. The other teams often said: to win the match, someone has to break Jonas's leg. So they'd stick a really tall, muscular defender on him, someone who looks like they must be twenty already, though in fact all the players are about Lounès's age, never older.

I say to Lounès, 'If Jonas isn't playing for the Tié-Tié Caids and Mabélé's playing instead, I'm not going to support the Tié-Tié Caids, I'm supporting the Voungou Dragons and I want them to win this match!'

Now we're at the Tata-Luboka pitch, Lounès points out Mabélé from a distance.

'Look, he's over there. He's the one doing up his bootlaces near the goalkeeper.'

The stadium's already full. People are standing all round the pitch, which is full of holes. The smallest bring their own stools and climb up on them, otherwise they wouldn't see anything.

While I'm still looking at Mabélé and thinking there's

nothing he's got that I haven't, Lounès whispers in my ear, 'Look who's just opposite.'

'Caroline?'

'Shush! Don't look that way, she's looking at us.'

Caroline's wearing an orange jersey, the colour of the Tié-Tié Caids. So she's come to support Mabélé.

'You told me she was gong to your aunt's, and…'

'Yeah, she's still staying there. Maybe Mabélé invited her.'

'I'm going home, I don't want to see this match any more!'

'No, stay, I'll take care of Mabélé, just watch what I do in front of everyone. Maître John's already taught me some advanced katas you only learn when you've got your orange belt. Just you wait!'

'No, I'm going.'

He holds me back by my shirt. I struggle, manage to break loose, but I hear my shirt rip.

I'm already two hundred metres away from Lounès and I'm running like a bullet. People yell after me when I push past them. I don't care, I just keep on running.

I hear Lounès's voice in the distance.

'Michel, come back! Come back! Come back!'

I don't go down the Rue des Plateaux, I cut through the yard of Placide's house – he's one of my classmates. It's a short cut I know well, Placide's big brother, Paul Moubembé bars my way.

'Michel, stop, why are you running like that, have you stolen something?'

I pretend to run to the left, then duck back to the right and manage to dodge Paul Moubembé, who stands there, like a post, watching me run. I go through Godet's parents' yard – he's another classmate. This is a short cut too, that brings you directly onto the Avenue of Independence. I'm sweating like

Uncle René when he's talking about Engels, Lenin, Karl Marx or the immortal Marien Ngouabi. I wipe my forehead with my right arm. My shirt is flapping where it's torn, as though I've got wings on my back. I might just take off, running this fast.

I'm on the Avenue of Independence now, and at last I turn round. Lounès hasn't followed me, he'll watch the match even if I'm not there. I don't know what will happen between him and Mabélé. Will they fight? Will Lounès do the karate Maître John taught him? What are these advanced katas his teacher's shown him? Does Lounès take off like Bruce Lee when he lays into people who are bigger than him? I don't actually want him to fight Mabélé, Caroline will only blame me.

Lounès likes me being with his sister, but when he yells at her to go and see me, Caroline screams like she's having her throat cut. He's told me now, it's our business, no one else's. He's not going to mention it to her again. Caroline is too complicated and Lounès says that whenever she cries, Monsieur and Madame Mutombo blame him and stop his pocket money for a week.

I get back home, and bump into Maman Pauline who's just packing a big bag. I turn my back on her so she won't ask me why my shirt is torn. She'll think I've been in a fight, though in fact I'm afraid of fights because I've never won one yet.

'Is the match finished already?'

'No, I'm hungry, and it's too hot there.'

I'm staring at her bag. It's a travel bag, so she must be going somewhere.

'I'm going in two weeks' time, but I'm preparing my bag now, otherwise I'll forget things.'

'I'm coming with you.'

'Oh no you're not. I'm going into the bush to buy bunches of bananas, then taking them to Brazzaville to sell. The bush isn't safe for children.'

At last Papa Roger has given her the money for her new business, I think.

'I'll go and make you something to eat.'

'I'm not hungry now.'

'Michel, it's a surprise: beef with beans, I've made it specially for you!'

'I'm not hungry.'

I go to my room and lie down on the bed with my eyes shut, but I'm not asleep yet. I hear a slight noise: rain drops on the metal roof. A voice inside me exclaims, Oh no! Not rain! I don't want it to rain – if it does the Tié-Tié Caids will postpone the match. That's how they win so often. They go and see a fetisher, and he promises to bring rain to wipe out the other team's fetishes. If the Tié-Tié Caids win, Caroline will carry on being crazy about Mabélé because it's always the number 11 shirt that gets to dribble, always the number 11 people love, and cheer for, always the number 11 shirt the girls come to see after the match.

The Shah of Iran's become a kind of vagabond, wandering from country to country, while the Monster, Idi Amin Dada, is fine, no one's after him, he's just chilling out in Saudi Arabia. He used to be swimming champion of Uganda, so perhaps he's got a great big pool and goes swimming every day. He must have a room where he does boxing, because he also used to be Ugandan boxing champion. The people running his country are saying: let him stay there in Saudi Arabia, we haven't got time to go running after him, but if he does come back we're going to put him away, he can pay for his crimes. And I think: Even if he can't read and write, is he really going to be stupid enough to go back to a country where they'll kill him? So he'll just go on swimming up and down his pool all day, and doing his boxing training with his cook and gardener.

The Shah still hasn't found a place where he can live with his family without being threatened from Iran. He left his Prime Minister behind, but now he's done a runner too. He might get executed by the new government, who have it in for anyone who worked with the Shah. Besides, Papa Roger says that since the Ayatollah Khomeyni returned from exile in France he's been ruling with an iron fist and the only thing he's interested in is catching the Shah and sentencing him, not governing his country for the good of the suffering Iranians at home.

While my father's busy talking like Roger Guy Folly, I try to count in my head the number of countries the Shah's been to. Every time the American journalist named one, I made an effort to memorise it. First of all he went to Egypt to see his great friend the Egyptian president, called Anouar el-Sadat. His friend wouldn't allow him to become an international beggar, him and his wife, the empress Farah. Out of the question. So Anouar el-Sadat said to the Shah: Don't you worry, my friend, you come and hide out here in Egypt , it's your country too, you're my life-long friend, a friend of all Egyptians, I won't let you fall into the hands of those who seek to put you on trial and execute you, like they're executing your former ministers.

But then Iran made it clear to Egypt that they weren't happy about them sheltering the Shah. Anouar el-Sadat wanted to keep his friend anyway, and said to him: I won't hand you over to the Ayatollah Khomeyni, you're my friend. But the Shah chose to leave Egypt, so as not to be a nuisance to his Egyptian friend.

The Shah went to Morocco, where he had another friend, a king called Hassan II, who offered to take him in.

I'm still counting the countries when I hear Papa Roger yelling at the radio like he's really angry with Roger Guy Folly, who's still speaking. My father turns the sound down and turns to us: 'The American president has abandoned the Shah! How can he do that? That's what they're like, these Americans! What do they think they're doing? It's them that's screwing everything up in Angola, because they're so scared of the Communists, and it was them and the Belgians that plotted to kill Patrice Lumumba and put that thug Mobutu Ses Seko Kuku Wendo Wazabanga in power, who for years has been making speeches and robbing the people of Zaire. Maybe the Shah should have been a dictator like Idi Amin Dada, maybe then they'd have helped him!'

So then the Shah turned up in Morocco, but he didn't stay long because the Iranians warned him that if Monsieur ex-President didn't clear out of Morocco, they'd assassinate all King Hassan II's family. So the Shah himself said to King Hassan II, 'Don't worry, I'll leave Morocco, I don't want them to kill your family.'

So then he left Morocco and went to some islands called The Bahamas because there wasn't a single country left brave enough to welcome him. And he didn't stay there long either, because Henry Kissinger (the American minister for what goes on abroad) suggested he should go and live with the Mexicans.

At this point I said to myself, 'It's strange, why don't the Americans take in the Shah, why do they keep sending him to this country or that? Maybe it's because they're scared of eating hot potatoes, as Papa Roger puts it. The Mexicans are like us, my father remarks. They suffer as we do, but at least they're better than us at football because they've already hosted the World Cup, even if Brazil actually won it. I don't even know if one day we'll qualify to go and play with the best players in the world. If we can't even invite the Shah to come and live with us, how's anyone ever going to trust us to host the World Cup?'

Next Roger Guy Folly says that the Shah's adventures are not over yet. Soon he's going to have to leave Mexico because he has cancer and he really needs to be cared for in a country where he has a hope of recovering. Otherwise he might die.

So, some time in the next few days, the Shah will be sent to the United States for care. The Mexicans, who are very kind, have promised to have him back again after the operation. At

least this piece of information cheers my father up. Just now
he was refusing to eat, and was about to go off and listen to the
singer with the moustache under the mango tree, but now he
asks Maman Pauline, 'Is there any more to eat, a little piece of
grilled meat, perhaps, with some cassava?'

'm trying to read a book off my father's shelves. I've chosen this one because it was on top of the others and the smallest. On the cover there's a picture of a young white man. To look at he seems very clever, as though he knows about things even old people won't know till their dying day. He looks like an angel, with his left hand propping up his chin. His smile makes me smile too, even if it's just a photo I'm looking at, not a real person. I say to myself, 'Like all white people, this young man has a lot of hair, and his hair grows faster than ours because they have a lot of snow where they live, and we don't. Very strange.'

On the back of the book they explain what it's about, and who wrote it. Then they tell you about the life of the young man with the face of an angel. When I read that I think: But how did he have time to do the things they say here, he's still so young? For example, they say his father abandoned his mother. That his mother looked after all five children on her own. That he wrote poems when he was very young and that even a grown up called Paul Verlaine loved him so much that he almost killed him with a pistol. He and this grown-up had some other kind of relationship, but they don't explain that clearly here: you get the feeling it would be shameful to go into it. This man Paul Verlaine hurt the poor young man with a pistol and he got put in prison for it. They also say the reason this Paul Verlaine behaved badly was because he had problems with his wife and had drunk a lot of alcohol the day he was seeing the young man with the face of an angel. When you're drunk you can't control what you're saying or doing to people, you say stupid things, you do stupid things, you can't walk straight because you think the roads have gone all wiggly and that the cars going by are just plastic toys like the one Uncle René gave me to get me to play at farming at Christmas or on St Michel. Now when you're drunk you have long conversations with people who don't exist, invisible people that the people who make the alcohol that goes in bottles. You may also laugh out loud and shout rude things at passers-by who've done nothing. I know all this because Monsieur Vinou, one of our neighbours, is the biggest drunk on the planet. When he's been at the bottle, he directs his remarks over towards our house – you'd think it was us that drove him to drink his corn spirit or his red wine in the bars of Trois-Cents. The alcohol has turned his lips red and he's always getting into fights, though he's not a strong guy. He's always shouting, 'Why's the whole neighbourhood turn against me when I have a tipple?' If he ever gets hold of a pistol like that Paul Verlaine, he'll shoot at anything that moves. But since he doesn't have a pistol yet, he shouts at his six children, calls them bastards, bush toads, West African crickets etc. He tells his wife she's not his wife, she's a public rubbish bin, where the men from Trois-Cents have dumped their waste and the waste is rotting her body and making it stink. When he needs to piss or do other stinky business, Monsieur Vinou leaves his yard, pulls down his trousers and does it all in the street, even though there's a toilet at the end of his yard. Would you say that was the behaviour of a normal man? If someone starts forgetting they've got a toilet in their yard, it must be the alcohol that makes them do bad things, and that's maybe why Paul Verlaine fired a shot at the young man with the face of an angel.

The title of the little book I'm looking through is *A Season in Hell*. There's a title in it I really like: *Bad Blood*. It sounds like an expression we'd use around here. In lingala, *bad blood* means *makila mabé*. When Maman Pauline says in lingala that someone has bad blood it means they were born all wrong, luck's against them, they've got no hope, even the birds passing overhead crap on them. I don't know if that's what the young man with the face of an angel meant too, but he must have been very angry to choose a title like that, it could be bad luck for anyone who reads the book.

I choose a page, I read out loud, almost as though I'm praying:

> *I abominate all trades. Professionals and workers, serfs to a man! Despicable. The hand that guides the quill is a match for the hand that guides the plough.*

On the back cover it says it's a book of poems, but there are no separate lines, no words that sound the same at the end of each line, like in the poem Lounès recited. Does that mean I don't have to follow what Lounès told me? There are some words and expressions in this poem I find really difficult. I'll have to ask Lounès what they mean, or Lounès can ask his teacher at school. For example, I don't know what 'the hand that guides the quill' means. Perhaps it's the hand of a white sorcerer who dresses up as a bird at night and comes to snatch children and take them to hell for a season. Yes, that's probably it, because just before that the young man talks about his ancestors the Gauls, who were real gangsters, he says. He says that as 'flayers of beasts, burners of grass', they were the most inept people of their age. Which is odd because our ancestors were like that too. Maybe they are distantly related to these people called the Gauls. Now I understand why my father told me once that in his day, at school, they taught them that our ancestors were Gauls.

In the poem in question, I find the words 'the hand that guides the plough'. I've already heard Uncle René use the word 'plough', when he talks about farming. When I want to get something done quickly, or I do it sloppily, he tells me off and shouts: 'Don't put the plough before the ox!'

The plough was always behind the oxen, so they could pull it. Now, the young man is talking about 'the hand that guides the plough'. That really does make it tricky, what with the hand that guides the quill and the hand that guides the plough, I'm really confused.

When you go into Monsieur Mutombo's workshop it's really like going into a tunnel, with clothes hanging up above your head. Lounès's father has two silent young apprentices working away at the back, doing the same thing over and over again, like two robots. Their job is to put the buttons on the shirts and trousers once Monsieur Mutombo has finished sewing them. I've never seen them put a piece of cloth on the table, pick up the scissors and cut it up. I do rather wonder if they'd even know how to make a pair of shorts for a child at infant school. If you try to talk to them they just look at you with these huge eyes, if they dare open their mouths Monsieur Mutombo will shout, 'Lazy good-for-nothings, I'll send you back to your parents and you'll have to pay them back the money they've spent on your training!'

The thing they like best is taking the women's measurements. They tell them to take their clothes off, including their underpants, and they take a look at lots of other things that women normally only show their husband or their doctor. They measure the women up at the back of the shop, on the right. You can't quite see what the apprentices are doing. You can just hear one of them saying to the woman, 'Take your top off, and the bottom half, and your pants, stand very straight, hold your head up, close your eyes.'

It's different for the men: they take their measurements in front of everyone. When that happens I always close my eyes, because most of them have great big bellies, even though they're not bosses or proletariat-exploiting capitalists. They have long hair under their armpits, sometimes they're all white, like they've put ash on themselves, or powder, that's been there for at least a week.

It's always dark in the workshop. It used to be the place where the priests from the Church of Saint-Jean-Bosco used to store their spades, their rakes and their picks. Besides, since the church is only a few metres away, when the bells ring, Monsieur Mutombo tells everyone to observe a minute's silence because the priest gave him this little building free of charge. I don't know how he manages in the dark not to prick his big fat fingers with the needle of the Singer sewing machine. Since he's very bald, with only a few grey hairs around his ears, it feels like it's his head that lights the place, because when he goes out for a smoke it gets even darker inside, and when he comes back it brightens up a little bit again. I've never seen anyone's head shine like that, not round here. Maybe he puts palm oil on it or maybe Madame Mutombo rubs a special cream into it every morning.

The reason I'm in Monsieur Mutombo's workshop this morning is I've come to get my shirt mended, the one Lounès ripped when we were at the Tata-Luboka stadium and I ran off before the start of the match. No, I'm not going to tell Monsieur Mutombo it was his son who did it. Lounès didn't mean to do it. He just wanted me to stay with him to watch the match, even if Caroline had come to support the Tié-Tié Caïds, who won in the end. I heard it was Mabélé who scored all three goals in the match. In any case, I knew their team would win because their sorcerer made it rain, so the fetishes of the Voungou Dragons would get wet and not work. And apparently whenever the ball got in front of the Tié-Tié Caids' goal, the sorcerers put invisible players on the pitch, who blew on it, and the ball flew off somewhere else, so the goal couldn't be scored. On the other hand, whenever Mabélé, proudly wearing his number 11 shirt, found himself face to face with the goalie for the Voungou Dragons and was about to shoot, the poor goalkeeper saw a javelin instead of the ball, and stepped to one side immediately because he didn't want to die pointlessly, and then the goal went in.

If I was a football referee for this *quartier*, I'd give red cards to the sorcerers sitting behind the goals, because they are the ones who decide which team will win, or if it's going to be a draw. And a draw happens when both teams have chosen sorcerers with exactly the same powers, i.e., the same *gris-gris*.

I've just handed my torn shirt to Monsieur Mutombo at long last, and he's looking at it as though it was an old duster, when in fact he made it himself last year.

'What's happened here? You've been in a fight at school and Monsieur Mutombo here has to sew up your shirt, eh?'

'I wasn't in a fight, Monsieur Mutombo.'

'So a ghost tore your shirt did it?'

The apprentices are pretending to work. I can tell they're going to burst out laughing any moment. They've come a bit closer, so they can get a look at my shirt.

'Who did this?' Monsieur Mutombo continues.

I say nothing.

'All right, if you don't tell me who did it, I'll keep your shirt and I'll show it to Roger and Pauline this evening. You'll have to go home with no shirt on!'

I don't want to go home with no shirt on, people will laugh at me in the street. And I don't like people seeing I haven't got any muscles yet. Especially the girls will laugh. No, I'll have to say something.

'I'll tell you who did it.'

'Ah, at last. So, who was it?'

'Me. Myself.'

'Very interesting! And how did that happen?'

'It's hard to explain. I was sitting like this, I put my back against the wall and there, all of a sudden, was this nail, out of nowhere. So just when I'm about to stand up to…'

'Michel, cut it out! I understand that you are fond of Lounès and to protect him you're prepared to take the blame yourself. But he's already told me everything. Everything! It was him that grabbed your shirt…'

Now I understand why the two apprentices had started laughing earlier. They knew, too, that it was their boss's son that had torn my shirt.

Monsieur Mutombo turns to them.

'Longombé, fix the boy's shirt, right now. And Mokobé, you do the turn-ups on Monsieur Casimir's trousers, he's been on at me since yesterday, even though I keep telling him he's not very tall and turn-ups will make him look even smaller than the president of Gabon.'

I go up to Monsieur Mutombo and whisper in his ear.

'Actually, I've got a bit of a serious problem…'

'Well, what is it, this bit of a serious problem?'

'Your apprentices…'

'What have they done to you?'

'They only do buttons and I don't want them to spoil my shirt. My mother will be cross with me if they do.'

Monsieur Mutombo bursts out laughing. His apprentices have heard me, and they have a good laugh while they get the chance, because they've been holding it in for ages. Since all three of them are killing themselves laughing, I start laughing too, and then I can't stop. Now when I laugh, it always makes other people laugh too, because I often laugh like a little jackal with a bad cough. So all four of us just go on laughing till a woman appears at the door of the workshop. It's as though she can't get in, frontways or sideways. She's so enormous that it's as though the door had just been blocked by an extraterrestrial. Even Monsieur Mutombo's bald head casts no light now. The woman's cheeks are all puffed out like someone blowing into a trumpet, or who has two mandarin oranges stuffed in their mouth. The sight of this makes me split my sides even more, it's too much, I'm going to choke laughing, I point my finger at the woman, I tell myself the others in the workshop must surely laugh with me. But suddenly everyone else has stopped. They're all looking at me. Monsieur Mutombo clears his throat and nods his head at me, as if to tell me to stop laughing. I stop laughing suddenly and wipe my tears with the end of my shirt.

Longombé stands up like a schoolboy who's been caught chatting and has to go up to the board and write out a hundred times: I must not talk in class. He walks past me, still holding my ripped shirt in his hands and goes over to the woman, who has now moved away from the door. When she moved I thought they must have switched on the street lamps in the Avenue of Independence. While Longombé and the woman are talking outside, Monsieur Mutombo leans over to me: 'You shouldn't have laughed! Do you know who that woman is? It's Longombé's mother. She comes every day to ask her son for money.'

Now Longombé's coming back into the workshop. He walks past me again, and gives me a strange look. I say to myself, 'Oh heck, he's angry, now he's really going to ruin my shirt, to get his own back.'

The cleverest person in our class is called Adriano and he's from Angola. He's very light skinned because some of his grandparents had children with Portuguese people. That's why no one teases him about his skin because it's not his fault he's not really black like us, it's the Portuguese people's fault.

The very first day Adriano arrived in class, the teacher told us that his father had been killed in the civil war going on in his country. Adriano and his mother came to take refuge in Pointe-Noire, so they wouldn't be killed too. In their country, at night, the militiamen who follow a wicked Angolan called Jonas Savimbi attack the army of the president, Agostinho Neto. We were all scared when the teacher reminded us that Angola is not far from our country and that you can get here from there on foot, via a tiny country called Cabinda, which, like us, has loads of petrol. What really scared us was the idea that Jonas Savimbi and his militiamen might turn up in our country, just to annoy our President as well, and push us into a civil war. We learned that there are lots of Cuban and Russian soldiers in Angola, to help president Agostinho Neto stay in power, because he's not just under attack from Jonas Savimbo, poor fellow, there are other enemies too, and they've formed the Front National de Liberation d'Angola, or FNLA, and their leader is a certain Holden Roberto, who doesn't mess about. Agostinho Neto is caught between Jonas Savimbi and Holden Roberto, who are supported either directly or in secret, by the imperialists.

After these explanations, the teacher was happy to be able to tell us that our country likes President Agostinho Neto because he's communist, like us. Adriano was very pleased about that.

In the classroom we sit in order of intelligence. When you come in, the first row, facing you, is made up of the three best pupils in the class: Adriano, Willy-Dibas, and Jérémie. The second row is for the fourth, fifth and sixth best pupils. And it carries on like that, right to the back of the class. The stupidest are in the back row. They get left at the back so they can chat and throw ink pellets at each other.

The second the teacher asks a question, Adriano has the answer, as if he'd dreamed it in the night, like that criminal Idi Amin Dada, who dreamed of what he would do to the Asians. And every time our teacher says to Adriano, 'Don't you answer, give the others a chance to answer and show their intelligence for a few minutes of their lives at least.' Adriano doesn't like that, he wants to answer all the questions. But why should we bother coming to class if there's an Angolan who knows all the answers, even about things to do with our country, like rivers and lakes? Adriano doesn't like it when someone else behind him gets it right. But when no one knows the answer – which is usually the case – the teacher has to say to him, 'Adriano, now you can answer.' When he's told us the answer, everyone has to stand up and clap for five minutes or more. His face goes all red like a tomato, and the teacher gives him a present: a box full of chalks, a notebook and a textbook containing all the speeches of the President of the Republic.

Those of us in the middle of the class, the average ones, dream that one day we might move up to the front row beside Adriano, but it's not easy. If you get a better mark than someone in a higher row, you go and sit in his place, and he moves back to your row. Occasionally I've got as far as the third row, but the next day I always got moved back because the person whose place I'd taken had gone and worked really hard all day Sunday, so he can get his place back among the top ten. It's only the front row that never changes, because Adriano, Willy-Dibas and Jérémie are so clever, they confer with each other so no one else can come up to their level. If the three of them are cross with you they pass a little piece of paper to someone in the class who doesn't like you. They write down the answers to the question on this piece of paper, and the classmate, who you don't like either, just copies them down. When you get into class the next morning, the classmate in question has changed places, now he's just behind Adriano, Willy-Dibas and Jérémie. And you're hopping mad.

I try really hard not to get moved to the back row, to stay in the middle of the class. In my row no one bothers you, and no one sees you either, because the teacher usually only notices the front and back rows.

Us boys wear khaki shirts and blue shorts, and the girls wear orange shirts and blue skirts. Every morning, to be allowed into class, you have to recite the first four articles of the law of the National Pioneers Movement, the MNP. I know them by heart now. Sometimes I dream that I'm reciting them in a stadium that's even fuller than the Revolution Stadium. Every evening before I go to bed, and every morning before I get up, I recite them. I close my eyes, I imagine I'm someone about to serve his country, that thanks to me capitalism won't reign victorious in our country, and I murmur the four articles, like a prayer:

> *Article 1: the pioneer is a conscientious and effective junior militant. In all things he obeys the orders of the Congolese Workers' Party.*
>
> *Article 2: The pioneer follows the example of the immortal Marien Ngouabi, founder of the Congolese Workers' Party.*
>
> *Article 3: The pioneer is thrifty, disciplined and hardworking, and completes his tasks.*
>
> *Article 4: The pioneer both respects and transforms nature.*

There's a boy in our class called Bouzoba who is not very bright. When I say he's not very bright, I'm being nice because Bouzoba is the stupidest boy in the whole class, so he sits in the back row, in a corner, where he can get on with being stupid without being seen. It was him that invented the famous 'mirror game' which is the craze at the moment in the playground. During break, he goes around with a little mirror in his pocket and when the girls are playing he comes up behind one of the girls who's standing up and puts his little mirror on the ground between the girl's legs to see the colour of her pants. Then he comes and tells us that the girl standing over there is wearing red pants and the one beside her has green pants with a hole in. And when the girls walk past us, we say, 'Marguerite, you've got red pants on! Célestine, you've got green pants with a hole in!' The poor girls start whimpering and go and tell the teacher that we've seen Marguerite's red pants and Célestine's green pants with a hole in. The teacher also goes to tell the head teacher that some of the children have seen Marguerite's red pants and Célestine's green pants with a hole in. And the head teacher comes personally to beat the boys in our class, because no one dares tell on Bouzoba, because he's strong and muscular and he'll beat us up in the playground and make us pay a month's fine: we have to give him our pocket money every day, and scratch his backside when he's got an itch.

The head teacher's very crafty and he really wants to know who made up the mirror game. First of all he gives us all a good hiding, and then he goes up onto the platform and says, 'Who can tell me what colour Célestine's pants are?'

The class sits in silence – you can hear the flies buzzing. The head teacher repeats his question with a broad smile, as though promising not to belt anyone who can tell him the colour of Célestine's pants. This is when that idiot Bouzoba puts his hand up at the back of the class and yells, 'Sir, sir, Célestine's pants are green!'

'Really? And how do you now that?'

'I saw it with my pocket mirror!'

He gets out his pocket mirror, waves it in the air. Then he adds, 'I'm not lying, sir, look, here's my mirror!'

The head teacher grabs Bouzoba by the ears and drags him into his office to beat him even more, and make him tidy the books and clean the windows as a punishment.

Our desks are too small, so we're all squeezed up together. You can easily read or copy what the person next to you is writing if you haven't done your homework. Everyone does it. I've stopped looking at what the others do, because every time I end up copying their mistakes. When someone's writing quickly, as though he knows what he's doing, you don't imagine he's making a mistake. So you copy off him, without thinking, because if he was writing rubbish he wouldn't be writing that quickly, he must be really clever, like Adriano, Willy-Dibas or Jérémie.

The teacher says, 'Anyone who finishes quickly can go home before the others.'

I know it's a trap to catch out the idiots. I'm not going to fall for it, I work at my own pace. Besides, it's better to write slowly, even if you're the last to leave. At least the next morning, when the teacher does the corrections, he won't beat you. He'll remember you weren't in a rush to get home to eat and sleep, like some capitalist's child. He'll think you love school so much you didn't want to go home. So he won't hit you hard.

It's chaos in Teheran at the moment. The Iranian students have taken hostages in the American embassy, even though America's the world's number one country. Papa Roger reminds us that it's usually the Americans who help out when there's a world war against the Germans. The Americans always head off to Europe, to some place called Normandy, where there's a beach. They get out their sophisticated weapons and they go on shooting till there are no Germans left trying to occupy France and massacre the Jews. I wonder how the Iranian students dare go and provoke a country like America by imprisoning fifty or sixty Americans in the basement of the embassy. Can the Ayatollah Khomeyni be stronger than the Americans' president?

Roger Guy Folly explains that the Iranian students won't release the hostages unless the Americans hand over the Shah of Iran, who's in hospital in their country. And the Americans are at their wits' end, and agree to have talks with the students. And since they really want to talk in order to save their fellow countrymen, Yasser Arafat's going to arbitrate between them. Papa Roger points out that he has already told us about Yasser Arafat, who was the witness at Idi Amin Dada's wedding, when he got married for the fifth time. Yasser Arafat is the president of Palestine, a country which people refuse to recognise as a proper country like ours. He must be very pleased to be arbitrating in the American hostage affair. If I was him, I would say to the Americans: 'If you want to negotiate, ok, but I'm happy to help you get the Iranians to free your fifty or sixty countrymen that they've shut up in the basement of the embassy. But I have an important request: first everyone must accept that the country of Palestine does exist, I want it to be accepted right now, straight away, or else I will tell the Iranian students to go on holding your citizens hostage in the cellar!'

Yesterday afternoon this guy was bothering the wife of Yeza, the joiner who lives over the way, and things went badly wrong. The nuisance guy, the one they call 'the Lady Whistler', because he's always chatting up married women, you'd think there was a shortage of single women in this town, though according to the people who know about these things, there are more women than men in our country, which is why men often marry three or four different women.

The Lady Whistler didn't know Yeza was in his workshop, busy making a coffin. He makes them in advance so he doesn't run out if there are ever several deaths in one day. Besides, there are also people who order a coffin as soon as their relative goes into hospital, because it works out more expensive afterwards. If you argue over the price of a coffin when someone's already dead, the joiner will look you up and down and say, 'Well go and make the coffin yourself, then, if you don't like my price.'

As soon as Yeza's wife heard whistling outside, she quickly went out and followed the Lady Whistler down to the end of the Avenue of Independence. At that moment I saw Yeza come out of his workshop with a hammer in his hand and I said to myself, 'Oh-oh, now the Lady Whistler's going to end up in that coffin the joiner's making.'

I followed the crowd that was walking behind the joiner and already shouting '*Ali bomba yé! Ali bomba yé! Ali bomba yé!*' Round here, if someone shouts like that it means there's a fight brewing. It's a way of working up the crowd and urging the people quarreling not to change their minds. Papa Roger thinks that the first people to shout *Ali bomba yé!* were the people of Zaire, the year Mohammed Ali and George Foreman came to fight on our continent, as if there was no room left back home in America. They were both black Americans, and apparently they came to Zaire to fight so as to be near to their black ancestors. The man who did the publicity for the fight was called Don King, another black American with such a big shock of hair on his head, a bird could have mistaken it for a tree and come and settle there to make its nest and lay its eggs. According to Papa Roger, this Don King guy had been paid millions and millions by the dictator, Mobutu Sese Seko to organise the fight, but the black American didn't realise that the reason the President of Zaire had put up all this money was to get publicity for himself so the whole world would think he was a good man, when in fact he was bad, and frightened his own people, and stole money from the State and hid it in European bank accounts, and was one of the people who assassinated Patrice Lumumba, who had done everything to try to free the Belgian Congo.

Every time my father talks to me about that boxing match, I move out of the way a bit because he always tries to copy Ali's hard right-hand punch that knocked Foreman out. If you're too close to my father his punch may land on your jaw. He says that to start with the Zairians were all for Foreman: his skin was darker than Mohammed Ali's, therefore he was the real African. Ali was too light-skinned, like our classmate Adriano; the Zairians were suspicious of someone with skin like that claiming to be black. But when Foreman arrived at the airport in Kinshasa with his great big dog with its tongue hanging out and its ears sticking up like the antennae at Radio

Congo, everyone was afraid. The Zairians said, 'That dog has the same face as the dogs of those Belgians who ordered us about during colonisation! How can a black man have a dog from the same family as the dogs of the colonisers? How can he bring a dog here that reminds us of the dogs that were trained to pick up the scent of a Black, and find him in the bush, at dead of night, when he was trying to escape from being hassled by the Whites?' The people of Zaire said to themselves: 'This Foreman guy isn't a real Black like us, he wants to become like the Whites, Ali must get the knock out to avenge our parents and our grandparents who were bitten by the Belgians' dogs. Besides, look how straightforward Ali is, off jogging with the little kids along the river, and in the streets of Kinshasa while that traitor Foreman stays in the gym punching away at a bag full of sand like a madman. Ali is a man of the people. Ali's like us. We have to help him win, even if Foreman's never been beaten in his life. The fetishes are on our side. Our ancestors are on our side. We'll ask the fetishes and our ancestors to support Ali. And our fetishes will fight the fight for Ali, and our ancestors will make sure Foreman gets tired quickly, so he can't see where Ali's punches are coming from.'

On the day of the fight, at the 20th May Stadium, Ali was dancing round the ring, with his amazing footwork. Our ancestors helped him keep supple. Foreman was tired of jab, jab, jabbing away. Ali set to work, listening to the ancestors, following the advice of the fetishes. Instead of hitting with his left, though he's a left hander, he hit with his right. And in the eighth round – bam! – he let his punch fly. Foreman didn't see it coming, his legs went from under him, he fell to the ground like a sack of potatoes. By the time he got up again the fight was over. Ali had won. And it started to rain. That meant our ancestors were pleased, that they were celebrating Mohammed Ali's victory.

So when I heard the crowd following the joiner shouting '*Ali bomba yé! Ali bomba yé ! Ali bomba yé!*' I started shouting too, like everyone else. But I didn't know who was going to be Ali and who would be Foreman in this fight. Meanwhile the wife of the joiner had disappeared.

The Lady Whistler saw Yeza coming with his hammer. He tried to run but the crowd quickly caught him.

Someone said to him, 'You can't run away like that, you've got to fight! You're not going to cheat us of our fight! Come on, fight!'

He replied, 'Oh no, I'm not fighting unless my opponent puts his hammer down.'

The crowd turned to Yeza.

'Put your hammer down! Put your hammer down! Put your hammer down! Put your hammer down, if you're a real man, if you've got any balls!'

And since the joiner was not prepared to put his hammer down, a big man, as strong as a hundred-year-old baobab took it off him. They made a circle round the two men. The man who was as tall and strong as a hundred-year-old baobab said to the two combatants, 'Yeza the joiner can be Foreman because he's got more muscle. The Lady Whistler can be Ali because he's better looking.'

That really annoyed Yeza, who wanted to be Ali because Ali always wins.

'Who says the Lady Whistler's better looking than me?'

The Lady Whistler sniggered, and everyone sniggered with him, which Yeza did not appreciate.

'Why are you all laughing with him? Are you on his side

or what? Can't you see he just goes round making trouble in other people's lives? Well I'll show you I'm Mohammed Ali, not him!'

With one leap, the joiner fell upon the Lady Whistler, who, like a cat, flipped him over and got on top. The two men were biting the dust. I couldn't make out who was on top now, and who was underneath. Fists were flying everywhere. When Yeza was doing well, a hand from the crowd would push him, and he'd suddenly be underneath again. The fight which had started in the middle of the Avenue of Independence was now right down the far end and everyone was jostling the two men. No one could separate them.

After they'd been fighting for over ten minutes, I saw people start to run away, jumping over the fences between lots. Police sirens could be heard. I said to myself: 'When the police arrive they always thump the witnesses before they work out who's fighting.' So I ran off like everyone else. I came to a stop in front of our lot and from there I saw Yeza going back into his house with his shirt all torn and blood on his face, looking as though he'd fought a pack of lions and an army of pygmy chimps all in the same day. He went straight into his workshop with his hammer in his hand. He banged away so hard at the coffin, I felt like he was hammering on my chest.

Deep inside I was thinking, 'What's going to happen when his wife gets home?'

What is it that Mabélé's got that I haven't, that makes Caroline love him, not me? I wouldn't mind fighting it out with him, to get him to leave her alone. I can imagine how it would go: I'd be Ali and he'd be Foreman. I'd fly like a butterfly, and sting like a bee, Mabélé couldn't even land a punch on me, you can't hit what you can't see. I'd be too fast for him, I'd rise up into the air, and there goes his fist – missed! Mabélé would stay with his feet planted flat on the ground like a builder's trowel. And by then Lounès will have taught me the katas of Maître John and I'll have lift-off, like in the films of Bruce Lee.

The first time I saw Mabélé at the Tata-Luboko football ground I said to myself: 'Call that a boy? Is Caroline blind or what? Can't she see I'm better looking than him? Can't she see Mabélé's knees are like misshapen yams growing in the Mayombe forest? Can't she see that when he's standing up he looks like a turkey with his neck wobbling about the whole time?'

True, I haven't got any muscles yet, but that will come, and then I'll be even better looking than I am now. What's she looking for, anyway? Doesn't she realise if she has her two children with Mabélé their children will be as ugly as their father? Ok, maybe their children will be clever but they'll still be ugly, there's no way round it.

Caroline must love Mabélé for some other reason. He must be able to sweet talk her, like a grown up. Grown up people know how to talk to women and make them laugh and show their teeth and their tongue, because whatever it is they're hearing interests them. I'm not very interesting when I talk. To be interesting you have to have things to say, things that women like to hear. But what kind of things? Mabélé's just a cheat, he goes and finds things in books by Marcel Pagnol and comes and bewitches Caroline by whispering them in her ear. There's no point trying to charm Caroline with Arthur's poems. I think, for example, I should try and get her attention by hiding a guinea fowl feather in my pocket, then when I see her, I could tickle her in the ear with the end of the feather. I'm sure that would make her laugh, and then she'd think I was more interesting than Mabélé.

Another thing I could do to interest Caroline would be to do what Louis de Funès does in *Le Gendarme et les Extra-terrestres*, a film Lounès really loves – he's seen it three times already. He says in this film the extra-terrestrials change shape, so they look just like policemen and everyone else looks so similar, no one knows who's an extra-terrestrial and who's a human being. I could turn myself into Mabélé so Caroline thinks it's her beloved Mabélé beside her, when in fact it's me, Michel, I just look like Mabélé. And when I turn back into myself – because I'm actually better looking than Mabélé, Caroline will crack up laughing. It could really work, because Lounès says this actor Louis de Funès makes everyone laugh – girls, boys, children, old people, animals etc., and I don't want to make everyone laugh, only Caroline.

When my mother's in love she feels like her heart is in her stomach. I've never felt that in my whole life. My heart is virtually immobile. Even if I jump, it stays exactly where it is.

When I asked Lounès if he'd ever felt his heart in his stomach he thought I was mad.

'Can your heart fall into your stomach?'

I didn't want to say that's what happens when you're in love. I've never seen Lounès chatting up girls. Usually it's the girls that chat him up, and he acts like he wishes they wouldn't, or like he hasn't noticed. And when he acts like he wishes they wouldn't, or he hasn't noticed, that's when the girls all run after him. And he comes to me and says proudly, 'You see that girl? She's been after me for ages but I'm going to leave her to be unhappy for a bit, then when I do go and talk to her she'll be all over me!'

I wouldn't dare act like that in front of Caroline, if I act like I'm not interested in her and leave her to be unhappy for a bit, she'll just say, 'You've only yourself to blame, Mabélé loves me, and he doesn't make me unhappy like you do!'

Our school is this old red-brick building with a roof that's going to fall in if they don't fix it in the next few months, maybe even in the next two or three weeks. The parents have meetings every month about mending the roof. Papa Roger won't go to the meetings any more. He thinks people just go along to talk big and say nothing, in French, so everyone will think they've been to France, like Uncle René, when they haven't. At the end they vote to decide the date of the next meeting. And they'll come back again to talk big in French while the school roof continues to get worse and worse. Also, there are some bad people who've stolen the wood for the windows to take home for firewood. When it rains, the water comes into the classroom, and we have to move all the desks into one corner so as not to get wet. That's why we come to school with our waterproofs and why our schoolbooks are covered in plastic. There's already the water that comes in through the roof, and if it's going to come in through the windows as well it won't be a school any more it'll be a swimming pool, like in the houses of the capitalists in the town centre, who buy all their food at Printania.

The reason it smells bad in our classroom is because the pupils wet themselves while the teacher's whipping them. If you talk too much, the teacher tells you to get up and go and kneel down on the platform with your arms folded, in front of all your classmates. The teacher goes on with the lesson while you stay there thinking: What's going to happen after the lesson, when he comes over to me? So you cry in advance. Which is actually a waste of tears, because it's afterwards you should be crying, once you've been whacked. And when you cry in advance, everyone hears you. And because they can hear you it means you're disturbing them when they're meant to be copying out the lesson. So you just make things worse for yourself. The teacher turns to look at you, he's very cross now. He goes to find a brick outside. He tells you to hold it high above your head and not move till the end of the lesson. If you drop the brick he gives you double punishment. You have to make really sure it doesn't fall, even if it weighs more than you do. You start sweating, snot comes out of your nose. And since you don't want to be snotty, you sniff it in, and it makes a strange noise like a ravenous chameleon swallowing insects. The teacher turns round again, and he's even angrier than last time because you're making a noise like a chameleon swallowing insects. He tells Adriano the Angolan to step up on the platform. Our top pupil's very pleased because he already knows what's going to happen.

The teacher says, 'Adriano, recite the speech given by the immortal Marien Ngouabi on the 31st December 1969, the day our brave Congolese Workers' Party was formed.'

Adriano stands to attention. He looks up in the air, and starts to talk like the immortal Marien Ngouabi, the same voice we use in our Revolutionary theatre class.

Adriano yells, 'Pioneers!'

The class replies, 'We serve!!!'

Adriano: 'All for the people!'

Class: 'And only for the people!!!'

Adriano: 'Victory or we die!'

Class: 'Victory or we die!!!'

Adriano: 'Who do we die for?'

Class: 'We die for the people!!!'

Adriano: 'What do we die for?'

Class: 'We die for the Revolution!!!'

And now the class is warmed up, Adriano recites the speech of the Immortal: *The year 1969 is drawing to a close. A year at whose end we can measure the length of the road that we have travelled, the pitfalls encountered, our sorrows and our joys. In short, one more year after which to take stock of our efforts and above all our failures. In the course of this very year our most dangerous enemies briefly entertained the hope that the National Revolutionary Council would give its approval to an executive conference bringing together a group of renegades in an attempt to lay the foundations of a national unity based on pro-ruling class, pro-colonialist factors: tribalism, regionalism and sectarianism. This hope, recently much nurtured in reactionary circles, was quickly dashed. Better still, after a glorious victory over imperialism and those who have betrayed the nation, our young and dynamic people had the courage this very day to found the boldest creation in the history of our Revolution: the Congolese Workers' Party. The Congolese people have thus revived the flames of the Three Glorious Days of the Revolution of 1830. Today and from this day onwards we shall no longer sing the Internationale out of tune. On this day, 31 December 1969, Congo-Brazzaville has entered the annals of the great global proletarian Revolution...*

The class applauds. You kneel there crying with your brick over your head, and the teacher turns to you and orders: 'Put the brick down, now you recite the speech of the immortal Marien Ngouabi, like Adriano.'

And since you can't recite it like Adriano, without stammering or forgetting a single word, you cry even harder. So the teacher takes the strap he has hidden in his bag and hands it to Adriano: 'Here, Adriano, give him twenty strokes with the strap, since he can't recite the most famous speech of the immortal Marien Ngouabi.'

So Adriano wallops you while the rest of the class counts to twenty and you call out for your poor mother, who is fortunately unaware of what's happened to you.

There's a map of the People's Republic of Congo pinned up by the blackboard, just next to the map of Africa. We have to chant that the People's Republic is a country in Central Africa, surrounded by Zaire, Angola, Gabon, Cameroon and the Central African Republic.

I often say our country is really small, but you mustn't say it in class, or the teacher will get mad and beat you even though everyone can see on the map of Africa that our neighbour Zaire is one of the biggest countries on the whole continent. No, you mustn't say that either, or the people of Zaire will start to wake up; at the moment, they don't even know their country is bigger than a lot of countries in Europe or that their president-dictator Mobuto Sese-Seko gave millions and millions of dollars to Don King so George Foreman and Mohammed Ali would go and fight there, when the people of Zaire are living in poverty.

The teacher insists we memorise all the names of all the regions in our country, from north to south, east to west. We especially have to know exactly where to find the village of the immortal Marien Ngouabi. His native village is Ombélé, it's up in the north, in the Owando district. It's where there's a red cross on the map. During our citizenship lesson we learn that the Immortal's mother is called Maman Mboualé and his father is called Osseré Dominique. And even though the Immortal was murdered by Northerners like himself, who wanted to take over from him, we've been taught what to say about these sad events. We have to say: *The immortal Marien Ngouabi, founder of the Congolese Workers' Party died fighting on the 18th March 1977. He had been murdered by the cowardly forces of Imperialism and its local lackeys.*

The teacher told us that in the end the government had managed to catch and imprison the local lackeys of Imperialism who killed comrade Marien Ngouabi. The Immortal fought hard but there was nothing he could do because it was a plot that had been hatched in Europe and the Europeans are brilliant at selling their plots to the Africans. The local Lackeys of Imperialism who killed our Immortal are black like us, Congolese, like us. The government promised that they will be tried and judged and sentenced to public hanging at the Revolution Stadium. The people must understand that you don't mess with the Immortals. So, for the moment all we have to do is put Imperialism on trial. It will be hard to catch it and put it in prison because it doesn't live here, unlike its local lackeys. And anyway, it's White.

According to Lounès, he and his classmates at secondary school study subjects that we can't learn yet at primary school because our brains haven't finished growing. We mustn't put anything too difficult in them, or they'll explode, and we'll probably go mad and start talking to invisible people and picking up rubbish in the street. That's why the mad people in this town all write arithmetic on the walls of houses, and sometimes poems too, thinking they've made them up themselves, when in fact it's just their madness doing it. The mad people round here have the strangest names, I don't know where they get them. Lounès told me about one of them called Athena. The police arrested him because he'd make up problems and write them on the walls of houses in the Avenue of Independence. Athena also gave the schoolchildren all the answers, so they just had to copy them down. And since it so happened that the problems went up during the exams, the children from the high school went looking for Athena in the streets of Pointe-Noire. When they found him, they brought him things to eat and drink, and sang him songs from when he was a tiny baby in his mother's arms. Athena wept when he heard these songs, and they knew that crying would help his imagination even more. The pupils offered him new clothes, cut his hair and his beard for him, and led him to a huge wall opposite Vicky's Photo Studio.

'Athena, you have to help us, write up the problem on this wall, then tell us the answer.'

Athena trembled with fear because, Lounès says, mad people always think children are giants, so they're more afraid of children than of grown-up people. Anyway, Athena thought for a bit, then began scribbling away on the wall. The pupils all scrambled to write it down. After that they all said: 'Athena, are you sure that's the right answer? Athena are you sure this is the problem we'll get in the exam?'

Then there's another madman over in Savon, they call him Archimedes, and another in Bloc 55 called Mango. Archimedes wanders around naked, likes to bathe in the river Tchinouka and fart in the waters to see the bubbles go Pop! Pop! Pop! Mango sits under any mango tree he can find at the side of the road. And when anyone asks what he's doing there he'll say he's waiting for a mango to fall on his head.

Lounès thinks Archimedes and Mango went mad because they were taught things in their childhood that their brains were too young to understand. Then the things all rotted inside their brains, and then the poor men started talking to invisible people and picking up rubbish in the streets of our town, as though they worked in Refuse Disposal.

So complicated maths is for the big boys and girls at high school, and we do mental arithmetic, geometry and so on. First of all we do rectangles, then triangles, then squares, then circles, then cubes. With all that, our brains will gradually get used to the exercises you do at high school.

But I don't agree with Lounès. I think the stuff we do at primary school's pretty difficult too. Once they gave us a problem I'll never forget because instead of trying to find the answer I just kept thinking: 'Is that the way it is in real life?' This was the problem: a shopkeeper has bought ten hectolitres of red wine at thirty CFA francs a litre and a hundred and fifty litres of palm wine at twenty-five CFA francs a litre, how much must he pay? The whole class watched while Adriano, Willy-Dibas and Jérémie worked out how much the shopkeeper had to pay. I just sat there in the middle of the class, watching. They looked like hunchbacks looking for a needle they'd dropped on the floor. They were writing away furiously, while the rest of us just kept reading the exercise over and over. I was thinking: Why should we work out what the shopkeeper has to pay? Why can't he do it himself, instead of bothering us when we're still too young to be shopkeepers? Do Maman Pauline and Madame Mutombo think about bizarre sums in their business? Still, the answer had to be found, and only Adriano, Willy-Dibas and Jérémie found it. They got out of class before everyone else and I was the last to go.

The next day, after the teacher had given us all a taste of the strap, he finally explained how to work out what the shopkeeper had to pay.

'Now do you understand?'

We all answered:

'Yes sir!'

'Really?'

'Really!!!'

We didn't really understand at all, we had no idea, we'd just copied down what the teacher had written on the board. I know if he ever gives us the same problem again, only Adriano, Willy-Dibas and Jérémie will find the answer.

Lounès's school is called Trois-Glorieuses, after the Three Glorious Days of our Revolution. It's near the Adolphe-Cissé hospital, not far from the sea. You can't get there on foot, you have to get a bus from the Savon *quartier*. But the children don't want to pay for their tickets, they want to keep the money to spend it on doughnuts at break. So they take the Workers' Train which leaves directly from Savon, in the centre of town. It's the TO, an old train with four carriages, and it's normally used by the railway workers. But they let the schoolchildren take it, because if they work hard at school then one day they might become bosses in the national railway company, the Congolese Ocean Railway.

Lounès thinks the high school kids cheat a lot on this train because they've seen the film *Fear Over the City*. There's a white actor in it called Jean-Paul Belmondo who's got problems because there's a guy robbing banks in the city, and Jean-Paul Belmondo has to find him. But while he's looking for the bank robber there's another gangster called Minos going round killing single women. He says he's bringing justice to the city. Isn't that a bit weird, if someone wants to bring justice, to go round killing all the single women? So now Jean-Paul Belmondo has to go out and find Minos. He climbs on top of a moving train so he can chase the murderer, who's already up there. Lounès swears that Jean-Paul Belmondo never falls when he's fighting with Minos. The high school kids must have thought: If someone can climb on top of a moving train in a film without getting hurt, we can climb on top of the TO to avoid the ticket inspectors.

So when the TO arrives at Savon station, the high school kids are there, waiting to climb up. First of all they check out where the inspectors are. And as soon as the train starts up, they run and cling on to the doors. Within a few seconds there are at least a hundred of them up on top of the carriages. Lounès says it's called train-surfing. Once they're up there, they hang on tight and duck when they go through a tunnel, like in *Fear Over the City*. The inspectors can't follow them up there because they're scared they'll fall and be killed. Besides, they're already too old, and old people can't train-surf like high school kids. The inspectors get the TO to stop, and call the police. But by the time the police arrive it's too late, the kids have already run off and are walking the rest of the way to school. Tomorrow they'll be back, and they'll train-surf again.

One day I asked Lounès what makes a good train-surfer.

'First of all – you must be fearless. Jean-Paul Belmondo was never afraid, in any of his films. In *Fear Over the City* it wasn't him that was frightened, it was the city. Train-surfing's easy; you wait till the train sets off, you run for a bit, then you run a bit faster and you grab hold of the door. Then you climb on to the ladders between the trucks and you're up!'

Maman Pauline asked me to go and buy some sugar from Diadhou the Senegalese, who has one of the biggest shops on the Avenue of Independence.

I've only been walking for a few minutes, but it's so hot this Sunday afternoon that my feet are burning. I ignored my mother when she said I should put my sandals on. When you walk barefoot on the tarmac out of the shade it's like walking inside a wood burning stove. Sometimes I stop by the side of the road and shelter under a mango tree to cool my feet, but when I step back onto the tarmac my feet start burning again. So it's better to stay on the tarmac, then your feet get used to the heat and you won't even feel them. You just have to grit your teeth and try to forget you've got feet. It's a bit like when you're desperate for a pee and you're a long way from home. If all you think about is having a pee and how good it will feel when you've had one, the pee is quite likely to burst out suddenly while you're still in the street, and you'll wet your pants. But if you try to forget it for a moment, you can hold on for another few metres.

So I'm walking along and thinking about nice things, not my poor feet. I'm thinking of Caroline. I'm thinking of the red five-seater car. I'm thinking about the little white dog. I'm thinking about the radio cassette player. I'm thinking about the book of Arthur's poems and his angel face. And it works.

Now I'm outside Diadhou's shop. And who do I see inside? Oh

no, I don't believe it! I want to turn round and go home. It's Mabélé inside the shop, and he's waiting while Diadhou butters his slice of bread. It's the first time I've seen him close up. My heart falls into my stomach. I think: So when you're frightened it's like being in love, your heart falls into your stomach.

Mabélé turns round and sees me too. Now what do I do? I've no idea. I go up to the counter and stand behind him. I keep about a metre's distance between us. If he throws a punch at me, it won't reach me, I'll just step back a few centimetres.

Mabélé acts like he hasn't seen me. He watches while the Senegalese goes on buttering his bread. After a while Diadhou hands him his bread, he pays and turns round to leave the shop. He walks past me, shoulders me out of the way and says quietly, 'Asshole, I'll wait for you outside. Let's see who's tougher, you or me. And when I've smashed your face in, Caroline won't even look at you again!'

He leaves the shop. I can see him outside, gobbling up his bread. I'm so frightened I forget what I'm doing here.

'What do you want, Michel?'

I don't answer, just look out at the road. Diadhou asks me again, 'What do you want? Have you got a problem outside, or what?'

The Senegalese has just noticed Mabélé outside waving his fist, and can see he's waiting to beat me up.

Diadhou shouts from behind his counter, 'Hey, you out there! You get away from my shop. I don't want fighting outside my shop. I don't suppose your parents are paying for my license, are they?'

Mabélé's gone, and I remember now that I've come to buy some sugar for my mother. I pay, and tiptoe towards the door. I stand there looking up and down the street. I sense Mabélé's hiding somewhere. I can't see anyone. Perhaps he's behind a tree or behind the cars parked on the avenue.

I get ready, counting in my head, ONE, TWO, THREE! Then I shoot off like a rocket.

I don't look over my shoulder, I just run, run, run. I run so fast that when I get back to our lot I go running past it and fall into the yard of the neighbour, Monsieur Vinou, the old soak without a pistol, unlike Paul Verlaine. He shouts abuse at me, calls me a thief, little gangster etc. I jump over the barbed wire between the two lots, and I'm home, drenched in sweat.

I take a look out of the window: Mabélé is standing outside our house. This time he shakes his clenched fist three times in the air and leaves. I think: When he does that it means he'll get me next time, next time I won't escape like I did today.

'm cross with the Mexicans. They didn't want the Shah back in their country after his operation in America, so now the poor ex-president is in Panama. It's not right.

Papa Roger can't tell us where Panama is. He just says it's close to Costa Rica and Colombia – a country which plays football as well as Mexico, but hasn't hosted the World Cup yet like Mexico. Still, it's good that Panama have welcomed the Shah. He must be very tired and he needs rest.

My joy is short-lived, though. Because my father also tells us that the Panamanians have been influenced by the Ayatollah Khomeyni and want to send the Shah back to Iran. When I heard this I felt like roaring with rage, but I made myself calm down because Maman Pauline gave me a cross look. She thinks I encourage my father in this business of the Shah looking for a country to take him in.

The radio's playing up today. Sometimes the sound cuts out for a few minutes at a time. My father thinks it's the government doing that to prevent us being informed about what's going on in the world and make sure we go on believing the immortal Marien Ngouabi was assassinated by Imperialism and its local lackeys. Why is the government so determined to talk about this assassination as though it hadn't been involved in the death of our Immortal itself?

The sound's come back on the radio, and I hear the

American journalist say a very complicated word I've never heard before: *extradition*. It's very hard to pronounce, you have to pretend you're about to sneeze then clear your throat. I look at my father, he's leaning towards me, he says that *extradition* is when you capture someone in one country and send him back to where he came from so he can be tried. Lots of countries all over the world have signed an agreement to catch people they're looking for like the Shah and send them back to their country of origin for trial.

Papa Roger is furious: 'It's shocking that Panama are sending the Shah back to Iran! You never know what might happen there. Thankfully the Egyptian president has asked him to come back to Egypt, where he'll be safe! But for the Shah it's back to square one. What choice does he have? He has to go back to Egypt! His cancer is getting worse all the time. I'm sure they deliberately messed up the operation in the States. I hope at least he won't die in Egypt like an abandoned dog.'

Papa Roger and Maman Pauline are out, so I can secretly go and get the book by the young man with the face of an angel. It's almost like he smiles at me slightly more each day, as though he's pleased to see me. I've left him on his own for too long. When I look at his photo it's like meeting up with a friend. I'd like to tell him all about Mabélé, who wanted to smash my face in the other day, even though he's the one who's pinched my girl and talks to her about that annoying Marcel Pagnol guy and his castles.

I'd like to talk to him about Lounès too, how we're always together, he's my friend, we love each other like brothers, we tell each other everything, but I'm not going to tell Lounès that Mabélé nearly beat me up, or he'll try and get back at him with his advanced katas that Maître John teaches him. I just don't like fighting, that's why I'm not going to go to Lounès' karate club with him.

Arthur doesn't speak, he just goes on smiling at me. What do I know about him, apart from the thing about the 'hand that guides the quill' and the 'hand that guides the plough'? Who is he?

They do actually tell you more about him at the beginning of the book in a part called the 'Introduction'. It says there that Arthur came to our continent, and traded in ivory, gold and coffee. That means he liked trading, like Maman Pauline and Madame Mutombo. It says that sometimes he liked to party with beautiful African women. Who wouldn't like partying with beautiful African women? I don't quite understand why they make out he was really bored when he was travelling when in fact he was partying with beautiful African women. A bit further on I find out that Arthur made money – perhaps even a lot of money – with his business and that he deposited this money in a bank in Egypt.

Egypt? This piece of information startles me because that's where the Shah is now, suffering from cancer. It's odd to go and hide your money in a place where people who have been driven out of their own country have gone for a rest, to help them get over the cancer of extradition.

Oh no, I can't imagine Arthur selling arms like they say he did in this book. Arms are for killing people, for waging world war. The person who sells arms is as guilty as the person who uses them. Why was he selling arms when he himself had almost been killed by his friend who only missed because he was so drunk?

Still, that's not the thing that really bothers me. What makes me really sad is when I discover that he was ill and in the end they had to cut his leg off, or it would have rotted. They just went chop! And took it off. After that he had a worse limp than Monsieur Mutombo. After that, instead of a leg he had a stump of wood. After that he got really sick, towards the end of his all too short life. That makes me think of the Shah, who's sick with cancer. Arthur had cancer, like the Shah, and Arthur's cancer ate up his leg so badly that it came all the way up to his right arm. Cancer's always like that, it gets worse and worse, and ends up slowly killing you. That's what Papa Roger said when he was talking about the Shah, not about Arthur; I'm sure he doesn't know the young man with the face of an angel had the same illness as the Shah. He can't know that yet, he'll only know when he's retired and opens the pages of this book I'm holding now.

Further on still I read that Arthur never stayed long in one place. He was always on the move. He wasn't like the Shah, who couldn't find a country that would have him. He did it for the adventure. He loved it. The reason the Shah moves about is so the Ayatollah Khomeyni doesn't catch up with him. But Arthur moved about so his past wouldn't catch up with him. Even when he was dying in France, he said to his sister that he'd like to go off exploring to Egypt. Egypt again! I begin to wonder about this country with all those pyramids and mummies. Is Egypt the best place to die, perhaps? Even so, I don't understand Arthur's behaviour: you get back home to France, and then instead of dying there, you want to go back to Egypt! Fortunately he did die in France. And was buried there. In his native land. If the Shah dies he might not be able to be buried in Iran. That's why I pray for him, and not for Arthur, who rests in peace, in his native land.

Last year, when the teacher gave me my school report, I said to myself: 'If I show it to Papa Roger, he'll tell Maman Pauline what's going on, they'll see that the teacher has written things about my behaviour, that I behaved badly, and then they'll shout at me, like two people beating the same drum, on and on.'

I put the report in a plastic bag and hid it in an abandoned house not far from where we live. No one goes there, except rats and dogs. Because of them I decided to dig a hole and bury the report. Then I went back home, like a nice good boy who's come top of the class. Every day I was terrified they'd ask me: Michel, where's your report?

The first week, Papa Roger was worried because he hadn't seen my report, though my brothers and sisters at Maman Martine's had all shown him theirs. I told my father that the teacher hadn't finished filling them in yet. The second week, I said the same thing. The third week, I lied and said everyone else had had their reports but they'd forgotten mine.

Papa Roger was not pleased.

'I shall go and tell your teacher that's no way to treat my son!'

And off he went to the school. He didn't go to work that morning, he considered it was too serious a matter.

We were in class when I saw my father peering through the window. The teacher went out to see him, they stood outside talking for a few minutes. Then the teacher came back into the classroom and pointed his finger at me.

'Michel, stand up!'

I stood up, while my classmates behind me all murmured, 'It's a serious matter! A serious matter! A serious matter!'

As I was looking at the floor, the teacher lifted my head up.

'Now then, Michel, just repeat what you said to your father! Is it not the case that I gave you your report over three weeks ago?'

I lowered my head again.

'Repeat what you said to your father!'

My classmates, who'd heard the teacher's voice, jostled each other at the window to see what was happening.

This time it was Papa Roger who lifted my head up.

'Right let's go. I want to see this report today! Go and get your school bag!'

I went back into class and collected my things while my classmates went on muttering, 'It's a serious matter! A serious matter! A serious matter!'

We walked down the street, me in front, my father behind. After half an hour or so we arrived at the deserted house. As soon as we pushed open the door the dogs started barking in their own complicated language and disappeared through the holes in the wooden slatted walls. Papa Roger put his hands on his hips and glanced around him. Then he turned to me.

'Is this the place? Where's your report then?'

I knelt down in a corner of the house and started digging, while my father watched. I went on and on digging. When I felt the plastic bag it was a bit wet, as though bags sweat too, like people. Papa Roger snatched it from my hands and undid the knot. There was the report, inside the bag. When my father started reading it I thought: I'd better run for it, soon he'll get to the bit where the teacher writes remarks about the pupil's behaviour.

I took two steps back, turned around and scarpered, like the rats and dogs living in the deserted house. Every now and then I looked back, but Papa Roger wasn't behind me. As I ran I was thinking: Pretend I'm Carl Lewis, the black American that Roger Guy Folly's been talking about. Carl Lewis is still only a student at lycée, but already he can run and jump like an adult, and within two or three years he'll be the fastest runner in the world.

I got back to our house, panting. I went straight into my bedroom and hid under the bed, wondering, 'Will Papa Roger thrash me? If he thrashes me it will be the first time ever since he decided I'm his son too, like the children he had with Maman Martine.'

'Michel, come out of there! I know you're hiding under the bed!'

I came out with my face covered in dust and spiders' webs. I was already starting to cry. I could hear noise outside: it was Maman Pauline coming home from the Grand Marché. Since I was now standing there like a chicken waiting to have its neck wrung on New Year's Day, my father signalled to me: 'Sit down there, I need to talk to you. I am not pleased about what you've done.'

I sat down where I sit when we have beef and beans and I peer at the big shiny piece of meat on my father's plate.

'What is it this time?' asked Maman Pauline, who had come to stand behind me.

'I've found Michel's school report at last.'

'Where?'

'He'd buried it in a deserted house, the one just on the edge of the *quartier*.'

My mother sat down while my father opened the report. Impatient, as usual, she said, 'Well then?'

'Michel has worked well. He's made the grade, and the teacher has written, "Very assiduous pupil".'

Now I was really confused. The reason I'd hidden the report was because I thought 'Very assiduous pupil' meant a pupil who behaves badly, who talks all the time in class and is stupid, like Bouzoba.

So now Papa Roger was congratulating me, and Maman Pauline was starting to prepare my beef and beans. But my thoughts were elsewhere. I had just realised that 'very assiduous pupil' meant a very good pupil, who behaves well, who turns up to lessons and listens to what the teacher says.

Whenever Maman Pauline goes into the bush for her business, like now, I go and stay in my father's other house along with my seven brothers and sisters: Yaya Gaston is twenty-four, Georgette's eighteen, Marius is thirteen, Ginette is eleven, Mbombie is nine, Maximilien's six and Félicienne, the last of all, is two.

This is my home too, my sisters and brothers never say that Papa Roger's my foster father, they consider me their real brother.

Yaya Gaston is the oldest child in the family. Even at twenty-four he already looks like a proper grown-up. He has a little moustache, which he clips, like on the film posters at the Rex cinema. He looks like Papa Roger, except Yaya Gaston is taller. They nickname him 'the Frenchman' because he always answers in French, even if you say something to him in munukutuba, lingala or bembé. Also, he only ever wears French clothes. He buys them at the port in Pointe-Noire, where he works in Customs. Sometimes he doesn't buy his clothes, people give them to him, if they want to collect a big parcel from the customs office without paying anything. He has a big gold bracelet, which he wipes with a cloth dipped in something called Mirror. It stings your eyes like Flytox and smells stronger than wild cat's piss. Every morning he polishes his bracelet standing outside the door of his little studio, which is on the side of the road, but attached to the main house where the rest of the family lives.

Georgette is very pretty, everyone's always telling her, and since she knows already she spends all her time looking at herself in the mirror, asking her girlfriends what the boys think of her. She puts red lacquer on her nails at the weekend, but she has to take it off during the week because you're not allowed it at school. Last year when she was seventeen, Papa Roger nearly sent her off to live for good with a young man who often stops outside the house to pick her up and take her for a walk in the dark. This guy's called Dassin and he acts like the Lady Whistler who had the fight with Yeza the joiner.

Yaya Gaston got hold of him once and said, 'Dassin, if you don't stop hanging round outside our house, if I hear you whistling one more time to get my sister to come out, I'll smash your face in.'

Dassin was trembling, there was sweat dripping down his face, because our big brother's as strong as Tarzan. The whole neighbourhood is scared of him. But Dassin wasn't born yesterday, or the day before. He's found another way to confuse us: he sends the kids from round about, he pays them twenty-five CFA francs if they can get our sister Georgette out of the house.

Papa Roger isn't a bad man, but this was serious, Dassin had got our sister pregnant. The only reason we never saw the baby was because it went straight to heaven, without ever coming to earth.

Marius is an old man's name, that's what people say around here. Papa Roger likes the footballer Marius Trésor – he's a black who plays for the French team – so he called one of my brothers after him. Sometimes he gets called Trésor, which he likes. Marius dreams of going to France one day, so he can become a footballer like Marius Trésor who, according to him, is the first black captain of the French team, when there are players like Michel Platini and Didier Six in the team, who really ought to be captains, not him, because after all, you don't expect to find a black ordering whites around.

Marius knows how you smuggle your way to Europe. He's only thirteen, but he already knows that stowaways make their way through Angola where there's a civil war, and no one has time to keep checks on things when there's a war. The stowaways get the plane from there to Portugal, then make their way to France. He knows because his best friend, Tago, is Jerry the Parisian's little brother, and Jerry the Parisian's a young man who comes back home every dry season and tells us how in France you can get everything without working, including suits and ties. Jerry the Parisian's a Sapper, so Marius wants to be one too, it was him that told me Sapper stands for *Société des ambianceurs et personnes élégantes*. Sappers are people who dress really well, that's all they care about, they walk elegantly and wear expensive clothes made by European tailors, not by Monsieur Mutombo. Maybe that's why Monsieur Mutombo doesn't like them and is always criticising them. He says the Sappers are thugs that come from Paris to get our girls pregnant then abandon them and their children and go back and live a comfortable life in Europe.

Marius plans to leave our country the day he turns eighteen. So that means, if I've worked it out right, that in only five years' time, he'll go off to be a Sapper like Jerry the Parisian. Now at eighteen I don't think he'll be able to become a footballer, because the king, Pelé, started playing when he was fifteen. I think my brother's more likely to become a great Sapper than a great footballer like Marius Trésor, Didier Six or Michel Platini. You can be a Sapper at any age, you don't have to do lots of fitness training, go running every morning or work up a sweat training. But first Marius needs to find the money to get to France. Lots of money. That's why he works at the Victory Palace Hotel in the school holidays, putting out the bins and watering the flowers. Papa Roger got him this little job, but he doesn't know that the reason Marius works is so that one day he can leave us all and go and live with the Whites in Europe. So Marius is saving up his pocket money in a little wooden box he hides under the bed and checks before he goes to sleep and when he wakes up. He thinks there are jealous people in the neighbourhood who might cast spells to stop him going to Europe and becoming a great Sapper, or footballer. The jealous people might send rats to get under his bed, and they might eat all his money, even the coins. So every night he sprinkles this stuff round the box, called Death to Rats. Any rat that comes round trying to eat his money is going to die an instant death from the poison.

People round here always find the name Ginette surprising, but I think it's really pretty. It's the name of the owner of the Victory Palace Hotel. Our father wanted to please his boss, who'd given him his job and held on to him for years. Apparently the boss was pleased my father had called his daughter after her. The result was, Madame Ginette increased Papa Roger's salary by 130 CFAs a month. In December she gives our sister Ginette a bigger present than she gives the other children of the hotel workers who were not clever enough to call their daughters Ginette.

Ginette's a tiny little thing. You wouldn't think she was eleven, she looks more like eight. I guess she won't be very tall because Papa Roger's short. But you mustn't tell her she's too short or she'll get mad and refuse to eat her lunch or supper. If we want to really annoy her and eat her food we tell her she's really small, that she looks like she's only eight. If she's very hungry she'll eat anyway, and swear she won't eat tomorrow, at lunch or supper. By the next day she's already forgotten that we told her the day before that she was really small.

When he saw that his boss was really happy that he'd called our sister Ginette after her, Papa Roger decided he'd do the same again when he had another daughter. He planned to call her Marie-France, after Madame Ginette's older sister. But this time, Madame Ginette was not pleased. She said enough was enough. That it was getting ridiculous. Papa Roger was very disappointed. In the end he named his daughter after his late mother. So the sister who's nine is called Mbombie like our late paternal grandmother. Otherwise she'd have been called Marie-France and she would have always had a big present at the end of the year. Sometimes Papa Roger calls her Marie-France anyway, because he really likes his boss. But Mbombie doesn't like that name and she won't answer when you call her by it.

'Don't call me Marie-France! Have you ever heard of anyone called Marie-Congo or Marie-Zaire?'

Maximilien is a boy who never says no, where most people by the age of six have long since learned to refuse to do things that grown ups want. So at home everyone asks him to go and buy this or buy that, close the front gate, go and see if the pan is boiling over in the kitchen. As soon as you ask him to go and buy something he runs off like the world 100 metres champion. Then after a little bit he stops, comes back again and asks you all wide eyed, 'What was I meant to go and buy? Where do I have to go to buy it?'

Often we send him to get doughnuts, or sweets, or a Gillette razor blade for Yaya Gaston, ribbons for Ginette's braids, palm oil for Maman Martine. But when he gets back he gets shouted at because on the way home he's lost the change the shop-keeper gave him. We know he's lost it when he starts crying and pointing back at the street, as though the street had stolen his money. Sometimes he forgets to come straight home with the shopping and stops at the crossroads to watch a row between some prostitutes from Zaire who are fighting with forks and pan lids because the younger one has stolen the older one's client. Maximilien is determined to stop them fighting so that afterwards the older one, who's been beaten up by the younger one, will give him a bit of money for saving her life.

Félicienne is the baby of the family. Maman Martine looks after her as though she's her only child. As a result she still acts like a spoilt five month old baby even though she's two. It's as though she doesn't want to grow up. She still crawls, even though she can walk fine when she chooses, especially when she's coming to me. And she looks like she's going to hang on to her bottle for a while yet. Once I came across her fixing her own milk. As soon as she saw I was watching her she stopped and started crying, as if she'd been stung by a wasp. Maybe because she realised I had found out her little game.

Félicienne likes me to take her on my knee, but when I do I always feel something hot on my belly: she's wee'ed on me, and now she's laughing. She does it on purpose. So whenever she holds her arms out to me with a big smile to get me to pick her up and carry her on my shoulders, I look the other way. Because I know it's me she wants to wee on, no one else. It's not really naughty, it's just her way of playing with me, and perhaps it's also her way of telling me she loves me as much as her blood sisters and brothers.

love it when Yaya Gaston lets me sleep in his studio, even if it makes my brothers a bit jealous. Yaya Gaston knows I won't gossip about what goes on in his studio, though honestly I could tell all sorts of stories, because I see all the pretty girls who come to visit him and even bring him food. The food they bring is so good, they must make it extra well to make Yaya Gaston love them even more. I listen to them talking, boasting about how pretty they are, prettier even than film actresses, when it's not possible, in fact, to be prettier than an actress. They try to be nice to me so that Yaya Gaston will love them. But it's just a smokescreen really because when Yaya Gaston's back is turned there are some of them that stare at me with these big mean eyes; they want me to get out of the house so they can be alone with our big brother. I don't go, unless Yaya Gaston tells me to go take a walk outside. It's not their house, it belongs to us.

Out of all the girls who are crazy about Yaya Gaston, my favourite is Geneviève. She doesn't stare at me with big, mean eyes. She doesn't ask me to go and take a walk outside so she can do rude things with my big brother. No, she asks me to stay with her, she asks me what I've been learning at school, what I like doing best, and what I want to do when I'm older, when I'm twenty. And I rattle on and on, I'm chattier than a whole family of sparrows, that's all I do, just talk. I tell Geneviève that I want

to be this, that I want to be that and that I want to be this and
that both at the same time, if possible. I want to do everything.
I want to be a movie actor so I can kiss the actresses in Indian
movies; I want to be President of the Republic so I can make
long speeches at the Revolution Stadium, and write a book all
about how bravely I faced the enemies of the Nation; I want
to be a taxi driver so I don't have to walk on the hot tarmac at
midday; I want to be the director of the Pointe-Noire port so I
can get free stuff that comes from Europe; I want to be a vet, but
I don't want to be a farmer because Uncle René wants me to be
a farmer. I also want to write poems for Caroline. I tell her this,
and she smiles and says life is too short to do all those things.
You have to choose just a few, and above all, do them well.

When I'm with Geneviève my heart beats really fast. I want
to be in her arms, to smell her perfume. She's not very tall, which
is a good thing, because Lounès says a woman shouldn't be tall,
or no one will want to marry her. If her husband's smaller than
her, he'd be embarrassed to walk by her side.

Gaston calls Geneviève 'My Black Beauty' because her skin
is very dark. She doesn't straighten her hair with white people's
products like the other local girls, she combs it so it stands out
in a big 'Afro', and you want to touch it. It looks like a black
American woman's. She always wears white, which means she's
someone who takes care her clothes aren't dirty.

Sometimes I think the reason Yaya Gaston loves her must
be her eyes. When she looks at you, you want to give her everything, even a house with an upstairs or a huge piece of beef,
even when you've been really hungry for two days. I've never
seen eyes that colour before. They're like a calm, green river,
with bright little diamonds sparkling round the edges.

. . . . .

I love it when I'm with Geneviève and we're walking down the street. I hold my head high and walk like a big boy, so people will respect me. When a car comes up behind us it's me that says to Geneviève, 'Look out, there's a blue Peugeot 504 coming up behind us!'

She laughs, we stand aside, the car goes past and we continue on our way. We walk for a long time, in silence. I know that she's not talking because she's thinking about lots of things, she feels low because of the other girls who've slept in Yaya Gaston's studio.

We're still walking. Now we're at the road that runs parallel to the Avenue Félix-Eboué. Suddenly she turns her back to me, as though she were going to go back the way we've come. I stop too, and I see her wiping away tears. I ask her why she's crying, she says she's not crying, she's just got a bug in her eye. I offer to blow in her eye to get the bug out.

'It's ok thanks, it's gone now.'

I know they're tears, she's crying because Yaya Gaston makes her unhappy.

Why don't the other girls who stay over in the studio all have bugs in their eyes? It must mean they don't love Yaya Gaston. If you love someone and you're unhappy because they're behaving badly, it must make a bug fly into your eye so it starts watering.

We set off again. I think about Geneviève being unhappy, about the other girls who say she's too black, too small, that she doesn't know how to cook, etc. And as I put myself in Geneviève's shoes, I find I've got a bug in my eye too. I turn my back on her, like I'm going back the way we've come, but it's too late, she's seen.

She stands still and asks, 'Do you want me to blow in your eye to get the bug out?'

And remembering her reply, I murmur, 'Thanks, but it's ok, it's gone now.'

And we both laugh. I never want to be apart from her. I never want her to let go of my hand. I never want to go back to Yaya Gaston's studio. I feel good with her. I squeeze her hand tight. She squeezes mine. I'm sure I feel like I love her, does she love me too? I'm in love with her. I want to tell her, right now. But how? She might laugh at me.

I tell her anyway: 'Geneviève, my heart is falling into my stomach, I want to marry you.'

She isn't at all surprised and asks with a little smile, 'Why do you want to marry me?'

'Because I don't want you to go on being unhappy. I don't want bugs to keep getting in your eye.'

She touches my head, I look into her eyes: her green river has more and more diamonds sparkling round the edges. I dream I could be one of those diamonds. The biggest one of all. I shine brighter than all the other diamonds and I make sure the river always stays green.

'Michel, you're not grown up yet, you can't marry me...'

'I'll be grown up one day!'

'Then I'll be like an old lady to you.'

'No, you could never be an old lady, and I...'

'Michel, you already have a girlfriend, you told me last time. What's her name again?'

'Caroline.'

'She's the one you must marry, you're the same age and...'

'We got divorced.'

'Already?'

'It was her idea, not mine.'

'Why?'

'She's going to marry Mabélé and they're going to have a red five-seater car and two children and a little white dog...'

'Do you want me to talk to Caroline?'

'No, I'm too useless. I can't play football, and anyway, I haven't read Marcel Pagnol yet, the one who writes about the four castles Mabélé's going to buy for Caroline.'

We arrive at the Senegali's shop, opposite the bar called Le Relais. We go inside and Geneviève buys me two Kojak lollies.

We get back to the house, the other girls have left. They've left their things in a mess everywhere. Geneviève's going to be spending the night with Yaya Gaston and she sorts out the mess in the studio.

First of all the three of us eat, then I go to say goodnight to Maman Martine, and my sisters and brothers, in the main house. Papa Roger's reading the newspaper in the bedroom, I hear him cough. Deep down I know he's missing the radio cassette player back in the other house. He'd like to be listening to the Voice of America, Roger Guy Folly, the one who reports on the Shah of Iran. And he'd like to be listening to the singer with the moustache weeping for his tree, his alter ego. But that's our secret, in the other house. I'm not allowed to say, not even to Yaya Gaston, that we've got a radio cassette player that can record what people say.

Yaya Gaston and Geneviève sleep in the bed, and I sleep on a little mattress on the floor. There's a black sheet hung between the walls to separate us. It cuts the studio in half, but they've got more space than I have. And when there's a light behind the sheet wall, I can see their silhouettes blend into one, and move together, like I'm watching a film in black and white. I hear little noises, like a little cat crying because its mother's left it all alone in the street. But it's Geneviève's voice. Why is she laughing now, though, instead of crying for help?

Before I close my eyes, I think hard about my two sisters in heaven. My Sister Star and my Sister No-name. Is it night in paradise, or is it always sunny there? I ask them to watch over Maman Pauline, who's all alone in the bush and will be alone again in Brazzaville surrounded by bad people who look at women in tight trousers.

Maman Martine's got white hair growing on the sides. She realises I've seen them, that I'm thinking she's older than Maman Pauline, who is probably her younger sister, but really much younger, her daughter maybe. But I'm thinking something else: would she possibly agree to have a seed from my mother's insides and keep it in her insides, so that Maman Pauline's children wouldn't go straight to heaven without coming down to earth? If she'd do that, Maman Pauline would stop being unhappy, there'd be another child in our house, because Maman Martine's children don't go straight up to heaven as soon as they arrive. Also, if Maman Martine agrees to my plan, we could keep it secret, we would tell people that the little seed really came from her insides. One day I must talk to Papa Roger about it, because I don't really think this doctor can sort things out inside my mother, even if he's white and white people never get anything wrong. At the same time, I'm sure there must be loads of women like Maman Pauline, loads of women looking for a child the whole time, and who can't have one and never will, even if they're cared for by white doctors.

We're sitting outside the front door. Maman Martine is scaling the fish we're going to eat this evening when everyone's here. It doesn't matter if it's not beef and beans. I eat everything here, and I pretend I like everything. I can be fussy with Maman Pauline but not with Maman Martine, it would really upset her.

At home there's only Mbombie, Maximilien and little Félicienne, who's just pissed on me when I was being really kind and giving her her bottle. I don't know where the other children have gone. Yaya Gaston left early this morning for the port, and Papa Roger won't get back till sundown. My other brothers and sisters ought to be here too, because it's the end-of-year holiday.

Seeing I can't stop looking at the white bits in her hair, Maman Martine says, 'Ah yes, I'm not young like your mother Pauline, now. She must be the same age as one of my little sisters, the youngest, she's just twenty-seven, she still lives in Kinkosso.'

She looks up at the sky, murmuring, as though she's talking to someone else. She begins to talk, and she tells me how she grew up in Kinkosso and that to get to the village from the district of Bouenza you have to go in an Isuzu truck which takes four or five days. You go through other villages, across bridges that are just two trees laid side by side from one bank of the river to the other, so the trucks can pass. The only time they ever replace the trees is when there's an accident, and lots of people die. That's where she and Papa Roger met.

I like the way Maman Martine's voice sounds when she tells the story about her and Papa Roger. Somehow she puts a bit of magic into it. I sort of believe her, but sometimes it sounds a bit like one of those stories from the time when animals and men could talk to each other about how to live together in peace.

When Maman Martine talks about when she met Papa Roger, she has a smile that lights up her whole face, and smoothes out the little lines – she looks young again, like Maman Pauline. Her face is all smooth, her skin is like a baby's, her eyes shine and you forget about her grey hair. I imagine her as a young girl, turning boys' heads. Somehow she manages to forget I'm there, and to imagine it's someone different listening to her, her eyes are somewhere above my head, not focussed on me directly. She's talking to someone who doesn't exist, and I think: That often happens, it happens all the time, grown ups are all like that, they're always talking to people from their past. I'm still too little to have a past, that's why I can't talk to myself, pretending to talk to someone invisible.

Maman Martine doesn't realise that for a little while now her lips have been moving, her head gently swaying, her eyes growing moist, as though she's about to cry. Sometimes she misses a few scales on the fish in her hands and I point out to her that there are still some scales left on the fish, that we might choke when we come to eat it.

She speaks very quietly. 'Roger was a real little heart throb! I can see him now, as he was that year, back then in the village they still called him Prince Roger.'

Then she suddenly gives me a look as if to say she's finished talking to the people from the past, now she's talking to a real person. And that's when I learn that aged twenty, Papa Roger was the best dancer in the Bouenza. In Ndounga, his home village, he was respected. When the rhythm of the tam-tams really got going he could actually rise off the ground and dance in mid-air while the crowd applauded and the women looked on adoringly, including the ones who were already married. When it came to dancing no one could get a win over him, or even a draw. He was famous then, and that was how he got his nickname 'Prince Roger'. When there was a burial in that part of the country, they summoned him urgently, like calling a doctor when you're sick. He'd turn up with his group of dancers – there were ten of them, all strong and handsome – and they danced all through the night, so that the deceased would not be sad on their journey to the other world, where the road doesn't run straight, and there is no music, no dance.

The year he met Maman Martine, Papa Roger had been asked to go and dance in the village of Kinkosso, whose chief had died, aged one hundred and ten. Everyone, from all the villages in the region, had come to his funeral, because it wasn't every day someone died aged one hundred and ten. When he got to Kinkosso, Prince Roger announced to the villagers, who were showering him with presents, 'This evening I will dance more then ten centimetres off the ground because it's our grandfather's grandfather who's died.'

The old sorcerers of the village threatened to make *gris-gris* against it, because they didn't want the other villages in the Bouenza to think Prince Roger was the best dancer in the whole world. The old sorcerers knew the secret of the levitation dance but ever since its invention, no one had seen a human being dance ten centimetres off the ground.

Prince Roger insisted: 'No one's going to stop me paying my respects to our grandfathers! I *will* dance ten centimetres off the ground!'

The old people went a long way off from the village and held a big meeting against the rude young man who was poking fun at them. They nearly started fighting among themselves in the meeting. They all accused each other of inviting that rude Prince Roger. But in the end they reached agreement: they must make sure that the stranger's dance went no higher than ten centimetres off the ground.

That evening when Prince Roger turned up in the village with his troupe, to find the women weeping over the corpse of the chief, he walked past three of the fetishers, and the oldest one came close to jostling him: 'Hey, son, this isn't just any village you know. You're in our village here, and here we have rules that date back to the time when our ancestors walked about naked and didn't yet know the word made flesh. You've got no grey in your beard yet, you're too young to understand certain things only those with four ears and four eyes can grasp. You'd better watch out, you mark my words. You may not respect our village, but you'd better respect my grey beard and bald head.'

Prince Roger replied: 'Grandfather, I accepted your invitation to come to Kinkosso because the man who just died is someone special. He's not just the chief of the village, he's our grandfather's grandfather.'

'Yes, but if you dance more than ten centimetres off the ground, you're done for! You dance how you want, but no higher than ten centimetres! Don't disgrace us in front of our people!'

Another unpleasant old man threatened: 'Who d'you think you are anyway? Why d'you take this tone with us, when you've no grey beard and no bald head? Where were you the day the first white man set foot in this village, offering his mirrors, his sugar and guns, and taking our strongest men far away, across the sea? There's Maniongui, who just asked you to show respect for his grey beard, his bald head, do you have a gold war medal too, like him? Old Maniongui's seen every French president, since Emile Loubet at the start of the century, to General de Gaulle! Anyway whoever gave you the title of Prince, you don't deserve it! We're the ones who give titles! I'm giving you one last warning; if you dance more than ten centimetres off the ground, we'll be burying you next, after our grandfather's grandfather! And your corpse won't find its way home, you'll be buried in the bush like a wild beast!'

The third old man spat on the ground. Which meant that he

wasn't going to waste his words like the others.

Prince Roger moved away from the old men, but they went on threatening him behind his back. He called together his ten dancers to give them their instructions: 'These old men are afraid they'll look stupid, no dancer from this village has ever gone higher than ten centimetres, even though the levitation dance first started here in Kinkosso. We won't be influenced by a handful of old goats who fancy themselves the guardians of tradition. We've learned their technique, we've mastered it, and now we're the best in the region. And tonight we'll prove it again, so get yourselves ready and don't lose heart. You beat your tam-tams, as usual, and I'll look after the rest.'

Maman Martine is scaling the last of the fish, and she almost cuts herself with the knife when she cries, 'Prince Roger! What a fine young man! What a stubborn young man!'

When she saw I was waiting for the rest of the story, she cleared her throat and continued: 'The evening of the grand-father's funeral the men of Kinkosso lined up on one side and the women on the other. And between the two, Prince Roger danced bare-chested, with a wrap made of raffia, and cowries round his waist, bells on his ankles and white clay on his face and in his hair. The bravest of the women were meant to step into the area left for Prince Roger, and dance along with him. But none came. Now the crowd was growing restless, this wasn't the kind of show you put on to say goodbye to the chief of the village. You could hear angry whistles, people shouting for a proper show. There had to be dancing, so everyone could get into a trance. Prince Roger whispered something to one of his dancers, who then yelled a challenge to the audience, and I can still hear that low voice shouting: "Prince Roger is very disappointed in this village! Have you no women in Kinkosso, or what? Is this the way to salute the memory of the grandfather of our grandfathers? If that's the way it is, Prince Roger is stopping right now, he's going home to his village. And he swears he won't be coming back to help you next time someone dies." At this, one skinny young village girl shot out of the line of other women, like an arrow. Prince Roger's dancers all applauded, the crowd clapped too, and the drums went wild, as though the hands of ghosts were drumming. You could hear them the length and breadth of the district, they even woke the animals sleeping in the forest. The young village girl kicked up the dust as she danced. The wind blew so hard now, it lifted the pagne round her waist up to her chest, and you could see her red pants.

'Everyone stepped back, and slowly the levitation dance began. The old men of Kinkosso shouted for joy, and they danced too, happy to see that the dance was led by a girl from the village, and not that rude Prince Roger. One of the old fetishers who had threatened Prince Roger earlier in the day asked his colleague: "Tell me, whose daughter is that? What's her family name again?" Another replied "What does it matter? Who cares who it is and what her name is, I just know she's a girl from Kinkosso, and she's leading the dance! So let's dance with her! That rude little guy who claims he's a prince is finished now! Shame on him!" Everyone booed Prince Roger. They all said he was useless. All this time, he was watching the girl with his arms folded. He turned to the chief drummer of his group. "Hey, who's this stick insect coming on to me, who is she, she dances like a sparrow that's just fallen out of her parents' nest." The chief drummer almost shouted, "We don't know her, but she's got to almost five centimetres off the ground, you'd better do something or it'll be a disgrace for us and the village of Ndounga!" Prince Roger made his mind up. "I'll just have to go higher myself. After all, I'm the prince! Give me ten bars of *muntuntu* beat, the one Mubungulu used to play when he was alive, when he played for the dead in the Batalébé cemetery!" One of his dancers was afraid. "You really want us to play that? It's too dangerous! The last time we played that rhythm it almost got you killed!" Prince Roger was adamant. "I'm telling you, it's an order!"

'And so the rhythm of the tam-tams suddenly changed. Even the sky started to stir, as though something might fall on our heads any moment. When the drummers beat their rhythm it was as though the skin of the drums was bursting and the clouds were parting. The villagers' eardrums were fit to burst with the unfamiliar rhythm, and they covered their ears. Up went Prince Roger, up off the ground. He reached six centimetres, then seven, then eight. He never got up to ten, because the three old fetishers who'd been on at him earlier that day were upon him, tearing at their beards in anger. He came back down to earth, the old sorcerers sighed with relief. Now, behind them, the skinny little village girl from Konkosso had started dancing again, and now she was ten centimetres off the ground and all the villagers were applauding. Furious, Prince Roger pulled himself up to his full height, span round in a circle, nodded to the drummers, who doubled, then tripled then quadrupled the speed of the lamented Mubungulu's *muntuntu* rhythm. And there they saw Prince Roger begin to rise, pedalling now, then up he rose, then pedalled again, then rose again, then pedalled harder and harder. We knew he must be over ten centimetres by now, but because no one believed it, there was now total silence in the village. They said it was the

spirit of the grandfather of our grandfather that had hidden
inside Prince Roger's body. The villagers were frightened and
fled from the wake with their mats rolled up under their arm
pits, with their wailing children. The dogs ran off into the bush
with their tails between their legs, like wild beasts. Even the old
men who'd challenged Prince Roger and his dancers had gone.
The corpse of our grandfather's grandfather was abandoned,
and Prince Roger had come back to earth, panting as hard as
if he'd been lugging great sacks of potatoes for miles. He fell
into a coma, the people in his group brought him round by
throwing cold water over him. As soon as he opened his eyes
he asked the drummers, "How high did I get?" And they all
replied in chorus, "Over fifteen and a half centimetres!" He got
to his feet, murmuring, "Let's get back to Ndounga straight
away, I don't know what's happened here. I've never been that
high before, I wasn't alone, a spirit was pushing me, and I could
have died, I couldn't breathe properly up there." It was already
past four in the morning when Prince Roger and his group set
off again for Ndounga. On the road they heard a strange noise
behind them. They turned round, each one ready to run for it,
as you do when you meet a devil out in the bush. The dancers
had already scattered, but Prince Roger stayed where he was
and saw someone coming towards him. He shouted after the
men who'd disappeared, "Come back! Come back! It's no devil!
It's the skinny little dancer from Kinkosso."'

Maman Martine said, with a broad smile, 'And that skinny
little girl from Kinkosso was me...'

Then she burst out laughing.

'Prince Roger, what a gangster! He took my hand, all I said
was, my name was Martine, but straight away he answered,
"There's a reason you followed me all this way. You are the

future mother of my children. We'll leave Bouenza, otherwise the old men in your village will be after us for the rest of our lives. We'll go and live in the town." And so I followed Prince Roger because I knew he would be the father of my children, too, and that the grandfather of our grandfathers had given me a sign, because I'd never danced the levitation dance before that night and I don't know what it was that pushed me to step out of the line of women and start out-dancing your father. Destiny, that's what they call it, it's destiny.'

She finished scaling the fish and put them on the board. I can see her dusting them with flour and salt.

'I'll grill them in a while with palm oil, and I'll make you a nice little tomato sauce. You'll see, you're going to love it.'

Before going to tip the bowl of water mixed with scales and blood into the gutter, she said, 'I could have been someone different, you know. But perhaps this was the best life I could have had. I only stayed at school till the fourth grade; your father had his lower school certificate, and even studied at the high school in Bouenza till seventh grade. That helped when we came to live here: the Whites wanted people who'd been to school, especially with diplomas, like him. A few weeks after everything that happened in Kinkosso, Prince Roger and I secretly boarded an Isuzu truck bound for Kouilou, making for Pointe-Noire. We needed to leave Bouenza without telling anyone. So we left just like that, each of us with a little bag. I was already pregnant, that father of yours is a real rabbit. I knew our life was going to change, and Prince Roger got a job at the Victory Palace Hotel, just after Yaya Gaston was born. That has to be fate, don't you think?'

My little brother Maximilien's sweating. He's been running so fast, someone must have sent him to buy something more than ten kilometres away.

He's still quite out of breath as he tells me:'There's someone looking for you outside. He's giant, he's taller than you, he bends over a little bit so people will think he's a child like us, but really he's a great big guy like Tarzan! Who is he? Does he want a fight with you? Did you steal his marbles in the playground?'

I don't answer. It's Mabélé after me again, he's come to smash my face in.

While I'm getting ready to leave our house, Maximilien shouts: 'Michel don't get into a fight, the giant will win! He's got these huge muscles!'

I stand by the entrance to our house and look out, but I can't see anyone. Where can he be hiding then, this giant? Behind the tree opposite? I have a good look, but there's no one. So I decide to go back inside the house to shout at Maximilien for teasing me. Just as I turn round to go, I hear someone whistling loudly, three times, from the house belonging to Jerry the Parisian's father.

It's Lounès. He couldn't bear us not seeing each other for a few days.

'So you're the giant that scared Maximilien! Why don't you come on inside?'

'It's better to talk outside, then we can see the planes go by.'

We go on down to the river Tchinouka. You have to take the road as though you're making for the Voungou *quartier*. It's a new *quartier*, where, instead of building proper houses, people build houses out of slats. They say that later, when they've got lots of money, they'll break up these houses and build proper, permanent ones. But that's just lies, because if you've got money you don't mess about, you build a proper house straight away and have done with it. Everyone calls these buildings 'houses just for now'.

The river Tchinouka divides the Savon *quartier*, where my father's house is, and the Voungou *quartier* where one day he hopes to buy another plot. There are some young boys fishing by the river. I wonder what they find there because there's more rubbish than fish in that water. People dump their rubbish there, they shit in it, sometimes they throw their old furniture and mattresses into it. No one says to them, 'Don't do that, it's wrong to behave like we were still in pre-history, when man still wasn't quite sure whether to stay as a monkey or turn into a creature that walks on two limbs and talks with real sounds.'

We lay stretched out in the grass, listening to the water flowing close to our feet.

'I asked my teacher what *saligaud* and *alter ego* meant,' Lounès says.

'But there's no school this week. Where did you meet him?'

'He came into my father's workshop to pick up his jacket.'

'So?'

'A *saligaud* is someone dodgy, someone who does bad things, and an *alter ego*'s like if you were me and I was you. If you're *alter egos* it means you can tell each other everything, anything you say, it could have been me that said it, and anything I say could have been said by you.'

'So the tree of the singer with the moustache is…'

'Yes, it's his *alter ego*. The singer wishes he hadn't left his tree like a bad person would, when the tree's his friend.'

After a moment's silence he goes on, 'You know what the teacher told my father? Don't laugh! He told him to buy me a dictionary, then I could find the definition of every French word there is…'

A plane is just going past. Lounès says: 'Guess where it's going to land.'

'Iran. The capital of Iran is Teheran…'

He's amazed. I don't usually answer that fast.

'How did you know that?'

'The Shah… He's the ex-president of Iran, and the Ayatollah Khomeyni wants to put him on trial and he's in Egypt and he's sick. And the Iranian students want him sent back to Iran and they've taken the Americans hostage in a basement of the embassy in Teheran. It's called extradition. But if the Shah gets sent back there they might kill him!'

I stare at Lounès in silence for a while.

'Why are you looking at me like that? Have I got a spot on my face or what?'

'No. But those little hairs there, on your chin… Is that your beard? Have you put beer froth on your chin?'

He touches his chin. 'Can you see from a distance, then, that I've got hair there?'

'A bit.'

'It's not beer froth, it's hair growing.'

'You'd better cut it quick, or people will think you're really old.'

'No, my father says if I cut it now then bigger hairs will grow back, and they'll be really hard.'

He closes his eyes. I know he's thinking. I can tell he's going to come out with something serious. That's perhaps why he's come to see me.

I try and think what could be serious, but I can't. I mustn't disturb him, though, I must let him concentrate.

At last he opens his eyes: 'Michel, I've always told you everything, and now there's something really big you haven't told me, it's almost like you lied to me…'

'Me, lied to you?'

'I was at my aunt's house, I saw Caroline, she told me Mabélé nearly beat you up and you ran away like a coward instead of putting up a brave fight. If I don't know what's going on how can I help you? Why don't you come to Maître John's karate club with me?'

I want to tell him I don't like doing press ups because they make you sweat and afterwards it really aches. And anyway, when you get into a fight you forget your karate because the other guy you're fighting's not going to wait for you to do your advanced katas and fly through the air like Bruce Lee.

It's as if Lounès can read my thoughts, because he says, 'If you like we can both sort out Mabélé. I'll leap into the air while you grab his arm and when I land again I'll beat him till he bleeds, and…'

'No, he'll go and tell tales to Caroline. Your sister will go on loving him and she'll hate me.'

Lounès gets up suddenly, as though he's really surprised by my reply. 'Hey, you're right!'

The boys fishing on the other bank throw stones at us. They think they're not catching any fish because we're talking too loud and the fish can hear us. We lower our voices, and since we've stopped talking we feel like falling asleep. We'll be there for at least an hour, waiting for the planes to pass overhead.

I give Lounès a shake to wake him up, and tell him I have to go home because I'm worried they might be looking everywhere for me, especially since Maximilien thinks I'm having a fight with a giant. He'll probably tell them that at home and the whole family will come out to look for me.

Lounès comes with me as far as our place. Maximilien's been standing on the same spot all this time, in the middle of the lot, like a post. He runs inside the main house to call Marius.

Marius comes out to face us with a stick in his hand. Maximilien's hiding behind him like a frightened dog and he screams till he's hoarse, pointing at Lounès: 'It's him! It's him! He's the giant Tarzan that wants to beat up our Michel!'

Marius grabs Maximilien's ears and goes back inside the house where he was probably busy counting his savings so he can get to Europe one day and become an even more famous footballer than Marius Trésor or a star sapper, like Jerry the Parisian.

Lounès has just left. Maximilien's sobbing in a corner of the lot, still going on about Tarzan the giant.

He comes over to me and takes my arm and murmurs, 'You know, I really wanted to protect you from the giant, but I'm still too little. When I'm big, I swear I'll protect you against the bad guys round here.'

There are three girls arguing in Yaya Gaston's studio. Geneviève takes me by the hand and says, 'That's not for your ears, come on, let's take a walk outside.'

I've been hoping she'd say that ever since she walked in and sat down in a corner.

It's dark outside. In the street we pass old ladies selling fritters and saltfish and maize. You can hear music coming from the bar called Joli Soir, and the noise of people drinking and dancing inside. Sometimes I'd like to go inside and see how they drink and dance in there. I'm not very tall yet, I might get trampled on, they might not realise I was there. And also, if I get beer froth on my chin, I'll have little hairs like Lounès and they'll think I'm an old man, when it's not actually true.

We get to a street lamp in the Avenue Félix-Eboué. There are some people sitting about there, and I even see a man and a woman kissing each other on the mouth and touching each other, you'd think they'd no bedroom at home to do it in. If I was them I'd feel embarrassed for a year, or more.

Geneviève stops, opens her bag, rummages inside and pulls something out.

'I know you're going back to your maman's in Trois-Cents tomorrow. I've got a little present for you.'

She holds out a packet to me. It's not every day I get given something that isn't a lorry, a rake and a plastic spade for playing farming with.

I open the wrapping and there, inside, is my present.

'Is it a book?'

'Yes, *The Little Prince*. It's the first book my father gave me when I got my primary school certificate and I know you're going to get yours soon.'

We go into the shop and I choose two boiled sweets. I offer her one, she says no. I keep it in my pocket for Maximilien, who'll be very happy when I give it to him.

On the way back home, we go past the streetlamps again. The man and woman who were kissing have moved on now. They're a little bit further down the street, where there's less light. They're so stupid, what if a snake comes and bites them in the night, what will they do then?

Geneviève talks to me quietly. As though she hopes I'll keep what she says a secret, just between us two.

'I love your big brother, he doesn't realise, he's blind. He's strong and handsome, he can have any woman in the *quartier*. I'm nothing next to him, but in fact I'm everything, because I love him with all my heart. Besides, he's the only man I've ever known, and I'll never go with another man, unless he throws me out so he can live with one of those girls who come to his house to argue. I'll wait a hundred years for him if I have to, love knows no limits. But I'm hurt, really hurt, and I lick my wounds in silence. When I talk to you I'm talking to him as well. Am I wrong? Am I right? Oh, Michel, I don't know. Yaya Gaston's not a child like you any more. He's spoiled his innocence with pride and flirting.'

We find Yaya Gaston all alone in his studio. He tells us he's kicked out all the girls because he was sick of them fighting. Now this was not what I wanted to hear. I hoped he would say he'd kicked them out so as to be alone with Geneviève. This was probably what Geneviève was hoping he'd say too, because we glanced at each other and then she lowered her eyes and went to tidy up the mess the girls had left. She put a mattress down on the ground for me and took out the sheet and pillow hidden under my brother's bed. She put out the storm lantern and lit a candle, just by my head and then got into bed with Yaya Gaston. I'm not tired yet. I lie with my back against the wall and start reading the little book she gave me. And I start murmuring the first few lines as though it's a prayer:

> *I lived alone, with no one really to talk to, until one day six years ago, when my plane broke down in the Sahara desert. A part of the engine was broken, and since I had no mechanic and no passengers I decided I must carry out the repair myself. It was a question of life or death...*

I go on reading the book, and as I read a word echoes round in my head: *desert.* I try to picture what a desert looks like, because we've got loads of forest here. I love the word *Sahara*, too. Even saying it is really hard, you have to remember to say the 'h'. It feels like it's far far away, as though the people there don't know that the rest of us exist, that someone in this house is reading a story that takes place where they live. How can I imagine a place I've never seen? So now I think of the Sahara just as desert, nothing else. And I wonder why the funny little man in the book went there, instead of coming here where there's lots to see, and plenty of people to meet. He could have lived with me. We could have walked together down the streets and the avenues in all the different neighbourhoods, or along the banks of the river Tchinouka with Lounès. In the Trois-Cents *quartier* the little man would have been surprised to see us all playing, running about, sometimes getting into trouble. But maybe the desert is a wonderful, magical place. Maybe there the people have a forest in their imagination. An evergreen forest. Maybe in the desert there's more room to live and maybe it makes you realise you're lucky to be born in a country where there are lots of trees and rivers and streams, and even an ocean, like here. Even so, I'm a bit worried the desert's where all the dead people gather and wait for the day when God says: 'You're going to heaven, you're going to hell'. I don't want to go to the Sahara. All I care about is, tomorrow I'll see Maman Pauline again.

My parents are having yet another row. And as usual I can hear them from my bedroom. Maman Pauline's sobbing, she thinks the white doctor they've seen is no good because she's still not pregnant. My father is calm, he says they must be patient, babies can't be made to order, that they always take their time and come along if you don't think about them every day.

My mother's talking very loud, she wants to give up her business. She brings up the question of Maman Martine's children and the Mutombos' children again.

My father raises his voice. 'I'm sick of you always bringing up the other children! It's not Martine's fault you and I don't have children! Michel's a child isn't he? His sisters and brothers love him, they've never once said the kid isn't their brother. Why do you go and say things like that, when we're trying to find a way out of this situation?'

'I'm giving up the business! I don't care! Why should I spend my whole life working when I haven't any children? Who am I working for?'

'Great! Ok, then, you give up your business, and let's hear no more about it! Maybe then we'll have some children!'

Maman Pauline hated him saying that. I can hear her breaking things in the bedroom. I think to myself: If Arthur's listening to this and watching this performance, I hope he's not disappointed by it.

I sit on the bed for a few minutes. I must do something. I can't let them go on rowing all night.

I get up and draw the mosquito net aside and go towards the living room. They've heard me. Papa Roger half opens the door of their bedroom. 'You go and sleep now, little one, it's all ok, your mother and I are just having a bit of a talk, nothing serious, she's just telling me how things are going with her business.'

I go back to my room and hide under the sheets. I don't want to see my surroundings. My room's like a coffin that's too big for my little body, I think. I'm suffocating in it. If that happens I'll go back to the planet I came from. I'll be in peace, then, in my own world, I'll grow roses. I'll water them every morning with water as green as the river that flows in Geneviève's eyes. The drops of water on my roses will be diamonds, sparkling in the sun. I will be a happy gardener because whatever I plant, even in the desert, will just grow. I'll walk about my field of roses, and even the butterflies will be rose-coloured. I will live in a world full of laughing, playing children, children with no mother, no father. We'll all be children because that's what God made us, and God is our Father. He'll say to us: 'Now children, you be quiet, I'm having a sleep'. And we'll be quiet because when he's sleeping, God always dreams up nice surprises for children. But He'll never have to raise his voice to tell us. He'll never have to whip us, because He can't whip what He's created in his own image. And we'll live happily, far from adults with their problems which have nothing to do with us. I will be the big brother of all the children. I'll walk ahead, to protect them. And if anyone attacks us, my muscles will swell up, and my chest too, I'll grow taller than two metres, and my fist will be bigger than a mountain.

. . . . .

My father's calmed down and my mother's listening to him. I come out from under my sheets again and creep towards the wall. I want to know what they're saying to each other because when adults are saying mean things about someone they often lower their voices. I think: Perhaps if they're talking quietly they're plotting something against me.

'We'll try a different solution.'

'What?' my mother replies.

'There's a fetisher come to work in the Voungou district, just across the Tchinouka. Everyone say's he's very good. The wife of the local chief was sterile and he cured her. He even got a ten-year-old child who'd never spoken a single word to talk.'

'What's he called, this fetisher?'

'Sukissa Tembé. He's from the north. Apparently he was personal fetisher to the President of the Republic. That's the only reason the President and his wife have a child, thanks to Sukissa Tembé.'

'Except people say that child's actually the President's nephew, and…'

'Pauline, listen to me, people can say what they like! They're just jealous, and jealous people get what's coming to them! There'll always be people who speak ill of others in this world. Sometimes they're people we try to help, and they get sly and hypocritical and cynical to hide their unhappiness. What matters is that the President and his wife have a child now, thanks to the fetisher, and that's all there is to it! We'll go and see him on Saturday!'

'But it's only Monday today. Saturday's ages away!'

'I know, but you have to have an appointment.'

'What? You have to have an appointment to see a fetisher now, like for a white doctor?'

'Everyone round there goes to see him, even people looking for work and people who want their children to do well in their exams. Not counting the ones with chronic diarrhoea or painful periods and the rest. It's a difficult thing we're asking, we'll need a half-day appointment, at least.'

Maman Pauline's stopped crying. She's reassured by this suggestion. But I'm thinking: What's all this about? Can a fetisher catch children who go directly to heaven without stopping off on earth? Is a fetisher more powerful than God?

I'm frightened for Maman Pauline. I have a feeling she's heading for another disappointment. I don't want her to be disappointed yet again, and have her crying for weeks and months to come when no baby turns up in her tummy, which has not been lived in since I came into the world.

Outside there are dogs barking. I don't like that. They say that if dogs bark at night it means the bad spirits are in the neighbour-hood and that some of them are on their way to market to sell the souls of people who are about to die. People think there's no one at the market at night, but in fact the bad spirits are there with their goods to sell, waiting for customers till four in the morning, when they go back to the cemetery. If the bad spirits heard what my parents were saying they'd make quite sure no baby ever came to our house.

I say a prayer to my Sister Star and My Sister No-name under the sheet:

Dear Sister Star
Dear Sister No-name

Please make it so Maman Pauline stops crying
Make it so Papa Roger doesn't get tired of it all
Make it so the bad spirits don't hear what my mother and
*   father are saying*
Make the fetisher Sukissa Tembé do for my parents what he
*   did for the President of the Republic and his wife*
Let a baby come to this house
Make it so the Shah of Iran doesn't die, make it so he
*   recovers from cancer and the Ayatollah stops bothering*
*   him all the time*
Make it so no country in the world will accept the Shah's
*   extradition.*

This afternoon I'm alone in my parents' bedroom. Maman Pauline's gone to the Rex *quartier* with Madame Mutombo to visit a girlfriend whose father has died. She's bound to be very late back, which is fine because Papa Roger's over at Maman Martine's tonight.

My father's books are here in front of me. There's Arthur's face. He's smiling at me, so I can go on, he's encouraging me.

I'm kneeling down, and I've got a book in my hands. The title is *Do Things to Me* and the writer is called San-Antonio. A strange name, more like a nickname.

I look at a second book: *One Flew Over the Cuckold's Bed*. San-Antonio again.

I pick up a third book: *Give Me Your Germs, My Darling*. San-Antonio again.

A fourth book: *Put Your Finger Where Mine Is*. San-Antonio again.

And a fifth book, again by this San-Antonio guy: *Dancing the Shah-Shah-Shah*. Amazing: so this San-Antonio guy was interested in the Shah too? Anyone who writes about the Shah must be a good guy. On the back cover of *Dancing the Shah-Shah-Shah*, which sounds more like an exercise than a book, someone's written a resumé, but I think it must be San-Antonio himself speaking, because he says 'I' all the time:

To be honest, I had long dreamed of going to Iran. But not

in these conditions! This is the 20th century after all. A little
surprising, then, to find oneself in a sabre fight! But fear
not, your San-Antonio soon reveals himself an ace in this
discipline, and the sbires who try to rub him up the wrong
way, while not exactly eunuchs, are no Casanovas either. As
for the adventures of Bérurier in the land of the Thousand
and One Nights (thousand and one plights, more like), they
cannot be summed up in one short paragraph. Let it simply
be said that when it comes to giving your dancing the Shah-
Shah-Shah there are many ways of crumbling that cookie!
Some harder than others, as you will see!

What does he mean, there are lots of ways to crumble a
cookie and that it can be hard to dance the Shah-Shah? Is that
meant to be funny or sad? What's the Shah done to him? And
it sounds as if he's decided to go and fight in Iran, this San-
Antonio. Well, I don't like the sound of that one bit. So I put the
book down on the bed.

I don't know why, but I can't take my eyes off the cover of *One*
Flew Over the Cuckold's Bed. Maybe because there's a picture
of a bird on it. I like birds because they live on the earth and in
the skies. Birds can see forests, like ours, as well as deserts, like
the Sahara, in *The Little Prince*. They travel long distances and
sing, to make the sun shine on the earth. Birds are nice, they
never harm anyone. You won't find a bird going to Iran to fight,
like San-Antonio.

I also read the back cover of *One Flew Over the Cuckold's*
Bed.

This time, folks, the agency gets a call from Arthur
Rubinyol, the famous virtuoso. Oh my Lord, roll out the
red carpet, sing hymns of praise! Good job it was red is

all I can say. At least the wine stains won't show. To start with, there's the rabbi, Sly-ball, oops, sorry, Silas, who goes and gets himself stabbed. Not to mention Miss Yankee, who cadges a lift in my plane, and sets about who-know-what-ing your old friend! Throw in our Finnish jaunt, during which Béru has a sniff at the lumberjack's old lady, and I think you'll agree that there are some pretty odd goings on in this here opus! And all because of a vindictive old cuckold! Talk about horn of plenty!

San-Antonio writes a rude sort of French, I think to myself. It's like you're supposed to laugh at certain bits, because if you don't it means you don't understand his sense of humour, so you must be stupid. And what about this Arthur Rubinyol he talks about in his book, the one who's a 'famous virtuoso'? Might he be poking fun at my Arthur, even though my Arthur's never done anything to him?

I leave *One Flew Over the Cuckold's Bed* and read the back covers of the other books by San-Antonio. But I don't want to move everything, I'll only look at the backs, because Papa Roger has lined them all up so neatly, you can read the titles.

In this bookcase there are only books by San-Antonio, apart from the one by Arthur. Has San-Antonio written more books than anyone in the world? What's Arthur doing here then, lying on top of these books? I think: San-Antonio must be very famous, more famous than Marcel Pagnol, more famous than Arthur, more famous than the Shah of Iran.

I put back the five books. I try to remember what order they were in before, but I get in a muddle. Was *Give Me Your Germs, My Darling* on top of *Put Your Finger Where Mine Is* or underneath *Do Things to Me*? I can't remember now.

In the end I just put *A Season in Hell* on top of *Dancing the Shah-Shah-Shah*. Because the Shah San-Antonio writes about must be the same one who's sick and in Egypt. Because I think Arthur also needs to know that the Shah of Iran isn't well, that his cancer's getting worse, while that criminal, Idi Amin Dada, lounges around in the pool in his villa in Saudi Arabia.

The president of France is called Valéry Giscard d'Estaing. While the journalist, Roger Guy Folly, is speaking, my father writes the name of the president down for me on a piece of paper. French people's names are too complicated, they're never written the way they sound. But then the French think our names are too complicated. Odd, isn't it?

Roger Guy Folly informs us that Valéry Giscard d'Estaing is in deep trouble and may have to stop being president of the republic for the second time. He's pretty much had it now, he's all washed up. I think to myself: He's probably ill, or he's had an accident, poor man. But he's not ill, actually, and he hasn't had an accident. His problem is to do with some diamonds he was given by the president-dictator of the Central African Republic. And according to my father this dictator is as wicked as Idi Amin Dada of Uganda.

While Roger Guy Folly's explaining that the French president is being criticised by everyone in France, Papa Roger tells me, without looking over at Maman Pauline, that it's a very difficult business to understand because when Giscard d'Estaing accepted the diamonds from the dictator Bokassa, I was still a baby, and Giscard d'Estaing wasn't head of State, just the minister for a different French president called Georges Pompidou. According to my father, Pompidou was a fine, intelligent man, and no one was afraid of him, even if he did have enormous eyebrows like the Russian president, Leonid Ilyich

Brezhnev, and Giscard d'Estaing was the finance minister for this man Pompidou.

Seeing I don't quite follow what he's saying, and that I'm scratching my head with all the different thoughts swirling round in it, Papa Roger explains that the finance minister is someone who looks after all the money in a country, but the state keeps a careful eye on him, not like here, when the finance minister is someone who steals the country's money or helps the President and the members of his government to hide it in Swiss bank accounts. In our country the state can't keep an eye on the money because everyone's got his hand in the till, from the top all the way down, and everyone accuses everyone else. And since you can't send everyone to prison, they let it drop, and just carry on pinching the state's money.

The president of the Central African Republic who's just been driven out of his country has a lovely name. It's less complicated than the names French people have: he's called Jean Bédel Bokassa. But unless you want him to cut your head off you'd better call him Emperor Jean Bédel Bokassa. It was his own idea to make himself emperor; he threw a big party and lots of heads of foreign countries came to celebrate at his house and acknowledge he'd now become an emperor. Long before he got into the trouble he's in today, he was good friends with the French and now the French have dropped him like a dog with fleas, or rabies. Yes, he was a faithful servant of the French, because he fought alongside French soldiers during the Second World War, he got his military training from the French and they gave him a fine medal because wherever the French went to fight, he was always at their service, in Indochina or in Algeria. Jean Bédel Bokassa rose to the rank of captain in the

French army before going home to Central Africa, where he was able to take advantage of the muddle down there after a *coup d'état* by some of the military against the president, his cousin David Dacko, to become president himself. It was some other soldiers who organised the *coup d'état* against his cousin Dacko, but Bokassa's so clever, he managed to turn the situation round, take things in hand and end up becoming president of the republic, even though the *coup d'état* wasn't his idea in the first place. So he made a *coup d'état* out of a *coup d'état*, my father says. Now, in becoming president he had actually over-thrown his own cousin. That's why Papa Roger reminds me that our worst enemies are sometimes members of our own family. If I become president of the republic, I'm definitely going to watch out for my Uncle René, and place my trust in Lounès, and appoint him prime minister.

Apparently Emperor Jean Bédel Bokassa wept and wept at the death of General de Gaulle, who ran France before Georges Pompidou. De Gaulle was as tall as two men from round here, or as five and a half pygmies from Gabon. Papa Roger says people liked him in the Congo, because when the Germans decided to go and occupy France by force, General de Gaulle came to Brazzaville to announce that France was no longer in France, that the capital of France was no longer Paris, with the Eiffel Tower – Brazzaville was now the capital of free France. So the French all became Congolese like us. Besides, at that time, it was better to be Congolese than a Frenchman collaborating with the Germans, led by Adolf Hitler and his scary moustache. So we let the French all come over here, no problem. We said to ourselves: 'Things must be pretty bad over there in Europe if the Whites are running to hide here in Brazzaville, the

Germans and their leader Adolf Hitler must be giving them a hard time.'

Papa Roger also remembers that the year the great de Gaulle died, people in our country acted as if their own president had died. We had a long history with de Gaulle, because when he came here and then took the plane back to Europe, our prophet, André Grenard Matsoua disappeared too. And to this day lots of people in the Kongo tribe think the prophet isn't dead, that he'll turn up at Brazzaville airport again one day with General de Gaulle. That's why there's always a crowd at Maya-Maya airport, waiting for General de Gaulle and our prophet to return. As far as we're concerned, General de Gaulle's not dead. The French are lying to us. Our prophet, Matsoua, isn't dead, the French are hiding him somewhere with General de Gaulle. Some day, sooner or later, the two of them will come back to the Congo.

But then Papa Roger really confuses us by telling us that General de Gaulle really is dead and that he's buried in a part of France known as Colombey-les-Deux-Eglises, a village with two churches.

As soon as Maman Pauline, who had just picked up her glass, heard this weird-sounding name, Colombey-les-Deux-Eglises, she leapt from her chair and her beer almost came snorting out of her nostrils.

'How can they bury someone that important in a church? And how did they bury him in two churches?'

Apparently the day General de Gaulle died, the dictator Jean Bédel Bokassa wept as though his own Papa Roger had died. He made out like it was his own father who'd just gone up to heaven and left him alone on earth. And he wept so much for his father de Gaulle that even the Africans began to wonder: What if it's true? Now, it couldn't possibly be, because Bokassa the First was as black as the bottom of a cooking pot. And a famous White like de Gaulle couldn't have a black child. It's impossible, even in a nightmare. But the Emperor Bokassa I didn't care what people said, so he went to the General's funeral and there he happened to meet the French minister for finance, Valéry Giscard d'Estaing who, it just so happened, had family in the Central African Republic. His family loved to go hunting animals in our forests for fun, even though the animals are the spirits of our ancestors, and have never harmed anyone. Our animals are lovely, they make sweet little babies so that the bush will always be full of living creatures, and so that each generation of little Africans can see with its own eyes what a lion looks like, what an elephant looks like, what a zebra looks like, what a squirrel looks like. The Whites in Giscard's family played at hunting with these animals and killed them just for a bit of fun, and to take some photos. Then they stuck the heads of the animals on the wall so they could boast: 'I hunted in Africa, I killed that lion, I killed that leopard and I killed that elephant.'

Every time the minister for finance, Giscard d'Estaing, went to visit his family in the Central African Republic, he popped in to say hello to dictator Bokàssa I, now they'd met each other at General de Gaulle's funeral.

Papa Roger reminds us too that Giscard d'Estaing came to visit Bokassa I, who showed him round his lovely palace and gave him lots of nice presents, including a present with all these diamonds on it. Bokassa I was always very nice to his guests and he gave Giscard some more diamonds the day he came to see him in the château he owned in France. And then it turns out there were other presents too, which is why my father says it's a complicated business, and we don't know whether Bokassa I is exaggerating, telling lies, making stuff up, because he's angry with France now he's in exile. Or if Valéry Giscard d'Estaing is trying to hide some other diamonds, and prove to everyone that he hadn't been given real diamonds, just bling.

So now it's like world war between Giscard d'Estaing and Bokassa I. Bokassa must be sitting there in his country of exile thinking: Giscard, I gave you those presents, those diamonds, why did you go and attack my regime and put my cousin David Dacko back in power, when I'd already overthrown him in a *coup d'état*?

Yeah, Bokassa I must be really annoyed at being driven out of the Central African Republic, and having to go and live with the Ivoirians. He thinks France has betrayed him, he wants revenge, he wants to topple President Giscard d'Estaing. And now that all you ever hear about on the radio and all you read about in the papers is this business with the diamonds, Papa Roger can't see how the French can vote for Giscard d'Estaing. He's going to get pensioned off, even if he is still a bit young. Bokassa I down on the Ivory Coast's going to be happy about that.

Just as Roger Guy Folly finishes speaking and Papa Roger turns off the radio, it occurs to me that Bokassa I won't ever die of cancer. No, he didn't love his country like the Shah did. Cancer's for people who love their country or adventurers like Arthur. Also, Bokassa I could have chosen Egypt for his exile, instead of the Ivory Coast. When you're in exile, or adventuring, if you don't stop off in Egypt it means you're not a good guy, you're not very important. And I really don't like Bokassa I. So I really do want the French to vote for Giscard d'Estaing again. Then at least Bokassa I will get lost.

I go into my bedroom and put up the mosquito net. I can't stop thinking about Valéry Giscard d'Estaing. I fall asleep over the last few words I say to My Sister Star and My Sister No-name:

Let Giscard d'Estaing carry on being President of the French Republic for ever and ever
May this business about the diamonds not make the French vote for a different president
Let's hear it for Giscard! Let's hear it for Giscard!

I f Caroline thinks I'm going to apologise to her, she's wrong. She was the one who wanted a divorce, not me. Why should I go running after her? Since I'm not speaking to her, and she's not speaking to me, and Monsieur Mutombo thinks it's not right, he turns to Longombé and Mokobé and asks: 'What's up with our two little lovebirds?'

Caroline throws a fit and shouts that we're not lovebirds. We're not married, we never were married, her husband is a great footballer who wears the number 11 shirt and scores lots of goals and reads books by Marcel Pagnol. She goes running out of her father's workshop.

I've come round to bring Papa Roger's mohair trousers. They're brand new, but they're too long, so they need to have several centimetres taken off, otherwise my father's going to be sweeping the dust as he walks, like some other papas I've seen in the *quartier*. I see some of them who've turned up the hem of their trousers themselves and every time it comes down again, so you have to turn it back up in front of everyone, when it's really hard to walk, if you're always thinking you must be careful your trousers don't come undone. Who thinks about their trousers or their shoes when they're walking down the street? You think about other things, about where you're going and how you're going to get there in time.

As soon as I walked into the workshop with my father's trousers over my right shoulder, I saw Caroline sitting just by

Monsieur Mutombo and I nearly left, thinking I'd come back later. But I went in anyway because the two apprentices at the back had already seen me.

Longombé shouted, 'Hey it's our Michel!'

Mokobé added, 'Probably got his shirt ripped by his friend again!'

I didn't say hello to Caroline because she was looking at me already as if to say, 'If you say hello to me I'll shame you in front of these grown ups.'

The apprentices were busy sewing her a red dress with green flowers on it.

Monsieur Mutombo says to me, 'Go and see what your woman's doing outside, you should never leave your wife unhappy, someone else might cheer her up and marry her, and you'll be left weeping alone.'

I come out of the workshop. Opposite, there's a little football pitch. Caroline's sitting on the ground watching me walk towards her. Just as she's getting up to move away I call, 'Wait, don't go, I've got something to say to you…'

'No, it's over, we've been divorced for ages.'

I force myself to stay calm and say, 'I know, but at least let's talk about it and…'

'No, I don't want to talk to you, or I'll start loving you again and then I'll feel sad all the time!'

Now she's drawing things on the ground with a little twig. I look at her drawing close up.

'What's that then?'

'Can't you see it's a rose? Mabélé taught me how to draw it, and he's really good at drawing. He said I'm a rose, so now I'm drawing myself.'

The name Mabélé irritates me. I lose my cool and go on the attack: 'Does Mabélé know who Arthur Rimbaud is?'

'Who's that then?'

'He's a writer. He's got loads of hair, it all grows in winter…'

'Is he more famous than Marcel Pagnol? Has he got four castles and…'

'No, Arthur hasn't got all that stuff, he doesn't care about things like that.'

'If he hasn't got a castle, that means he's not rich and famous!'

'But he travelled at lot, so he can get to see all the castles in the world.'

'What about his own castles?'

'He built them in his heart. And I'll keep you in the castles I've got in my heart too, where no one can harm you.'

She looks up at me at last. It's almost as if she's got a bug in her eye.

'Where did you learn to say things like that, like some grown-up chatting up a woman?'

'It's thanks to Arthur.'

'Really? Have you met him then?'

'Yes.'

'Where?'

'In my parents' bedroom. And when I look at him hard he smiles and talks to me.'

A plane passes overhead. I can't ask Caroline to guess which country it's going to. That's a game between me and her brother.

So I look at the plane on my own and I think: It's going to land in Egypt. The capital of Egypt is Cairo. I don't want that plane to go and land in Saudi Arabia where Idi Amin Dada is, swimming in his pool and boxing with his servants. I don't want the plane to land in the Ivory Coast where Emperor Jean Bédel Bokassa the First tells tall stories about Valéry Giscard d'Estaing, who wants to be president of the French Republic again.

While I'm thinking about Egypt, Caroline takes my left hand and begs me, 'Can I meet your friend Arthur with the castles in his heart too?'

'Of course, he'd love that! But you'd better come to my house because my father will get cross if I take Arthur out into the street. And if my father gets cross, Arthur won't ever smile at me again.'

She's just rubbed out the rose she had drawn in the earth, and she's taken hold of my hand. We go back inside her father's workshop.

'You know, Mabélé's not actually very good at fighting. Why did you run off when you met him in Diadhou's shop? If someone attacks us one day in the street will you run off like that and leave me alone with the bandits?'

I don't answer. Because I don't want to have to hear Mabélé's name again.

Monsieur Mutombo's amazed to see me coming back with Caroline. Longombé and Mokobé want to laugh, but they stifle it. They know Monsieur Mutombo will probably shout at them. Longombé pretends to sneeze, then finally bursts out laughing, as do Mokobé and Monsieur Mutombo. As the three of them are now laughing helplessly, Caroline and I start laughing too. As usual, I'm the one laughing loudest, holding my sides. The more I laugh like that, the more it sets the others off. I collapse on the floor, laughing. I get up again, laughing. I lean against the wall, laughing. I lean against the table where they cut the cloth, laughing. I laugh and laugh and laugh and suddenly, without warning, the whole workshop turns black. Monsieur Mutombo's shiny head disappears. I turn round and see Longombé's mother blocking the doorway. As usual, she can't get in the door, not even sideways. I manage to stop laughing just in time. Besides, everyone else in the workshop has stopped. Longombé gets up and goes over to his mother, they stand and talk a few metres outside. I creep out to watch. Longombé's giving his mother money. Too late, she's seen me, and she calls threateningly: 'Hey you, Pauline Kengué's son! I'll get you one of these days! Why do you laugh every time you see me? Because I'm fat, is that it? How do you know you won't get fat when you're grown up?'

Off she goes, at top speed. When she walks the dust rises off the street. People she passes turn round as though they've seen an extra terrestrial. She shouts abuse at them, even though they've said nothing. I think: why doesn't Longombé's father ever come and ask his son for money? Has his father left his mother? Doesn't Longombé even have an adoptive father? I feel sorry for him, working so hard and paying for his mother's keep while I'm standing there laughing like an idiot. Would I like it if people made fun of Maman Pauline like that? No, I'd want to throw stones in his face.

So I'm very sorry I laughed the last time, that I didn't realise Longombé's mother's a brave lady, as brave as Maman Pauline or Maman Martine. Longombé comes back into the workshop and looks at me with red eyes, like an angry crocodile. Monsieur Mutombo tells him to hurry up and do my father's trousers. He's going to deliberately cut them too short and when my father puts them on he'll look like a hare wearing trousers in *Tales of the Bush and the Forest* that they read to us in the infant school.

Uncle René's house is the prettiest in Rue Comapon. My uncle always worries because it's so nice, and you can see it shining in the distance as you approach, that the local proletariats, who live in the clapboard houses, will break into his property at any moment and steal all his wealth. That's why his plot has secure fencing all round it, with barbed wire on top. Anyone who thinks: I'll just go and rob Monsieur René's house because he's rich, will hurt himself on the barbed wire, and bleed and scream like babies when they first come into the world, the ones that know already that they're going to have big problems in their lives, and that they'd have been better off staying in their mother's belly, or going straight to heaven without stopping off on earth, like My Sister Star and My Sister No-name. Also, it's not just barbed wire protecting Uncle René's plot, there's a great big iron gate as well. That's where everyone goes in. The other iron gate is at the back of the house – the entrance to the garage – which my uncle opens with a remote control.

When you arrive at Uncle René's house, first of all you ring the bell and wait in the street, then the houseboy comes to peer at you through a little hole that's so well hidden that you'd never think anyone was looking at you. If you look suspicious, if you look like a trouble maker from the Grand Marché, the houseboy won't open the door to you. If you won't go away he puts Miguel onto you, who, my uncle says, is the fiercest dog in the neighbourhood, not to say the whole town, and why not the entire Congo. When Miguel's excited he tries to bite his own shadow. The reason he's so fierce is that the houseboy gives him corn spirit to drink. Once he's had a glass of that he goes really quiet for a few seconds then he starts turning circles, chasing his own tail, but he can't catch it because when he turns left it goes right, and when he goes right it goes left. Then he gets really mad that he can't catch it, so he barks and rolls on the ground. The houseboy calms him down, puts a chain round his neck and ties him up to the foot of the sour sap tree in the yard. Miguel goes on barking, he's so angry his spit dribbles from his mouth the whole time.

Uncle René's put a sign on the gate in big letters that says:

BEWARE FEROCIOUS DOG 24/7.

When I see '24/7' I think: So when is Miguel ever NOT 'ferocious'? Does he ever sleep? I do a quick sum in my head. Given that there are 365 days in the year – sometimes 366 – and a day lasts 24 hours, and an hour lasts 60 minutes, and a minute lasts 60 seconds, and a second is divided into sixty degrees, calculate in seconds the length of time during which a dog which is 'ferocious' 24/7 is ferocious over a period of five and a half years…

So there I am, at the entrance to Uncle René's house. At Christmas I have to visit Uncle René with the truck and plastic rake and shovel he gave me a few days earlier. I play mostly with Kevin, who's eleven, and Sebastien who's nine. You can't play with Edwige, who's fifteen, and is always telling us off when we run around in the house, and climb on her father's armchairs without taking our shoes off.

I didn't want to come to Uncle René's house today, but Maman Pauline said her brother would be cross if I didn't go to see him; he'd think we resented the fact that he was richer than us. And besides, I do have his family name. Maman Pauline told me to go and take a shower, to scrub under my armpits, my backside and where I pee. I don't like it when she says that. Does any normal person ever have a shower without washing under their armpits, their backside and where they pee? If you don't wash there, why take a shower at all?

'When you were a baby and I washed those bits, you always cried,' she reminds me.

I gave them a good scrub. After that she picked out a pair of blue underpants, some black shorts, a nice white shirt, a black bow tie and rubber sandals. She put my truck and my plastic rake and shovel in a bag.

It was nearly midday, and it was already very hot, even in the shade. Just outside the door to our plot, Maman Pauline warned me, 'Don't get lost on the way. You go down the Avenue of Independence, turn right, then carry on till you get to the Savon *quartier* then you turn into the Rue Comapon. Watch out for cars and only cross the road when there's a grown up crossing. Walk directly behind them. Behave yourself, don't fall out with Kevin and Sebastien. I'll be here when you get back this evening, your father too.'

I nearly asked her why she's telling me where Uncle René's house is, when I know how to get there. I said nothing though, and set off walking down the Avenue of Independence.

I felt a bit scared when I got to Uncle René's gate. I was thinking: Is Miguel properly tied up to the sour sap tree? The reason I wondered that was because I've known that dog since he was a tiny little baby, but my uncle says that dog years and human years aren't the same thing. A dog's childhood is really short, they grow up much faster than humans. When a dog's six months old he'd be ten if he was a person. When a dog's one year old, he'd be fifteen if he was a person. When a dog's five years old he'd be thirty-six if he was a person. Now, Miguel is five and a half years old. If he was a human being he would be forty-six years old now, and that makes him an old man compared to me even though I knew him when he was really small, and gave him his milk, which he really liked. So I don't like the way he barks at me when I come to Uncle René's house like I'm some kind of evil spirit come to steal my uncle's riches.

The boy has seen it's me ringing the bell, and he opens the gate. He looks me up and down as though he's thinking: What's young Michel with his ridiculous bow tie got hidden in his bag then?

Miguel's barking at the back of the house, but he's firmly tied up. First I see Kevin, who's as thin as a reed, with his little head on top of a long neck, like a half-starved giraffe. We're outside the front door and Sebastien's just behind him. We say hello, and shake hands.

I go into the day room, I see they've got their toys out. Kevin's got a bicycle. Sebastien's been given a car that works with batteries and he's explaining to me that he can play with it without touching it. I don't believe him. He shows me a machine which controls his car, it's small with little buttons: 'That button's to switch it on. That one makes it go straight. That one makes it turn left. That one's to turn right. That one's to make it turn round and come back. And that one's to make it stop, and to turn off the engine, but you have to press it twice, or the car won't understand what you want it to do. Here, try and switch it on and see what happens.'

Just as I'm about to press the start button someone behind us yells: 'STOP! STOP! STOP!'

It's Edwige, who's just come out of the shower. Her hair's still wet. She looks really tall, but she's got spots all over her face, like someone with shrapnel in the World War. The last time I saw her she didn't have that. But it's true, I haven't seen her for ages.

'What are you doing? Papa says you're not to touch those presents now! Honestly! Who said you could open them anyway? You'd better put all that away! And stop jumping on that chair with your shoes on!'

Sebastien ignores his sister. He's still trying to hand me the machine that controls the car. I don't know if I should take it or not. Edwige has disappeared into her room, she comes back with a switch made of vine creeper. Sebastien runs to put his present back by the chimney and then dashes outside. Miguel hears us running about the grounds and starts barking his head off. He barks so loud that we don't even hear the car coming into the garage. Uncle René's arrived, with his wife Auntie Marie-Thérèse.

Now we've sat down to eat. I hate the way they eat in silence at Uncle René's. All you can hear is the sound of spoons and forks and you have to keep your mouth shut when you're chewing your food. Not only that – you have to keep your eyes on your own plate. If you look at someone else's plate, Uncle René kicks you under the table with his pointed shoes, it's like being poked with a javelin. It hurts for days afterwards. Several times he's got me on the shin, once or twice on the ankle, I was seeing stars for days. For the first few seconds it doesn't hurt, you even feel really surprised and pleased because you don't feel anything. Then all of a sudden, just when you thought it was over, the pain comes right up into your stomach, you feel it moving about in your small intestine and your pancreas, and your heart starts leaping about like a baby kangaroo in its mother's pouch. Then you throw up on the spot because how can you swallow your juicy piece of meat when you've got a pain going up from your ankle or your tibia into your stomach?

The trouble is, while I eat, I keep an eye on other people's plates to see if I need to eat more quickly than them to catch up or whether I should slow down a bit if I'm ahead of everyone else. Uncle René can't stand that. He says it's how a capitalist's child would behave, already accumulating wealth at the expense of the Wretched of the Earth. He thinks if I look at Kevin and Sebastien's plates, when they are the biggest eaters on earth, it means I envy them their pieces of meat. Even in the Russian films that come to the cinema Rex or cinema Roy, people don't eat like my cousins do. In Russian films they're only pretending to eat, that's what Lounès says, anyway. When the Russians eat in a film it's always faked. It's not real food like in French films, because the French eat for real. Besides, they talk with their mouths full, even though it's rude to behave like a savage especially since they're meant to be the Whites.

The photo of Lenin on the wall is crooked. The one of Karl Marx too. Perhaps it's the wind that does it, when you open the front door. Engels is sad because he never sees daylight. The immortal Marien Ngouabi is sad too, maybe because his photo is the smallest of the four. I'm sure his moustache has grown since the last time I ate here.

The photo of Victor Hugo's gone. I can't ask Uncle René

– children mustn't speak at table unless a grown up asks them a question.

'Michel, have you noticed anything about the wall opposite you?'

It's Uncle René asking.

I look up, and pretend to be thinking while I move my fork about, and I murmur: 'No, I haven't noticed anything.'

'Nothing? Look up properly!'

So I say: 'The photo of Monsieur Victor Hugo's gone…'

Auntie Marie-Thérèse gives me a nasty look. She tells me that when someone is dead you don't call him Monsieur any more, because they're no longer around to oblige us to respect them. But for me all these people in the photos are alive. They've been watching me eat since I was really small. So they're Monsieurs.

Uncle René is pleased with my answer. 'Bravo! Bravo! Bravo nephew! Your cousins hadn't even noticed!'

And we carry on eating, each with his nose in his own plate. I try to follow the rhythm. When they eat fast, I eat fast. When they slow down, I slow down. When they pause for moment, I pause too.

Edwige is on my left, Kevin is on my right. Opposite are Auntie Marie-Thérèse and Sebastien. Uncle René is like a president, because from where he sits he can keep an eye on all of us without moving his head or leaning forward. Kevin and Sebastien eat like pigs, you'd think they were in a race. Auntie Marie-Thérèse's not pleased with them, she thinks they should slow down.

My uncle comes back to the subject of Victor Hugo, who's been taken down from the wall: 'Michel do you know why I took down the picture of Victor Hugo?'

I shake my head.

He stares hard at the wall and begins: 'For years I loved that French poet stuck up there on the wall. He's a man of genius, Victor Hugo, he represents in one man the entire nineteenth century, not to say our own century. I would almost say that he's the only poet I love in the way I love Karl Marx, Engels, Lenin and the immortal Marien Ngouabi. But I'm going to show you something very serious now, which made me take down his photo from the wall.'

He stops eating, stands up and goes into the bedroom. None of us know what's going on. What's serious? What's he got against poor Victor Hugo, who's never done anything and who even wrote lots of poems you can recite out loud. We all wonder: Are we meant to stop eating too, or should we carry on without Uncle René, when there's something seriously up in the house?

Auntie Marie-Thérèse signals to us to stop. Edwige and I stop eating, but my two cousins carry on. Auntie Marie-Thérèse shouts at them: 'I said STOP!!!'

Sebastien had time to stuff a fat chicken wing into his mouth, and he's still chewing.

Now Uncle René's back. In his hand he has a very crumpled piece of paper, which he's smoothing out. 'I have photocopied the speech Victor Hugo made on Africa. He gave it during a banquet over which he presided in 1879. Sitting close to him was Victor Schoelcher, someone who fought for the end of slavery. And do you know what Victor Hugo said on that occasion?'

He puts on his spectacles, the kind that make him look like a doctor about to give a child an injection, and starts reading in the way the members of the Congolese Workers' Party do when they make a speech: '*"Oh what a land is Africa! Asia has*

its history, America has its history, even Australia has its history;
Africa has no history."'

He pauses for breath, as though he's just won a swimming
race in front of the dictator Idi Amin Dada. But we can see
he's skipping bits as he reads, that he's picking what he wants
to read to us. Why doesn't he read it all out so we can go on
eating our chicken in peace? When he pauses for breath he
looks like a buffalo that's escaped from some white hunters.
Why didn't he realise all this before he stuck up the photo of
Victor Hugo on his wall? And if someone only reads out a little
bit of something, and doesn't give you the bit that comes after,
how are you expected to put this bit together with the whole
thing and understand what's really been said?

He's off again: '*"Put all your surplus into Africa, and solve all*
your social problems, turn your proletariats into proprietors. Go
on, do it! Build roads, build ports, build towns; expand, exploit,
colonise, increase; and may the divine Spirit find its expression in
peace on this earth, and The Human Spirit likewise, in freedom,
far from the influence of priests and princes."'

'That's enough, René, the children are here to eat and
celebrate Christmas, not to listen to things that don't concern
them! And what happens if one day you discover that your
comrades Marx, Engels and Lenin have said things you don't
like about Africa?'

Auntie Marie-Thérèse is the only person in the world who
can talk like that to Uncle René. I don't know how she does it
because she's not a big woman, not like Longombé's mother
or even Madame Mutombo. She's very slim and short and her
voice is like the voice of a little girl who's afraid of boys. I can't
believe she talks like that to my uncle and that my uncle actually
stops reading from the piece of paper about Victor Hugo. She

must have some secret to be able to talk like that without my uncle getting angry.

Uncle René folds away his paper, looks at the space where Victor Hugo's photo used to be. Now there's just a square gap on the wall. Inside the square it's a bit lighter than the rest of the wall. You can tell there used to be a photo there.

'In any case', he says, 'tomorrow the boy will paint that wall, and then no one will ever know that Victor Hugo used to live here. I'll put up a photo of Ho Chi Minh or Che Guevara in its place.'

Uncle René wasn't angry when he saw the toys had already been unwrapped. I thought he would be because he's often the one who says when we should rip the wrapping off our presents. Even if I do get the same present every year, I take my present out of my bag and rip off the wrapping and pretend to be happy. That's why today, since I'm not visibly happy, he asks, 'Do you like your truck and your shovel and rake?'

I don't say anything, I just stare at Sebastien's car. Uncle René knows what I'm thinking and he adds, 'If you get your primary school certificate this year you'll get a car like Sebastien's. But you must come in the top five in the country!'

Has Sebastien got his school certificate? No, he's younger than me. So why did he get a car before he got his certificate, when I have to wait to get mine?

We play outside, behind the house. Edwige is in her room listening to music with the tape recorder Uncle René's given her. I mustn't tell them we got a tape recorder before Edwige. That's our secret. Papa Roger has said we must be discreet. We can listen to Roger Guy Folly talking every evening from

America. Edwige's tape recorder is only for putting cassettes into, and listening to music. That's all. And also, Edwige doesn't have the cassette of the singer with the moustache weeping for his alter ego from dawn till dusk. Why would I be impressed with her present?

Miguel's watching us from a distance. He's tired of being tied up to the sour sap tree. He lies resting, one eye shut, the other half open. I feel sorry for him because he didn't get any Christmas presents. He's always getting forgotten, when in fact he's the one who protects Uncle René's riches. I wish I could give him my shovel or my rake. The problem is, if I give them to him he'll probably bark, because dogs can't be farmers, they don't know that agriculture is the future of development in this country. They can't hold a rake and shovel with their paws. They're not to know you always put the ox before the cart. So there's no point my giving my shovel or my rake to Miguel.

I also feel sorry for Miguel because with every year that passes, every hour, ever second, every degree of a second that goes by, he gets older faster than us humans. It's not fair. And he looks at me with his one half open eye, as if he's understood what I'm thinking. Yes, he knows what I'm feeling deep inside. He knows because dogs see invisible things, like ghosts and evil spirits which we humans can't see in the flesh. Dogs can read men's thoughts, from A to Z. Just because they can't speak our language properly doesn't mean they're just idiots with a tail and fleas all over them. Besides, it's not as if we know how to speak their language, which is much more complicated than ours.

In any case, it's the first time I've seen Miguel this calm. Which means he's not ferocious 24/7 after all. We should change the sign outside and put a different one up, with the exact time when Miguel isn't ferocious. But if we put that on a sign maybe the bad guys from the Grand Marché will think: Let's go and rob Monsieur René while his dog's not being ferocious. Now I know the sign on the gate is a lie, it's just there to scare off bad guys.

I'm jealous of Sebastien's car. He let me try it and I thought: It's a great thing to have, a car that does what you tell it from a distance when you press on a button, whereas when you drive a real car, you have to hold the steering wheel, so as not to bang into other cars. I dream about this car the whole time, and I don't want to play with my truck, my shovel and rake. I'm sick of being a farmer. I really am sick of it. I think about Lounès. What present did he get? I think about Caroline. What did she get? Yeah, I want a car I can control from a distance. One day I'll get one…

At the end of the day, Uncle René tells his boy to walk me home. I don't even notice the cars going by as we walk. I don't even look at the people we pass. I just glide past them, as though they were shadows. My thoughts are far, far away. I think about My Sister Star and My Sister No-name. Do they get presents up where they are?

Please let me pass my primary school certificate this year, and let Uncle René give me a car I can control from a distance, a car that follows me everywhere I go.

I'm going to put my little dreams in the boot of that car and drive them about till I'm twenty years old, and Miguel's more than a hundred. Maybe he'll die, but he'll come back again as a little white dog, and then I can give him to Caroline.

One day I must ask Papa Roger why there's only ever bad news when we listen to the news on the radio. You'd think every day was the end of the world, that when you switch on the radio in the evening, anything might happen. Even if it's happening far from here, even if they're not talking about people who live in our neighbourhood, it's bad news for us too. I've never heard Roger Guy Folly laugh or make us laugh. Now I feel afraid every time I hear a journalist announce:

> It's twenty-one hundred hours, universal time, and you're listening to the Voice of America. Coming right up, the evening news, with your faithful servant, Roger Guy Folly...

There's a really bad guy in France called Jacques Mesrine who's just been killed. He'd been sent to prison for twenty years, but someone helped him escape like in *Lucky Luke*, when the Daltons are able to escape from prison till Lucky Luke catches them again and then we can read the next episodes. If the Daltons really did escape, how could we ever read the next *Lucky Luke* episodes? What would Lucky Luke do without the Daltons? He'd just wander about the desert with his dog Rantanplan and hunt little animals hiding under the cactuses.

Jacques Mesrine won't be having any more adventures now, particularly since he attacked a judge's daughter and held her hostage like the Iranian students who took the Americans hostage and shut them up in a cellar. Apparently they looked everywhere for Mesrine and no one could find him. People would say he was in such and such a place, but when they went there he'd left ages ago. Then other people said he was in this place that had been definitely identified, and then when they got to the definitely identified place they'd find Mesrine was already miles away.

So then the police killed him. They cornered him, the way you corner a palm rat in the bush. You ring all the holes, and the rats only have one hole to come out by, and you wait for them there.

Roger Guy Folly reports that Mesrine got away in his car and that's when the police shot him. His wife was in it too, and she was injured. Now the people of France can breathe a bit easier, because Mesrine was their most dangerous enemy. According to Papa Roger, this Mesrine guy was stronger and more intelligent than our own famous gangster, who we called Angoualima, who had six fingers on each hand, four eyes, four ears and two willies. Angoualima cut people's heads off, or stole from the Whites in the centre of town. But unlike Mesrine, he had no car he could escape in and get shot in with his wife. That's why he didn't get killed like Mesrine did. We don't know how our Angoualima got killed. Who knows if he is really dead? It's weird I get to hear the story of Mesrine just when round here people in the street are all starting to talk about Angoualima again, and some people are saying that there's a gangster by the name of Grégoire Nakobomayo who's following in the footsteps of our own public enemy number one. The problem is that Grégoire Nakobomayo is clumsy, he messes up his crimes and just makes the police in our town laugh.

Since Jacques Mesrine's death, the gangsters in the Grand Marché have been copying his name and refuse to be nicknamed Angoualima like before. When you walk down the street you see the name Mesrine written on the walls of derelict houses and: *I won't give up without a fight.* I don't know what that means, why they want to have a fight, no one wants a fight with them, that's what we're all trying to avoid! Our gangsters want to be just like Mesrine, but they've got no cars, no wives to go on the run with them and get shot down by the police. So they end up getting caught alive and dragged back to the police station, and being given a good beating up before being released, because there's not much room in our prisons which are pretty full.

What bothers me most isn't this story about Jacques Mesrine. What really upsets me is that Roger Guy Folly also talked about a new law in France which says that you can refuse to let children be born. The child in the womb thinks it's going to come into this world, but then they go to hospital and bang! the doctor makes it come out and chucks it in the bin. The word Roger Guy Folly uses for this is *abortion.* The journalist points out that in the past it used to be done in secret and lots of women used to die along with their children. The people who did the abortions were seen as murderers and were put in prison.

When Roger Guy Folly talked about abortion and explained the new law in France, which was championed by a woman called Simone Veil, Maman Pauline's expression changed. She listened for a moment without saying anything, then she got up from the table and went into her bedroom. Papa Roger quickly searched for another radio station and happened upon Radio-Congo, where the journalists were talking about the 'Day of the Tree', which has just been set up by our President. From now on everyone has to plant a tree somewhere and the police are going to come and visit every neighbourhood, every household, to check that the President's order has been obeyed. Anyone who doesn't plant a tree will be fined, and if they're members of the Congolese Workers' Party they'll have their card taken away. Poor old them, no more seats in the front row for the National Holiday processions.

My parents both ask together: 'Michel, what present would you like?'

I'm very surprised because at Christmas they already gave me several bags of marbles and a castle you have to build, which I still haven't managed to put together. I suspect they are hiding something from me, or have some very bad news to tell me.

Papa Roger adds: 'We'll go into town, just you and me! We'll eat apples! Afterwards you can choose your present.'

'Any present you like, whatever it costs!' finished my mother.

'Yes, any present you like, we just want you to be happy. Then you can come and see me at work, I'll introduce you to my boss, Madame Ginette. And you'll meet Monsieur Montoir too, who gave us the radio cassette.'

'And that's not all, Michel. One day you can come with me to the bush, and then to Brazzaville. Your first train journey!'

I don't feel like eating now. There's too much good news, all at once. And this is not how they usually talk to me. They're like two different people sitting opposite me this evening. They're smiling, but I can tell their smiles are hiding something. And when I look straight at them they lower their eyes because they know their Michel can read people's minds. When they give me a present they never ask for my opinion, they choose it themselves. Sometimes it makes me cross, but I always end up accepting because they're not going to go and take it back to the shop. Maman Pauline's always said her business trips were dangerous because of the bush and the gangsters in Brazzaville. That I was too little to come with her. So she goes on her own, and every time, before she leaves, she tells me off because I say I want to come to Brazzaville with her. Am I big enough to go with her now?

In the end, what have I got to lose by accepting what they want to give me?

'I'd really like a car like Sebastien's!' I tell them.

They are surprised. They look at each other and start to laugh. But I'm serious, I'm not laughing here. If I start laughing it will be like in Monsieur Mutombo's workshop, I won't be able to stop, I'll have to hold my sides and fall on the floor.

My father doesn't like this idea. 'A car like your cousin's! Is that really all you want? Think carefully, take your time, finish eating and then tell us what you want.'

We go on eating, though I'm only pretending, and they can tell because I've stopped peering at the largest piece of meat on my father's plate. Besides, he's just put it on my plate and I'm stalling before I eat it.

I can see they're giving each other looks. My father's even kicked my mother under the table, and his foot touched mine as well.

'What are you hiding from me?'

My father replies, 'Oh, Michel, we're not hiding anything! We've never hidden anything from you, you know that. We just want to make you happy, that's all.'

My mother asks me, 'Would you like a bit more beans and beef?'

I shake my head, even if beef with beans is my favourite dish. I like the way she makes it. She takes her time, washes the meat carefully, starts boiling the beans first thing, and lets them sit till the end of the morning. Towards midday I begin to smell it, I'm hungry, I can't wait, and it's her that says, 'Just five more minutes.'

But those five minutes are like five and a half centuries. And when it's ready I eat like tomorrow there's going to be a nation-wide famine. So today she can't believe I don't want a second helping.

'Wasn't it nice? Did I not make it right?'

'I'm not hungry now. I'll eat the rest tomorrow.'

'No, tomorrow I'll make you something else delicious.'

My father's impatient: 'So, what should we give you really, Michel?'

'A car like Sebastien's.'

'But what's so special about this car?'

'It's the best car in the world. If you press a button it starts up all on its own. And you can make it go left or right if you press different buttons.'

My mother wants me to change my mind. 'And what about a bike? A bike would be better, for a boy your age! You can go riding about, people will see you, they'll like that and... '

'I don't know how to ride a bike. I'll just fall off.'

'Lounès can teach you! I was at their house earlier, I had a long chat with Madame Mutombo.'

As soon as I heard that I thought: If Maman Pauline's been to see the Mutombo's, Lounès must know what my parents are keeping secret.

'I want a car like Sebastien's, not a bike.'

'All right then, we'll give you two cars and some new clothes,' says Papa Roger, getting up from the table to fetch the radio cassette from the bedroom.

. . . . .

I can't get to sleep. I can't breathe properly because of the mosquito net. It stops My Sister Star and My Sister No-name from seeing my face. I'll have to take it off this evening.

I get out of bed, push aside the mosquito net and get back in. An army of mosquitoes immediately attacks. But though they bite me all over, I feel nothing.

Just as I close my eyes, I hear my parents on the other side of the wall, as though in a dream. My father asks my mother, 'Pauline, do you think Michel guessed what's going on?'

'No, I don't think so. He couldn't guess, he's still too young to understand these things.'

Mother Teresa is the mother of all poor people. She helps children who have no family and have to hang out in the street down in India, especially in a town they call Calcutta, but she also wants to help poor people all over the world, so people can be happy here on earth. She works very hard. Since she has white globules, she'll go to paradise where God's waiting for her, so he can congratulate her in front of all the angels, and they'll all clap. She also helps people who are sick or are going to die. Roger Guy Folly says that today she's been given the Nobel Peace Prize. The Nobel Peace Prize is a present they give people who don't like it when other people do bad things. They give it to people who've done something important for humanity.

The American journalist reads out the names of the other people who have been given the prize before Mother Teresa, and I notice that the president of Egypt, Anouar el-Sadat, is on the list. I'm very pleased about that. Anouar el-Sadat got the prize along with another man called Menahem Begin, who's from Israel, the country that was angry with the Ugandan dictator/president, Idi Amin Dada. Roger Guy Folly also says that was a great event, because Anouar el-Sadat is Arab, Menahem Begin is Jewish and these two important people are trying really hard to get the Arabs and the Jews to stop hating each other and fighting.

· · · · ·

According to Roger Guy Folly, when Mother Teresa accepted the Nobel Prize in the name of all the poor people on earth, she said that abortion was the thing that would finish off our world. Now I know why Maman Pauline always talks about this woman as though she was a member of our family. Mother Teresa this, Mother Teresa that. Maman Pauline thinks this woman is right and France is wrong, because France voted to shut the door in the face of children. My father explains to her that this business about abortions is very complicated, that there are times when it is better not to allow a child to come into this world if it's going to suffer unnecessarily.

'For instance, Pauline, a woman can't keep the offspring of a rapist in her womb! Abortion also means freedom for women! In any case, if abortion is made illegal, people will always do it in secret. So, what's better: doctors who carry it out properly, or charlatans who make a complete mess of it and risk killing the mother as well?'

Maman Pauline thinks that abortion is a crime, that what they need to do is give the children they would otherwise throw in the bin to mothers like her.

So now they're rowing. My mother's not prepared to listen: 'Let's stop this discussion now! You always have to be right!'

One thing I know is, as long as she hasn't had another baby besides me, she's not going to agree with Papa Roger on this subject. Her view is, they should kill the rapist, keep the child and not tell him that his father was a bad man with lots and lots of red globules.

. . . . .

Roger Guy Folly is still talking about the life of Mother Teresa, who even sends nuns into Muslim countries where they read the Koran, not the Bible. Papa Roger changes radio stations and we listen to the President of the Republic on Radio Congo, making a speech congratulating himself on the success of the Day of the Tree, and announcing another plan he's got, called 'One school, one field'. Every school's got to have a field. If any school doesn't have a field, it will be closed. Too bad for the pupils and teachers, that's their hard luck. Our President congratulates Mother Teresa on winning the Nobel Prize. Our journalist says at the end of the President's speech:

'We hope that the jury of the Nobel Peace Prize will one day consider the exceptional revolutionary activities of our Revolutionary leader. It appears his name was cited this year as a possible laureate. These were credible rumours, and our leader has officially confirmed that he received a phone call from Sweden. But the Imperialists and their local lackeys made quite sure that the Congo and proletariats all over the world were deprived of this prestigious award, which would have furthered the cause of lasting peace on this earth. Be that as it may, our leader can count on our undying love, more precious than any Nobel Prize!'

That plane going overhead is going to land in Cairo, in Egypt. We're sitting by the river Tchinouka. Lounès knows if he asks me the question about where the plane's going to land I'll start talking about Egypt and the Shah, who's ill again. So instead he says, 'Your parents are going to buy you lots of presents.'

I'm so surprised I fall over backwards. 'How do you know?'

'Your mother ran into my mother at a fetisher's and...'

I interrupt him: 'I see, so fetisher Sukissa Tembé's behind all this?'

'Why, do you know him?'

'No, I don't know him, but when my mother and father were talking in their room I heard everything. And they mentioned that name.'

'Well your mother and father have already been to see him. My mother was there too, for her lung problem. I couldn't believe it either, when I heard my mother telling my father about it: the fetisher consulted his fetishes, and the fetishes said that it's your fault your mother can't have another child.'

'MINE?'

'Yep, yours. The fetishes say you're a child by day, but at night you're a grown-up person, with white hair, and when it's dark you get out of bed and go and meet up with other old people who don't like your mother and are plotting against her.'

'And you believe that? He's a liar, this fetisher!'

'He thinks you're going to be jealous and unhappy if you have brothers and sisters. So you've closed up Maman Pauline's belly. When children want to come, they find the door shut and they die just this side of it. So you're the one that has the key to your mother's belly.'

'That's not true! It's not true!'

'So the fetisher said to your parents that they have to give you lots of presents, any presents you want and apologise to you, till you're ready to give them the key to your mother's belly. The fetisher can't do anything for Maman Pauline, she'll never have another child before she dies, not unless she gets the key.'

'I don't want their rotten presents!'

'Michel, you have to take them.'

'NO!!'

'Are you glad your mother's miserable because she's only got one child? If you die before she does, what will happen to her? Have you thought about that?'

Another plane goes by.

'Where's that plane going to land?' Lounès asks me.

'In Calcutta, India.'

'Really? Not in Egypt?'

'No, it's going to India. There's a woman there called Mother Teresa who loves all poor people, and abandoned children. She got given a big present for it: the Nobel Peace Prize.'

Suddenly Lounès seems sad. When I look at him I can feel that he loves me, he wants to help me, but he also wants to help my parents. He speaks very slowly to me, as though he was almost begging me to do something: 'Michel, listen to me, tell me where you've hidden the key. I won't tell anyone else about it, I promise.'

'I haven't got a key.'

'You have, because you're the one that locked your mother's belly, the day you were born.'

'I haven't got a key!'

'Michel, that fetisher can't lie, he was fetisher to the President of the Republic!'

'Well, he's just told his first lie then!'

'Listen, give me that key and I'll give it to my mama, and she'll give it to yours.'

Since he's so insistent, and I've run out of answers, I agree.

'Ok, I'll give it to you.'

'Really?'

'Yeah. I've hidden it somewhere, the fetisher's right.'

'm in my parents' bedroom. Arthur's smiling at me. I want to talk to him, to tell him everything's getting on top of me. But instead I tell him I don't like riding bikes, I don't know how to pedal, I'm probably going to fall off and hurt myself. I also tell him I'd rather have a car like Sebastien's, a car you can control from a distance. I'll go left, then I'll go right, then I'll go straight on for a bit, then do a U-turn. If I meet people who don't have a car walking along in the midday sun, I'll give them a lift home in mine. No, I won't have an accident because I'll always drive slowly and I'll stop at the stop sign, or when people are crossing the road, especially old people and children. The others will just have to watch out because I'll have priority, and if I run them over that's their lookout.

I also tell Arthur I haven't got the key, it's not me that locked the door to my mother's belly. I try to think back, but there's nothing there, there is no key. If I had hidden it somewhere I'd definitely remember. So how come everyone's accusing me?

I have the feeling Arthur's saying: 'Michel, calm down, let them say what they want, and just admit it was you that locked the door to your mother's belly, you've got the key there somewhere, and if they still go on bothering you the whole time, pack your things and go and take a break in Egypt, to help the Shah recover from cancer. He'll be pleased to make your acquaintance. Yes, tell all those who accuse you that you do have the key, that you've hidden it somewhere. It won't cost you anything. You'll make your mother even more miserable if you don't listen to your friend Lounès.'

'What shall I do then?' I ask Arthur out loud.

He smiles at me again, and seems to be saying very quietly, 'Go and look for any old key in a rubbish bin, somewhere you're bound to find one. Give it to Lounès and he'll give it to his mother and she'll give it to Maman Pauline. After that you can go off to Egypt. I'll give you some addresses of friends of mine there, you won't be alone.'

'Arthur, what's "the hand that guides the quill"?'

He doesn't reply. I think maybe he doesn't like being asked about his book. He just wants to help me.

'And what's "the hand that guides the plough"? How much money did you leave behind in Egypt?'

He's not going to answer that. He's not smiling now. He's just a picture on the book cover now, but earlier he was almost alive, like me, I could hear his heart beating.

When I got to Maman Martine's house this morning, Papa Roger had already set off into town. He even works on Saturdays because that's the day when lots of people arrive at the hotel. The evening before, my mother had a long chat with Maman Martine. She told her she was going off into the bush, and then to Brazzaville for four days. She'd left a bit of money for Maman Martine, who refused it at first. But my mother insisted, so Maman Martine eventually accepted: 'We'll make a nice dish of beef with beans.'

Maman Pauline stroked my hair. When she put her arms around me I thought I might start to levitate! Then she let me go, and looked at me tearfully. She turned around, I saw her walk away, get into a taxi and wave from a distance. I knew she was thinking about the key to her belly. But she didn't know I knew about it now, and I'd already begun looking in dustbins in our neighbourhood, as Arthur had advised. And I really didn't want her to know. I still haven't found anything, I'll go on looking, and I'll find the key for her before she gets back if possible. After that I'll go and have a rest in Egypt, I'm so tired.

Yaya Gaston says: 'Geneviève's coming this evening. There won't be any other girls besides her.'

I'm so happy I want to laugh out loud, but if I laugh he'll ask me why I'm laughing like that. So I just act like it's normal that Geneviève's coming this evening, and no one else. I know Genviève's talked to Yaya Gaston, and that he knows now that I don't like the other girls, who make a lot of noise and talk about things that even us children find silly.

I think about what I'll say to Geneviève when she comes. I'll definitely talk to her about the business with the key to my mother's belly. I'll tell her the story about the madman I met when I was just beginning to look. Then she'll know that I've been wandering about all over the Trois-Cents, and I haven't found a single key lying on the ground. I emptied out the bins, but I only found old needles, broken glass, carcasses of dead dogs with maggots wriggling around in their eyes, old cooking pots with rotting food at the bottom, bottles full of urine and lots of things besides. No keys. What if I stole a key from one of the Lebanese or Senegalese shops? No, I can't take a brand new key to give to Lounès. A key that you've had hidden for a long time has to be quite old looking with rusty bits. When I came across an old lock in a bin over by the Savon *quartier*, I said to myself, 'If there's a lock in this bin the key can't be far away, it must be in this bin too.' So I turned over all the rubbish with a bit of wood. I poked around angrily in its belly, muttering, 'There's a key hidden in this rubbish, and I'm going to find it! I'm going to find it! I'm going to find it!'

Seeing me rooting around and talking to myself, a madman looking for food a few metres away burst out laughing. He said the world had really changed, that people were going mad in childhood now. In his day only grown ups were mad, not children.

'How long have you been mad, little one?' he asked me.

I was about to run off.

'No, don't be afraid. I don't eat people yet, though I may

start to if I don't find anything in these rubbish bins.'

I told him I wasn't mad like him, I was looking for the key to my mother's belly, I'm just a normal boy, I go to Trois-Martyrs school, I'm an average pupil, very hard-working, and maybe I'll get my School Certificate and go to Trois-Glorieuses secondary school. Then I'll be with Lounès, I'll joy ride the workers' train like Jean-Paul Belmondo in *Fear Over the City*.

He laughed again, and rolled round in the rubbish like a child playing in the sand on the Côte Sauvage.

'So you're not mad, little one, but you're rooting around in the rubbish with me, and *I'm* mad?'

I don't know what came over me. I said in a little voice: 'You're not bad, otherwise you'd have told me to clear off from your bin. So you must be mad, but only a bit, just a tiny bit. And maybe you're not actually mad, it's just that people think you are.'

He'd stopped rummaging now, he looked troubled. Close up I could see his big pink lips moving about, his red eyes like two peppers. His square jaw and the little moustache with a few white hairs.

He came up close to me: 'I'm going to help you, little one. Together we'll manage to find the key!'

So we both start sifting through the rubbish. We chatted, like two school friends.

He comes over to me: 'You look on the left, I'll look on the right.'

While we were looking through, he asked me over and over: 'Found anything?'

I shook my head.

'I'm not mad, you know, little one. People think I am but I'm not. I'm a philosopher, I've got my diploma in arts and philosophy. D'you know what a philosopher is?'

'No.'

'Then I'll tell you. A philosopher is someone who has lots of ideas that other people never have. That's why the fools that pass me by in the street think I must be mad. If I was in Europe, people would write down what I say and teach it in school to little white children.'

He stopped rummaging and threw his head back to look up at the sky. Tears rolled down his cheeks, and I felt a little bug come into my eye too.

In a loud voice he announced: 'Round here they call me Little Pepper, probably because of my red eyes. What's your name then?'

'Michel...'

'Well, Michel, today I want to talk to you, so listen, and don't interrupt, it's been a long time since I talked to someone who looks at me like a real person and doesn't think I'm completely off my head. You're looking for a key to open a door, I'm looking for one to get out of the place I've been shut up in for years. Maybe the same key will free us both. When I was a child like you I loved it when my grandfather told me stories. And there was one story I will never forget. I'd like to tell it to you, to teach you to respect all forms of life, human, animal, mineral.'

He'd stopped looking, he was sitting down now, with his long hands placed on his legs. I stopped too, and placed my own little hands on my legs.

'Well, Michel, my boy, I've always had this feeling that animals looked at me strangely, that they know I'm descended from their master, my grandfather Massengo. When I was a child I used to smile when grandfather taught me that this sheep was related to us, that goat was my maternal aunt, that pigeon was none other than my big brother who drowned in the river Moukoukoulou. I thought it was just nonsense from an old man who was cut off from the world, clinging to his ancestral beliefs. How could an animal be the double of a human being? Back then, Grandfather Massengo warned me: "My boy, you may play with any animal you like, except for that lone cockerel there. That's all I'm going to say, but believe me, if you truly love me, never touch that cockerel…" Who was my grandfather's double? It was the old lone cockerel with its crest at half mast. The cockerel was my grandfather, and my grandfather was the cockerel. Man and beast breathed the same air, felt the same pain, shared the same joy. The cockerel's feathers stood out like a porcupine's quills. Its thin, arched feet showed he was an animal from another time, he had faced all life's difficulties and dangers and now watched with indifference the passing seasons, people dying, children being born, marriages in the village. He was not really of this age. I would see this cockerel almost wherever I went, he might almost have been following me. I knew then that Grandfather Massengo was not far away, that he constantly sent his animal double to protect me against bad people in this world. In the evening the cockerel slept on one leg outside the door of our mud hut, with one eye open. During the day he hung around the yard, sheltering under the mango trees when it was hot or it was raining. When he moved around – always waddling because of his great age – all the hens in the village clucked to show their respect. The animal had lost all sense of time and could not tell night from day. Sometimes I had to chase him out of my grandfather's yard because he was always leaving his stinking droppings in the house. I'd no sooner shooed him out than he'd be back a few minutes later, giving me this look as though mocking my stupidity, my ignorance of the true meaning of things. I was angry too, and went chasing after him into the manioc and maize fields, where he managed to give me the slip. At least then I knew he wasn't in the yard, that he was lost in the bush somewhere. But when I got back to the village I was amazed to find him already outside the door of my grandfather's house, with his beak in the air, his wings up high – it was his way of being proud, of showing he wasn't afraid of anyone in this world. So how had he managed to get back to the village in only a few minutes? Was he faster than me? It was humiliating. Once I picked up a piece of wood off the ground to knock him out. Behind me I heard a deep, angry voice: "What do you think you're doing?" It was Grandfather Massengo, standing at the door of our hut. I had never seen him in such a rage. He jerked his head. "You come with me, grandson, I think it's time I had a talk with you about a few things, before it's too late…" He took my hand and we went round to the back of the hut. He told me to sit down on the ground, while he remained standing. He was suddenly sweating, and his breath came short and fast, as though he had just escaped a grave danger. "So, grandson, you thought you'd kill me with that piece of wood, did you?" And I replied: "No, I want to hit the lone cockerel, not you." He stroked his little grey beard and sighed: "Same thing! If you hit that cockerel, you're hitting me. You'll understand that one day when you're older, but will I still be here then…?" From that day on I gave up my war against the cockerel. I let him follow me everywhere, and leave his droppings in the hut. Sometimes I fed him and he liked that, because afterwards he'd come and rub himself against me to thank me and I'd stroke his crest till he closed his eyes and went to sleep, but with one eye open. I'd sleep too, beside him, and I was the happiest child alive. Whenever I showed the cockerel respect, fortune shone upon me, so that if I went fishing I'd bring back more fish than all my friends. At the village school I came top in every subject, I was the best pupil in the whole district, with the highest marks in the Primary School Certificate. All I had to do was think about the cockerel, and everything that the other pupils found complicated became as clear as spring water to me. But the world is full and always will be, of people who are envious, people who are starving, of hypocrites and cynics, and those people are the reason Grandfather Massengo is no longer with us. May his soul rest in peace. Yes, he died because of my Uncle Loubaki's greed. Loubaki, who lived a few hundred metres away from my grandfather, was determined to eat the lone cockerel. At the end of the old year, the family always met to discuss what they would eat on New Year's Day. It was to be a cockerel from grandfather's chicken house, the biggest in the whole village. Up until then, the cockerel had survived because he was so intelligent that he understood our language and listened at doors to find out what humans were plotting. At the end of December that wretched year when the cockerel was to leave this world, my Uncle Loubaki said to the rest of the family: "We must eat the lone cockerel, he's too old, he's no use to us any more. And besides, he stinks and he spreads disease among all the other birds in the village." My grandfather, who was present at this meeting, did not react to this. The cockerel, however, had heard everything. He slipped away quietly before dawn and only came back around the fifth of January. Meanwhile, on New Year's Day, they chose a different cockerel. Then the next year, Uncle Loubaki decided to play a deadly trick on the lone cockerel, who was hanging about eavesdropping on us: "It's decided, we won't eat the lone cockerel for the New Year, he's too old, he stinks, we'll let him die of old age, why spoil the party with old rubbish like him when there are lots of other cockerels and hens in grandfather's hen house. That lone cockerel is the ugliest creature on earth. He doesn't deserve to be eaten. So let's eat the two chickens we bought last year at the market in Mouyondzi instead." At that everyone laughed. Everyone applauded the decision. And since the lone cockerel was now quite sure he would be spared the pot once again this New Year, he stayed in the village on the evening of the thirty-first of December. On the first of January, at six in the morning, Uncle Loubaki himself caught him outside grandfather's door and slit his throat in one sharp movement. The feast was long and joyful. Only grandfather, they noticed, sat alone in his corner. He seemed distanced from our joy, and he began talking to himself about things no one could understand. We all drank to his health and long life, to all he'd done for his family and the village. We wished he might live as long as the prophets in the Bible. He thanked us several times. He accepted all the presents the family gave him. But when he thanked us he was weeping. I saw him turn away to wipe his tears, so no one would see. At the end of that day, the old man withdrew into his room murmuring: "I always thought you loved me in this family, but I've been wrong, all my life I've been wrong. I wish you all *bonne fête*, and hope you enjoyed the cockerel." No one knew then that these would be his last words. On the second of January around ten in the morning, Uncle Loubaki went to knock on grandfather's door, for usually he was up and about by six. He found him in the living room, lying on the floor, with his arms crossed. Scattered around him were the feathers of the lone cockerel, though we had buried them well the day before, behind the chicken coop, as was usual when one of the family's chickens was killed. And since that day, young Michel, no one in our family has ever eaten a cockerel. And even when I'm really hungry and I find a chicken thigh in a bin, I still don't eat it because I might see that old man's face as I do so, the man I loved more than anyone in the whole world. I think maybe that business drove me mad. When I sleep, I swear, I see headless cockerels in my dreams. I see feathers flying in the wind, and I fly after them, high in the air, till I see the face of Grandfather Massengo, where the sun should be. And if I hear a cock crowing somewhere close by, I run towards it, thinking I am going towards my grandfather.'

Little Pepper falls silent for a few moments. I've begun to look through the bin again, though since he told me the story of the cockerel I've had a little bit of a bug in my eye. Then suddenly, in great excitement, he plunged a bit further into the rubbish, shouting: 'That's it! I've found it! There's the key!'

I hurried towards him to look. But I was soon disappointed: 'Little Pepper, that's not a door key, it's far too small.'

'Well what is it then?'

'It's a key for opening tins of sardines, the kind without heads brought in from Morocco.'

'Yes, but you said a key, you didn't say what kind!'

He kept it in his pocket, and we went on looking for at least an hour. People who saw us thought I must be his child. My clothes were dirty, like a mechanic mending an old car engine. There were maggots climbing up my arms, and Little Pepper came to pick them off and eat them like roasted peanuts.

'As long as it's not chicken, I can eat it!'

It made me feel sick, which made him laugh like a little child. Then I realised he really liked this game and that we'd be spending hours in this bin if I wasn't careful, so I stood up.

'I have to go home, or my parents will be cross.'

'Oh come on, Michel, let's keep looking, the key's here, we'll find it, I promise.'

But even when people bought fresh rubbish, and stood a little way off, watching us rummage, we didn't find the key.

When the sun began to set behind the houses on the edge of our *quartier*, Little Pepper stood up and dusted his backside down with his right hand.

'You can go now, little one. I've just had the best afternoon of my whole life. I'll go on looking for that key for you. If I find it I'll keep it for you.'

He pointed over towards the cemetery of the Voungou *quartier*: 'I live down there. Yes, just by the door to the cemetery. It's quiet down there at night, I can sleep in peace, and talk with the dead and departed. They don't look at me like the living do. They tell me everything that goes on in this town…'

'Can you really talk with the dead?'

'Of course!'

'So have you seen my two sisters?'

'What are their names?'

'My Sister Star and My Sister No-name.'

'I need real names. You know how it is, I see so many people pass by.'

'I don't know their real names, I just call them that.'

'Well ask your mother their names and come back and see me whenever you like.'

I stood up too. I dusted down my backside like Little Pepper. I called goodbye as he watched me leave. I'm sure he was thinking I'd never come back.

I've just told Geneviève about what happened with Little Pepper.

'Have you really got a key you've hidden somewhere?' she asks.

'No.'

'Well find any old key, then! I'll help you. I've got an old key that…'

'No, Little Pepper's going to find it for me, he can talk to invisible people. And it will be a real key, to open up my mother's belly.'

'You should be careful. That man's mad.'

We've been walking down the street for a few minutes. We're going to the Lebanese shop, where she'll buy me some boiled sweets.

I look at her. 'The river in your eyes isn't as green as it was. The diamonds have gone from the edges.'

'That's because it's dark.'

'Diamonds shine in the dark, too.'

'I know, but sometimes they have to rest because they've been shining so much in the day. Tomorrow you'll see, the river will be green again, and the diamonds on the edge will shine once more.'

'Will they shine just for me, no one else?'

She smiles: 'Yes, they'll shine for you. No one else. But you should be looking at the river and the diamonds that sparkle in

Caroline's eyes. Have you spoken to her?'

'Yes.'

'And?'

'We're not divorced now, we got married again.'

'That's great!'

'I told her I had castles in my heart that were bigger and better than the castles of Marcel Pagnol. And I said I wanted her to come into the castles in my heart, and then I'll protect her.'

'That's beautiful! If your brother Yaya Gaston could talk like that, I think I'd be the happiest woman on earth... '

'I'll ask him to talk to you like I talked to Caroline!! I'll write down my sweet-talk on a piece of paper, and then he can read it to you when I'm not around, because he'd be embarrassed if I was there.'

'No, you can't force things with love, it has to come from the heart. Yaya Gaston could never talk as you just did, he lost his innocence long ago.'

Now we're standing outside the Lebanese shop. But I don't go in.

'Don't you want to go into the shop?'

'I want to ask you a question first...'

'You know I always listen to what you say!'

'I want you to tell me the truth, I don't want to go on and on feeling unhappy.'

'Ask me then. I'll raise my hand and swear to tell the truth, the whole truth and nothing but the truth.'

'Am I your little black prince?'

'I see you've finished reading *The Little Prince*! Of course you're my little black prince. Come on, let's go and get some boiled sweets and go home.'

· · · · · ·

We'd only just got home when we heard someone whistling outside. They whistled three times. It was coming from just opposite our house.

Yaya Gaston exclaimed: 'It's that Dassin, Georgette's stupid little pal. I told him not to come whistling after my sister. If Georgette leaves this house and goes to meet him, I'll give them what for!'

Dassin goes on whistling. Yaya Gaston's hidden behind the door to his studio and is watching to see what will happen. We hear the front door of the house open. Georgette comes out. She was already all dressed up before Dassin started whistling. Now she crosses the yard and goes out into the street.

Yaya Gaston wants to go after her. Geneviève holds out her hand to stop him, but he pushes her away.

'Let me go! I want to teach them a lesson!'

Too late, he's already out in the yard. We come out of the studio too, because anything could happen outside.

Yaya Gaston runs down the street like a robber. Georgette, who has seen him, slips off down a side street behind the bar called Joli Soir.

Dassin isn't running, he just stands there. He strikes a pose like a world heavyweight boxing champion. He thinks he's Mohammed Ali and that Yaya Gaston is George Foreman. People come running from all over now, because my brother and Dassin are exchanging insults.

'Fuckhead!' Yaya Gaston shouts.

'Pervert!' Dassin replies.

'Who are you calling "pervert"?'

'Who are you calling "fuckhead"!'

''Your mother's cunt!' continues Yaya Gaston.

'Your father's balls!' yells Dassin.

'Capitalist!'

'Local imperialist lackey!'

'Who are you calling "capitalist"? Me?'

'Who are you calling "local imperialist lackey"? Me?'

Geneviève pulls at Yaya Gaston's shirt, but someone in the crowd's just shouted: '*Ali bomba yé! Ali bomba yé! Ali bomba yé*'! They're going to have to fight now.

Yaya Gaston says, 'I'm Ali, because I'm the good-looking one, and you're Foreman because you're an ugly louse!'

Dassin replies, 'No, no, I'm Ali, you're Foreman!'

'How can you be Ali, a wanker like you?'

'You think you can be Ali with your face like something an elephant's sat on?'

Yaya Gaston takes off his shirt because it's from France and he doesn't want Dassin to tear it out of jealousy. He throws his shirt over to us, and Geneviève catches it before it falls to the ground, otherwise someone else will pick it up and run off with it.

Everyone in the *quartier* is outside. *Ali bomba yé! Ali bomba yé! Ali bomba yé!* I'd better do something, there might be people in the crowd who are against Yaya Gaston because he works at the port, because he's handsome, because he's got a shirt that comes from France, most of all because he has a gold chain.

I slip away from Geneviève, I get into the middle of the circle and I give Dassin a push in the back. He wasn't expecting it, and he falls to the ground. Yaya Gaston seizes his chance and jumps on him. He hits him, then he hits him again, and again and again. Everyone's excited now, and every time he hits him they cheer. When he hits Dassin's face, I kick him in the stomach because he's the baddy. He yells out, calls for his mama. I'm just about to bite Dassin's tibia like a wild dog when someone grabs me by the shirt. I turn round to hit them, but stop short because it's Geneviève.

'Michel', she threatens, 'stop that now, or you won't be my little black prince any more!'

I do want to be her little black prince. So I stop thumping. Yaya Gaston and Dassin are rolling about in the dust. Dassin's also trying to hit my big brother in the face. When he gets him, I feel like it's me he's hitting.

From a distance comes the noise of sirens and everyone scatters. Within five minutes the fight in the street is over. The police search for them both but can't find them.

We're already in Yaya Gaston's studio. Papa Roger is there too, and he's yelling at my big brother. He knew there was a fight going on outside but he didn't realise it was Yaya Gaston. So he'd said to my brothers and sisters, 'Go back inside the house and close all the doors and windows. No one's to go outside! There are thugs out there fighting in the street, just let them get on with killing each other, it's not our problem!'

Geneviève's looking after Yaya Gaston, who's got a cut over his eye. He asks her, 'Where's my Yves St Laurent shirt?'

I show him his Yves St Laurent shirt. Papa Roger's outside, yelling.

Yaya Gaston looks at me, 'That was fantastic, what you did, Michel, I'm proud of you.'

His words warm my heart. The bug goes straight into my eye and I start crying because Yaya Gaston might have to go to hospital, he might die, and for nothing. I'm really crying now, so Geneviève drags me out into the yard. Her face is set firm. She says, 'If I ever hear again that you've fought someone, or you got into a scrap in this *quartier*, you can stop calling yourself my little black prince. And if you're not my little black prince, you won't be seeing the green river in my eyes, and the diamonds at the edges won't shine for you any more.'

Maman Martine asks Maximilien to go and buy some milk from Bassène the Senegali. Just as he's about to dash off she grabs him by the shirt.

'Wait a second. What's your problem? Whenever anyone asks you for something you don't even stop and think, you just go running off like a sheep. And then you'll come back and say: "What was it again I was meant to buy? Where do I go to buy it?" You're to go to Bassène's, and you're to go with your big brother, Michel, or you'll probably lose all the money or not come home till tomorrow evening!'

So we set off together. Maximilien wants to run, I ask him to walk, not run.

He's not pleased. 'I want to run! Let me run!'

'But why do you always run?'

'Because if I don't run all the greedy people round here will drink up all the milk in the shop and we won't have any milk this morning, we'll die of hunger.'

I grab him by his shirt like Maman Martine, and I hold on tight. The Joli Soir bar is quite close to the house. You can often hear music, from midday till six in the morning, when it closes. Often you hear music coming from there from midday until six in the morning, when it closes. I stop and read a big notice outside, written in large letters, as if it's meant for people who are short sighted:

FROM 18H TILL DAWN, PAPA WEMBA IN CONCERT
WITH HIS BAND VIVA LA MUSICA
FROM MOLOKAI
LADIES: 600 CFA, MEN: 1000 CFA

I say to myself: 'Children can't be allowed at this concert, because there's no ticket price given for them.' I have actually heard of Papa Wemba. He formed his band two years ago. When you go past our local bars you hear him singing and we sing along, though we have no idea what he's singing about. And when he sings with his musician, Koffi Olomidé, you get girls weeping over it, because when the two singers blend their beautiful voices together you can't go past a bar without stopping to listen.

We get to Bassène's shop. We get two litres of milk and Bassène gives us the change, which Maximilien hides in his pocket. Now he's running already, I try to catch his shirt but I miss. I shout after him. Too late, he's gone already, and as he runs, his shirt billows in the wind.

I go back past Joli Soir and a read the poster. Why is the price for men's tickets more than for ladies? It's not a good idea because now there will be too many women and not enough men. The boss of the bar can't be very clever if he does that.

Oh well, at least I know I wasn't dreaming: Papa Wemba will be at the concert at the Joli Soir from six in the evening onwards. I really want to go, but I'm not twenty yet.

We have our breakfast in the yard. We sit in a big circle with a cup in front of each of us. Maman Martine pours out the milk, she won't let us do it ourselves, she thinks we'll finish it all up, and we need to keep a bit for tomorrow. Only Papa

Roger and Yaya Gaston are missing from the circle. It's Sunday morning and they've gone to the port to buy sardines for lunch. Georgette doesn't talk much now that Dassin's had a fight with our big brother. I remember how Papa Roger calmed Yaya Gaston and Georgette down. The day after the fight he said to our big brother, 'There's nothing wrong with Georgette going out with boys at her age.'

Then he said to our sister, 'Now, my girl, you don't have to carry on with your young men under your family's nose. This is a big town, go and coo at each other in some other part of town, even in the field down by the airport!'

And so the affair was sorted out, and Yaya Gaston and Dassin never fought again in our *quartier*.

Geneviève's stayed for breakfast with us. Maman Martine asked her to, just as she was about to go home to her parents'.

'Stay and eat with us, my dear girl.'

At first she says no, once, twice then three times, then after that she agreed to stay. She wanted to sweep the yard, wash the plates and put the rubbish out in the street, but Maman Martine snatched the broom out of her hand.

'No, Georgette will do that, it will teach her not to let men come whistling after her round this house. She can wash the plates and put the rubbish out too.'

Since Maximilien's sitting next to me, he gives me little nudges with his elbow. I know he wants to eat my bread. Maman Martine said everyone could have half a roll. But a half isn't enough for him.

While Maman Martine's looking the other way, Maximilien whispers to me, 'Michel, if you give me your bread I'll help you, and you'll be happy for the whole of your life.'

'No, no, no! You can't have my bread!'

'Well, that's your hard luck, then. I won't take you with me to Papa Wemba's concert tonight.'

'What? But you're younger than I am, how come you're going to Papa Wemba's concert?'

'I'm telling you, I'm going to that concert.'

I can tell he's just making it up to annoy me. I give him a shove and raise my voice: 'Liar! If you can go to the concert then I can too, I'm bigger than you!'

'Shush! Don't talk so loud, Maman will hear what we're planning.'

'How are you going to do it?'

'I know someone.'

'And where does this someone live?'

'Give me your bread first.'

'No, I'm hungry too!'

'Ok, we'll split it. We'll cut your bread in two, but you give me the big bit because it's thanks to me you're going to see Papa Wemba this evening.'

I draw away from him and start to nibble at my bread. He watches me like a dog trying to work out the size of the bone his master's grinding. I get almost halfway through my piece of bread, and I think: What if Maximilien's right?

Just as I decide to give him the rest of my bread Maman Martine makes me jump. 'Michel, what are you doing?'

'He's not hungry,' says Maximilien.

'You be quiet, greedy, I'm not asking you. Michel can answer for himself!'

Maximilien winks at me, and I help him out: 'Yeah, Maman, I've had enough and I want to give Maximilien my bit. He didn't ask me.'

My little brother swallows the bread in a few seconds, then whispers, 'Thank you! Really! You and me, we'll go and see Papa Wemba this evening!'

It's half past five in the evening. Maximilien comes to find me, looking very pleased.

'Let's go, or we'll be the last in the queue.'

'What queue?'

'No questions. Just follow me.'

We leave the house in secret and make our way to the Joli Soir. I think: How is he going to get us into this bar for grown ups? The way he walks, he's like an adult.

We arrive at the Joli Soir, but we walk straight past.

'Where are we going? Where are you taking me? The bar's back there!'

'Just follow me. You'll see.'

We turn down the street that runs behind the bar. Now we're on a bit of land where there are at least ten or so people between my age and Maximilien's. They are already lined up in front of a wall. It's taken me a moment to realise that the Joli Soir is just the other side of the wall, which smelled of piss, because that's where lots of the customers go to piss the beer they've drunk inside the bar.

A boy who looks older than me, but is about Lounès's age, comes up to Maximilien and asks him, 'Where's the money?'

Maximilien takes some coins out of his pocket and says, 'Here, there's twenty-five CFA francs for my big brother and twenty-five francs for me, which makes a total of fifty francs.'

The boy counts the money and nods his head: 'Go and stand in line with the others, you're eleventh and twelfth.'

We go and line up, and see other boys arriving, like rats

coming out of a hole. They each pay twenty-five francs and line up behind us.

Already, I'm getting worried: 'How are we meant to get into the bar?'

'Don't be in such a hurry. You'll see.'

The queue is now really long, like at the cinema Rex when there's an Indian film. A bit further down on the same scrap of land, behind us, I notice a big yard and a house that's lit with a Petromax lamp. On the terrace an old man and an old woman are eating in silence, almost like ghosts.

'Maximilien, who are those old people?'

'They're Donatien's papa and maman.'

'Donatien?'

'That's the name of the boy who took the money back there.'

'And his parents are ok with that?'

'No, Donatien will give them the money. That's how it works when there are concerts at the Joli Soir.'

'Hang on a minute, where did you find the money you gave Donatien?'

He replies calmly: 'When I get sent to buy things from Amin's or Bassène's, sometimes I say I've lost the change. It's not true though, I keep it in a box I've buried at the back of the house. And when there's a concert I take the money, I pay, and that way I get to see all the concerts. I've already seen Franco Luambo Makiadi and his group the All-Mighty Ok Jazz, I've seen Tabu Ley and his band Afrisa, I've seen Lily Madeira, the singer with a hump, and I've even seen the Cuban and Angolan orchestras!'

'But why do you waste your money on these concerts instead of spending it on sweets?'

'Because one day, when I'm grown up, I want to be a musician like Papa Wemba. I want to make it big like him. I want to play solo guitar because the guitar's what you hear most. If I only eat sweets and never go to concerts I'll never become a musician.'

Behind the wall we can hear guitars, drums and voices shouting: 'Mike 1, testing', 'Mike 2, testing', 'Mike 3, testing'.

The queue starts to get restless, people begin to squabble, Donatien calms everyone down: 'The concert hasn't started yet, you'd better all keep still or I'll give you your money back and you can get out of line and go home!'

The concert's just started. Donatien runs towards the wall of the Joli Soir and pushes aside the boy at the front of the line. He lifts a piece of plasterboard away from the wall and I see there's a little hole between two bricks.

'That's how we're going to see Papa Wemba, through that hole,' Maximilien says to me.

'What? It's tiny!'

'Yes, but you can still see what's happening in the bar! Just look through one eye and you'll see really well. Believe me. If you get tired with one eye, you change to the other.'

He presses his lips to my ear and whispers, 'See those ten boys ahead of us in the queue? They won't see anything of Papa Wemba!'

'Really?'

'They're new, those boys, you can tell. They don't know that the band leader never comes on first, he'll turn up later because he's the most important musician. So those boys will only see Papa Wemba's other musicians because after ten minutes Donatien will ask them to make way for the others. And since we're eleventh and twelfth we'll get to the hole just when Papa Wemba's about to take up the mike.'

He's very clever, our Maximilien. How does he know this stuff, when if he's at home and you ask him something he acts like he's really stupid, and we all make fun of him? When I think how he mistook Lounès for a giant who'd come to beat me up, it baffles me. Totally.

We've been standing in line for over an hour when Donatien comes and signals to us. It's our turn to go up to the hole.

Maximilien tells me, 'You get ten minutes, I get ten minutes, that's a total of twenty minutes between us. But we'll split the twenty minutes in four: you look for five minutes, then I'll look for five minutes, that way each of us gets two goes. And while you're looking, you tell me what's happening, and when I'm looking I'll tell you, ok?'

'Ok.'

'Right, you go first.'

I lean forward. Even though the hole is small, you can easily see what's going on in the bar because Papa Wemba is directly opposite, and his band is behind him.

I describe what I can see to Maximilien. I tell him, Papa Wemba's arrived, he's dressed in black leather from head to toe, he's just picked up the mike, he's singing with his eyes closed and he's already sweating all over. There are couples dancing, clinging onto each other, tightly packed together. They move up and down, from one end of the dance floor to the other. When they're dancing opposite me I can see them. But when they move to the left, or to the right, I can't, even when I swivel my eyes like a chameleon. Some of the couples get in my way, they dance too close to my eye. One woman's backside is so huge, it's like a second wall in my face. I need to find a long piece of wire and prick the great fat backside of the woman stopping me getting a good view of Papa Wemba. On the other hand, I don't want to prick it because the backside in question is moving to the rhythm of the music and it makes me want to dance. When the drummer hits his instrument really hard, the woman's backside bounces like a grain of sweetcorn in a pan of hot oil. And it makes me want to laugh, I didn't know you could dance like a grain of sweetcorn that's been flung into boiling oil. There's a man over at the back there holding on too tight to a woman in a really short skirt. He's put his head in between this woman's breasts and closed his eyes, like a baby that's just finished its bottle and has fallen into a deep sleep. Every time the woman breathes the man's head moves to the rhythm of the music and it makes me start to dance too, imagining it's me with my head between the breasts of the woman with the short skirt, that I've got my eyes closed and am fast asleep on the woman's chest, like a baby that's just drunk up it's bottle. That woman could be my mother, so I shouldn't be thinking things like that. I should be trying to imagine she's a girl of my own age. So I think about Caroline's chest. Caroline doesn't have breasts like the woman's yet, but perhaps they'll be that big when she's twenty.

Papa Wemba is singing now, with a musician I don't know very well. I've seen his photo somewhere. Who is he again?

'That's Koffi Olomidé, he lives in France,' Maximilien tells me, as though he's guessed I was going to ask him that.

When my five minutes are up, Maximilien takes my place, and describes everything. He tells me about the bass guitar, the backing guitar, the guitar solo. He says the big deep voice we can hear above all the other voices is a singer called Espérant Kisangani, alias 'Djenga K'. Maximilien would like to be able to sing like him, to play guitar solo better than Rigo Star and

Bogo Wendé, Papa Wemba's two guitarists. When did he learn those two names, names I don't even know, and I'm bigger than him? And he's dancing while he talks, dancing really well, all without taking his eye from the hole. His head sways to the right, his backside swings to the left. Then the same thing the other way round. He swings out his right leg, and shakes it when the drummer bangs out a quick rhythm. He does the same thing with his left foot, then he shakes his arm, as though he's imitating a bird in the sky. And when he dances like that, the whole line behind him starts dancing like him and imitating his moves.

I turn round to see how the other boys are dancing. That's when I notice that some girls have arrived in really short skirts, hair in braids, lipstick, and pointed shoes, like the high heels that grown-up women wear. They're with well-dressed boys who dance with them, with their head on their chest, even though they don't have big breasts like the women dancing in the bar.

Every five minutes, Maximilien and I swap over. When it's me looking through the hole, Maximilien yells in my ear: 'You mustn't keep still, you have to dance, or people will think you don't know how to dance and they'll make fun of us. Go on, move! Put your head on one side and move your body the other way. Imagine you're a turkey, a dancing turkey! It's the new dance they call *Turkey Cuckoo*.'

So I try to imagine I'm a dancing turkey. Maximilien sniggers because he can see I don't know how to dance the *Turkey Cuckoo*. I keep moving my head up and down instead of from side to side.

'Michel, you're meant to be a turkey, not a lizard. The *Lizard Cuckoo* was last year's dance! That's old fashioned now!'

The other boys are sulking a bit because we've been cleverer than them and split our twenty minutes into four. Every time my brother and I swap over they all shout: 'Plot! Plot! Plot! Cheats! Cheats! Cheats!'

Donatien looks at his watch and steps forward to move us away from the wall: 'Come on then you two, time's up now, off you go, let the others have a turn!'

Maximilien takes my hand, 'Let's go home, we've seen everything. In any case, it'll be mayhem in a minute, the musicians will be too tired, they'll have smoked their dope and they'll start playing rubbish.'

Our parents are very cross, even Yaya Gaston, who still has a cut over his wound from the fight.

Maman Martine says, 'Where were you then? Don't you know the thugs from the Grand Marché come and hang round here on concert days?'

We stare at the ground and she goes on, 'Since you'd disappeared, we finished all your food, so there'll be nothing for you to eat tonight! That will teach you!'

Maximilien murmurs in my ear: 'Don't you worry, I thought about that. We'll take the money that's left in my money box and go and buy some big dumplings and soup from Mama Mfoa in the street opposite the bar called Credit Gone West, that's open 24/7. Believe me, her soup is so good, you won't mind missing the sardines the others had tonight, besides, we had them for lunch anyway!'

This morning my big brother Marius and my little sister Mbombie are getting ready to go into town. They are going to get their vaccinations against tetanus and sleeping sickness. Until now, those two have always said: No, we won't have our vaccinations. But this time they can't say no: a boy from our *quartier* died yesterday from sleeping sickness, and in the evening Papa Roger reminded everyone, 'Tomorrow morning, all those who haven't had their vaccinations must go to see the Chinese doctors at the Congo-Malembé hospital! When I get back from work I will check your arms to see you've got marks from the injections. You must have tetanus jabs too.'

While Marius and Mbombie are crossing the yard, Maman Martine says to them, 'Wait, take little Félicienne to see the Chinese doctors too.'

I say to myself: 'Let them take her, I don't want her pissing on me again when I pick her up. When the Chinese doctors give her her jab at the hospital she'll yell so loud you'll hear it all over town.'

Maximilien, Ginette and I had our vaccinations last year, so we stay at home. We help Maman Martine sweep the yard and do the washing up and take out the big rubbish bin at the back of the house and put it in the road for when the refuse lorry comes. Sometimes the lorry doesn't come by for a month or more. That's why there are great piles of rubbish in the middle of some streets, and the cars have to drive round them.

. . . . .

Maximilien is running like a mad man. He comes up to me, his brow drenched in sweat.

'Get your breath back,' I say.

'No, I haven't time. It's too dreadful!'

'What's too dreadful?'

He glances back at the street.

'Don't you see what's happening out there? Look who it is, waiting opposite! It's him, the giant Tarzan who came to beat you up the other day. He's still there, I don't want you to fight with him! He's stronger than you, he's a great big giant! I'll give him my money if he'll leave you alone.'

'Take a deep breath, Maximilien. That's my friend, he's called Lounès, and he's come to see me because we haven't seen each other for a few days now. He's not a giant. He's just tall like big brother Marius.'

'Yeah, but he wants a fight.'

'No, he just wants to see me.'

I leave him standing there, and I go out into the street. I find Lounès and we walk together as far as the river Tchinouka.

There are no fishermen today. The river's calm. You can just hear a few birds, hidden in the trees.

'It's weird, there've been no planes for the last few days,' Lounès says.

'Perhaps they've changed routes. Because we've been staring at them. Or they're hiding in the clouds.'

Suddenly he changes the subject. 'Did you find that key to your mother's belly?'

'No.'

'You really have to find it.'

'I'm still looking. I will find it.'

'So it was you that locked it?'

'…'

'Where have you put the key?'

'Little Pepper's looking after it for me and…'

'Who's Little Pepper?'

'Someone who talks to people you can't see. We went looking for the key together because he'd lost it in the bin and…'

'Someone who goes looking through bins is usually called a vagabond. Is this Little Pepper a bit mad, by any chance?'

'Oh no, he's a philosopher, he has all these ideas other people can't have. That's what philosophers do.'

'He's just mad, then, let's face it, like Athena and Mango.'

'No, he's a philosopher!'

'Let's both go and see him, and ask him to give the key back!'

'I can't today…'

'Why not?'

'At lunchtime I have to go with Maman Martine to the Bloc 55 *quartier*, and after that I have to go home with my father, Maman Pauline's getting back from Brazzaville.'

At last a plane goes overhead, but it's way up in the sky. Usually it seems like the planes are passing just a few centimetres above the roofs of the houses in our *quartier*, and the dogs start barking, and the little children go running into their mothers' arms.

I say to Lounès, 'That's a strange plane, don't you think?'

'Why?'

'It's like the front bit's bent downwards, like it was going to fall on top of us.'

'That's just because we're lying down.'

'No, something bad's going to happen, I can feel it. It's strange that no planes have gone over since we've been lying here. And it looks like it's got to land really urgently somewhere.'

'So where do you think it's going to land?'

'In Egypt. The capital of Egypt is Cairo.'

The Shah of Iran has died. In Egypt.

Papa Roger is angry, you'd think it was someone in our family who'd died. Maman Pauline is still tired from her long trip and isn't listening, so my father turns to me and explains that the great man is going to be missed by the whole world. I already know everything he's saying. But since he's sad, because after all, the person who's died is someone he loved, he tells me once again about Egypt, Anouar el-Sadat and how he shared the Nobel Peace Prize with Menahem Begin, about Morocco, King Hassan II, Mexico, the Bahamas, Panama, etc. Each time he mentions one of these countries, I imagine a plane flying over our town and I think: The capital of Egypt is Cairo, the capital of Morocco is Rabat, the capital of Mexico is Mexico City, the capital of the Bahamas is Nassau, the capital of Panama is Panama City, etc.

'The Shah had had cancer for many years,' Papa Roger says again. 'He had lost his homeland, and when that happens to someone they get homeland cancer, and no doctor can treat that, except by helping the sick person live longer. When you lose your homeland you can't tell night from day, you're haunted by memories of what you've left behind, and if you're not in good health, your illness gets worse. And that's the kind of cancer that killed the Shah.'

While he's telling me all this, I see Arthur's face again, in my mind. I would like to go and tell him the bad news, but I remember that I'm never allowed in my parents' bedroom when they're at home. Only if my father says: 'Michel, go and fetch my wallet from the bedroom, I've left it on top of the books.' Or if my mother says: 'Michel, go and fetch that pair of red shoes from under the bed. And bring the earrings I left on your father's books.' Then I can go into my parents' room. And when I do go, I stay for a long time, because I try and get a quick look at Arthur. Sometimes it's me that goes to fetch the radio cassette, and if I forget the cassette of the singer with the moustache, Papa Roger says: 'Michel, the Georges Brassens cassette isn't in here, quick, go and get it.' I really like that, because I know I will see Arthur's beloved face, with his angelic smile, for the second time that evening. But one evening they don't send me into their room, I don't like it, I feel sad then, even when my father makes jokes about people he's met with Monsieur Mutombo in the local bars. My mother laughs at his jokes, but I don't, I don't get hysterics, like I do whenever I'm in Monsieur Mutombo's workshop and Longombé's mother turns up at the door asking her son for money. I sleep badly, and I can't stop thinking about Arthur. When I go to bed I tell My Sister Star and My Sister No-name everything. I don't feel the mosquitoes biting me, I don't even hear them because they bite my body, not my soul; my soul has already left the house, and gone to another world. Even if they do bite me, I've been vaccinated against malaria, I'm not going to die of that.

The Shah has been buried in Egypt, not in Iran. Once again, it's the Egyptians who've given him a decent burial, even though he wasn't their president. No other head of state, in the whole of the rest of the world, has had the courage to come and pay his last respects. And once again I wonder if Ayatollah Khomeyni is perhaps the most powerful man on earth now, because all the other presidents are afraid of him.

Roger Guy Folly said that the president of the Americans, called Richard Nixon, went to the Shah's funeral, and criticised the other world presidents because they were too scared to turn up too. All that's just a smokescreen. Words thrown to the winds. Why wait till someone dies to say that kind of thing? He irritates me, that Richard Nixon. He should have helped the Shah ages ago. He should have been criticising the presidents back then, instead of making a song and dance now. When people intervene when it's too late, Uncle René says they're 'calling the doctor after someone's died.' Richard Nixon's scolding isn't going to bring the late Shah happiness in the next world. I'm sure when he meets God personally he'll tell him the names of all the presidents who failed to face up to their responsibilities.

've got heaps of presents now. It's as though I've caught up on everything I've never had, since I was born. If you saw them you'd think there must be lots of children living in our house, when in fact there aren't. Bags of marbles. Plastic soldiers with complicated weapons that run off batteries. French castles that are really difficult to put together. Ambulances with paramedics dressed in red and orange. Footballs, rugby balls, hand balls. A Superman, and lots of other things besides that I sometimes forget all about, then when I find them again I think: When did my mum and dad give me that?

There's hardly any room left to put it all. Some days my parents don't tell me they've brought me presents, they put them straight under my bed, and when I go and look for a football or a handball, to go and play with Lounès and some other boys from round here, I find them, and shout for joy, you'd think I'd just got my Primary School Certificate, which I haven't. If I find the key to my mother's belly, will they still go on giving me presents?

My favourite toy is, of course, the car like Sebastien's, which my parents bought me a few days ago. They said it wasn't easy to find because Christmas was ages ago. They looked in all the shops in town, and there was just one car like it left, at Printania.

On Sundays I go into our yard and press all the command buttons on my car. It turns left, it turns right, then does a U-turn, it goes straight on then comes right back to my feet. Then I press the red button and it stops, and the engine goes off.

At first my parents wanted to buy two of these cars, but I said: 'No, first wait till this one breaks down. Besides, if it does break down I'll call Sebastien, he'll know how to repair it, because he's had a car like this for ages.'

That made them laugh, but not me.

When I play with my car, Maman Pauline and Papa Roger sometimes stand behind me, like they want to be children again, and play with me. They get down on their hands and knees and watch my car go all the way to the end of our yard and then come back to my feet. They cheer and I'm very happy that my car interests them so much. On the other hand, I know they are too big, really, to be down on their knees, crawling about in the dust. Grown-ups only get down on their knees to pray. So I think that if my father and mother are getting down on their knees it's not because they want to play with me, it's not because they like my car, it's just because they want something from me. They want the key.

They can see I'm happy playing, so they ask me: 'Do you like your car, Michel?'

I'm concentrating very hard because I don't want my car to bang into the mango tree or to go outside, where someone could steal it, so I just nod, and say nothing.

Then Papa Roger leans over to me: 'Michel, you need to think about us too, now. You need to think about making us happy, because we love you, and we aren't your enemies. We'll never be your enemies. We've given you lots of presents already. Just think, none of the children in our *quartier*, not in this town, even, have got the things you've got. Now you think about us, make us happy. Do you understand?'

I just act like I don't understand, and go on playing. Until Maman Pauline and Papa Roger tell me directly that I'm the cause of their misery, I'll act like I know nothing, and understand nothing, and am waiting for them to spell it out.

This Sunday Lounès and I have been playing with my car on the big football pitch in the Savon *quartier*. We don't even feel the late afternoon heat. He came and whistled for me outside the house and said: 'We need to run your car in properly, or it will never go very fast. Let's go to the football pitch in Savon, there's no match there this Sunday.'

The two of us are trying to see how fast my car can go and how many minutes, or hours it will run for. As soon as it sets off we start shouting as though it was a race between two cars when in fact there's only one. That's when I realise my parents were right to want to give me two cars. We could have had a real race between Lounès and me. I don't want to ask Sebastien to have a race with me, because then he'll know I've got the same toy as him and he'll be jealous of me.

The car's already done several runs out and back. Suddenly we hear a strange noise as though I'd pressed on the stop button.

I yell: 'It's broken down! We'll have to take it to my cousin's!'

Then, remembering that I don't want Sebastien to see my car, I press the start button again and again to make sure it really has broken down. It won't move. Panicking, I pick it up and turn it over. Maybe it's because of the dust. So I blow on it.

'Don't bother doing that, it's not broken, the batteries are dead,' says Lounès.

So I run over to the little bag I've brought with me, put

the car away, and get out the football: 'It doesn't matter if the car doesn't work, let's play football. We'll play penalties, since there's only two of us, you go and stand in goal over there, and I'll go first.'

Lounès doesn't move. He just stands there in the middle of the pitch like a pillar, looking at me.

'Why don't you go and stand in goal?' I ask.

'I don't want to, Michel. Here we are, just playing around, while your mother's back there feeling miserable. That's not right, is it? You need to think about her now. You need to find that key...'

This really annoys me, though usually I never get annoyed with him, because I know that if we have a fight he'll win, with his muscles, and his height, and his advanced katas that he learns in Maître John's club.

I go back and put my ball away and pick up my bag to leave the football ground. He runs after me: 'Wait, Michel. I just want Maman Pauline to stop being unhappy, that's all.'

We walk fast now, not speaking. We get to their house first.

'You coming in to say hi to my parents?'

'No. Another day.'

'Come on, you'll be glad you did. Caroline's there...'

I don't answer, just hold out my hand. He takes it, holds it for a while, and then says: 'Off you go then, and don't forget to change the batteries in your car, if that's what you really care about.'

These days my dreams take me far far away. I'm not just Michel these days, the little guy you see running round the *quartier*, or walking about in a khaki shirt, blue shorts and a pair of plastic sandals. I wear polyester trousers, linen jackets, white cotton shirts with a bow tie. I wear a hat, too, like the child in that film *The Kid* that Lounès has told me about, doing his imitation of Charlie Chaplin. But I'm older than the boy who gets left in a car by his mother and goes to live with Charlie Chaplin till his mother comes back rich and takes him back and thanks the adoptive father. Yes, I'm a bit bigger than him, I'm the way I'd like to be when I'm twenty.

In my dreams I walk with my head held high, my shoulders back, people respect me, they greet me, they raise their hats when I walk by, and speak other languages, not just ours. I speak very correctly, you'd think I was born in whatever country I'm in, though it took me only seconds to get here, when in fact it would take a day, or maybe two, to get here by plane. Maybe I'm speaking Chinese because earlier in the day Lounès and I were talking about the Chinese who built the Congo-Malembé hospital in the Trois-Cents *quartier*. Maybe I'm speaking Arabic because I heard Monsieur Mutombo talking about Algeria. Maybe I'm speaking some Indian language because Lounès told me about an Indian film where there was a prince and princess being mean to a poor peasant.

· · · · ·

Every night it's the same: before I close my eyes I think about far away countries. Once I'm asleep, I meet people who come from there and we get talking. They never ask where I'm from because in these dreams everyone is just the same, that's how come I can speak any language on earth, when in fact it takes years to learn them. I fall asleep smiling because I know I can touch the sun and the moon and the stars. Life seems easy. But when I wake up I feel sad because I can't speak a single word of any of the languages I knew really well in my dream. I've forgotten everything, everything's been wiped out. It all seems so far, far away.

'I've come to see Gorgeous Arthur.'

I'm a bit jealous because I was hoping Caroline was going to say it was me she'd come to see. I wish I hadn't told her about Arthur. Now she'll think about him all the time, and she won't look at me any more. But then I think, Arthur's just a picture on the cover of one of my father's books, and I calm down because a picture can't take someone's wife from them. And anyway, Arthur's dead.

We go inside, and I think I mustn't show her the radio cassette player. But I'd really like to. If she sees that I'll get lots of points over Mabélé. He's never shown her anything like that, and he can only talk about things that don't really exist.

I come out of my parents' bedroom with *A Season in Hell*. I've turned it over so Caroline can't see Arthur's picture.

'Close your eyes.'

She puts her hand over her face. Her fingers aren't closed up properly, she can see what I'm going to show her.

'You're cheating. Cover your eyes with both hands!'

She puts one hand on top of the other. Now she can't see anything. I come up to her and whisper in her ear, 'Now you can open your eyes, here's Arthur!'

At first she says nothing, then she snatches the book out of my hands. She touches Arthur's face with the index finger of her right hand, she sniffs at the book as though it was something to eat. She runs another finger over Arthur's hair and eyes. Finally, she opens the page I've marked and begins to read:

I abominate all trades. Professionals and workers, serfs to a man! Despicable. The hand that guides the quill is a match for the hand that guides the plough – What a century for hands! – I'll never get my hand in. And besides, there's no end to 'service'. The beggar's honesty distresses me. Criminals disgust me – men without balls. Myself I'm intact; it's all the same to me.

'What's "the hand that guides the quill"? What's "the hand that guides the plough"?' she asks.

That startles me because she's asking exactly the same questions I asked the first time I touched the book.

She's stopped reading now, she's waiting for my answers. I can't tell her I don't know or she'll laugh at me and think I don't know Arthur very well.

'Well, the "hand that guides the quill" is a hand with feathers, it's the hand of a white sorcerer who dresses up as a bird at night and snatches children and takes them to hell for a season. That's why it's called *A Season in Hell.*'

She takes another look at Arthur, as if she's really frightened of him now. She puts the book down on the table: 'And aren't you scared the feathered hand is going to take you down to hell too?'

'No. Arthur will protect me.'

'What about "the hand that guides the plough"?'

'It's the hand that guides the plough in a field, the hand of a farmer, and my uncle says you should never put the plough before the ox.'

Can she tell I don't actually know what it means? I speak

calmly, without hesitation. And under her admiring gaze, I feel cool air entering my lungs. I know I've just scored a thousand points against Mabélé. That Mabélé's of no account now. I'm so happy, I take the book from her, and go and put it back in my parents' room.

I come back into the living room with the radio cassette player. The cassette is already inside the machine. I press 'play'. The singer with the moustache starts weeping about his tree. When the song gets to the bit about *alter ego* and *saligaud*, I start to explain to Caroline what it means but she goes: 'Hush! Keep quiet!'

She listens, swaying her head. The song's finished now, I press on 'RWD' and it starts again.

Caroline stands up: 'Dance with me!'

'No, you can't dance to this sort of song, and...'

'I want to dance with you to this song! Come on!'

I'm standing facing her, but I leave a big gap between us.

'Are you frightened of me? Don't you know how to dance, or what? Come here, and hold me tight!'

I hold her really tight, and we move slowly. She's closed her eyes and it's as though she's not in the house with me any more, she's flying, far far away, further than Egypt. I close my eyes too, so I can fly in my thoughts as well, and I think of the concert I saw at the Joli Soir with Maximilien. I see the woman dancing in the very short skirt, her backside blocking the hole in the wall, her long legs, her great big breasts almost hanging out. My heart's beating really fast now. I put my head on Caroline's chest like a baby that's drunk up its bottle and falls fast asleep. Now, Caroline doesn't have big breasts yet like the woman I saw dancing. I can feel some little breasts though. I imagine that in a few years they will grow as big as a pair of ripe papayas.

While we're dancing and our two bodies are like just one body, she puts her mouth right next to my ear: 'Michel, you're still my husband, and I want to live in the big castle inside your heart.'

Her words make my heart race. I'm floating like a kite in the sky. I've never felt this happy, not even eating meat and beans. I never want this moment to stop. I want it to last till the end of time. I feel Caroline's hand touching my hair, her mouth close to my ear. I close my eyes again, till the moment I hear her say very quietly: 'Michel, where is the key to Maman Pauline's belly?'

I open my eyes, I stop dancing and I pull away from her. I lunge towards the radio cassette player on the table, and I press on the button that says 'STOP'. I can feel anger rising in me, I'm almost shaking with it, but Caroline stays very calm, and goes on: 'I'm your wife, and I don't love Mabélé. Do you understand that? But if you don't give your mother that key we'll get divorced again, and next time I'll go and live with Mabélé for real.'

She arranges her hair, looks at herself in the mirror and picks up her little bag.

She's already at the door when she says: 'I'm speaking plainly to you because you're my husband. Married couples shouldn't have secrets. They're meant to tell each other everything. And I'm afraid of you now, because if you can hide the key to your own mother's belly, the first child we have is bound to close up my belly and hide the key somewhere like you did. And then I won't have two children with you, like I want, I'll be an unhappy woman like Maman Pauline. Don't you see?'

'Have you found the key?'

'Hey, calm down, Michel, my boy…'

'I want that key – today!'

'To start with, you never say "I want". It's rude.'

I sit down, like him, with my back against the cemetery wall.

Little Pepper's lit a cigarette, his face disappears behind the smoke. When he coughs it sounds like the engine of an old truck that won't start.

He starts talking, in his broken voice: 'Last time I told you how my Grandfather Massengo died because my greedy uncle killed the cockerel for the New Year feast. Well now, after that I had to leave the village and come and live here in Pointe-Noire in one of the houses my grandfather had left. I lived with my other uncle, who died when I was twenty-five. This uncle's name was Matété, he suffered from amnesia, an illness that ends up with you losing your memory. I'd lost both my father and mother, and he was all I had. When he died I was devastated because the two of us had lived together with no one else, and he wasn't married, he had no children. I identified too closely with him, and I noticed I lost my memory too, just after he died. I was convinced he had passed his amnesia on to me, instead of taking it with him up to heaven, where my mother, who was already up there, would have blown on his brow and healed him. But it seems that the dead have to arrive in heaven

with their hair all tidy, sweetly scented, men in a three piece
suit, women in a white dress, and above all, in good health, and
that's why the illnesses stay in the cemetery and then go and live
in one of the descendant's bodies when the soul of the person
who's died finally starts climbing the stairway to heaven. I was
that poor descendant. Are you still with me, Michel?'

'Yes, I'm with you…'

'Now since I'd become amnesiac too, I'd forgotten to go to
my job at the Maritime Company where I was a manager. It
was me that took on the newly qualified staff. Only I'd stopped
going altogether and when my work colleagues got worried and
came knocking at my door all the time to try and get me to see
sense, I threw pepper water in their faces. I didn't recognise
them, and I thought they were garden gnomes come to trample
my poor little spinach plants, when the only thing I had left
to do was cultivate my garden in a corner of the plot my uncle
had inherited from my grandfather and I'd inherited from my
uncle. I could put up with anything, but not people coming and
treading on my poor little spinach plants, that I loved watering.
I told all my woes to those poor little spinach plants whenever
grief overcame me and I thought of my mother, my father, and
especially uncle Matété who probably still hadn't recovered his
memory even up in heaven. Those poor little spinach plants
were my whole existence: I'd jump out of bed early and check
no gnomes had been in the garden, jumping off the trucks of
the Maritime Company; I'd take a pick, a hoe, a spade, a rake
and a watering can, that I filled up with water from the river
Tchinouka. Then I'd dig the soil, scattering seeds, whistling.
Sometimes I'd spend the whole day just sitting in my vegetable
garden, hoping to catch sight of my poor little spinach plants
growing. I was afraid they'd pop up without me knowing. My

neighbour, Maloba Pamba-Pamba started to get worried, and came to see me one day, with a pitying look on his face: "Little Pepper, you've been sitting in your garden since this morning, and not once have I seen you adopt the noble gesture of the seed-sower! What's going on?" I replied: "I'm watching my poor little spinach plants grow." He was astonished: "You're watching your spinach plants grow?" I almost lost my temper: "There's one thing I'd really like to understand: why do those poor little spinach plants of mine only grow when my back is turned? Does that not seem unacceptable to you?" He looked at me in some surprise: "Yes, that is unacceptable, Little Pepper." I added: "It's not ok, I'd even say it was ungrateful of them, myself! After all, who is it waters the poor little spinach plants? Who looks after them? Who pulls out the weeds that stop them growing? They can't do this to me! I'm not leaving this garden until my poor little spinach plants are prepared to grow here and now, before my very eyes!" My neighbour, Maloba Pamba-Pamba murmured: "My dear Little Pepper, I am going to be frank with you: I think you need help. Things were bad before, but now they are desperate…'"

Little Pepper stops speaking, and when he looks at me I know he's wondering if I understand what he's saying. But since he has told me not to interrupt, I keep quiet. I act like I'm in class and the teacher's explaining something new. But I'd really like to say to Little Pepper: 'Give me the key. I want to set everything straight today, and go to Egypt, and I'd like to grow up, too.' But I mustn't order him about because he's a grown up, even if in his head everything's bouncing around, like marbles bumping into each other, all those screws that have been loose ever since his uncle died. If I go on asking for the key, and don't listen to him first, he'll get really cross and then I'll be going home empty-handed. Now, if I don't get that key today, I'll have to go and look through the bins again, tomorrow and the day after, and perhaps for the whole of the rest of my life, spend my whole life looking through the bins around here. I don't want a life like that. So I listen to him. He has to stop some time.

'But no, Michel, dear boy, now when I wandered down by the banks of the river Tchinouka, it was not for pleasure. It was the amnesia. I'd forget to stop at my own place, I'd carry on and on till I got to the river, convinced that I could walk on water, like Jesus. And when I tried to get across the river that runs through our *quartier*, even if I shouted three times over *"alea iacta est!"*, I'd still hesitate for a moment, because whatever it might look like, I don't actually have the courage of a Roman general about to face up to Pompey the Great. Even when you lose your memory, there's a red line you don't step over. Amnesiac, yes. A living coward, yes. A dead hero, no. So I didn't risk walking on the water, I hesitated, I told myself maybe it was too cold, or too polluted by the excrement of certain members of the local population who made out it didn't matter if they did their business in the water, because world experts had proved that running water had no bacteria in it. My neighbour, Maloba Pamba-Pamba looked all over the *quartier* for me, to take me to a fetisher. Which was extremely decent of him. But he never got as far as the river, where I stayed for hours, wondering what I had come looking for in the dark hours of the night, braving the street dogs and the gangsters from the Grand-Marché, dividing their spoils and threatening each other with screwdrivers. I talked away to myself, I made wild gestures in the air, I laughed with the shadows of the night, with people all around me, and ended up scolding the frogs who were all yelling angrily at me. Amnesia also made me walk strangely. I'd wander off to the left, then to the right, I'd come back several times to the place where I'd started, but not recognise it. And since I was going round and round in circles, like a snail caught in his own slime, I had to find a way, some little thing, not too complicated, a little trick to stop me getting dizzy: I'd draw a cross of Lorraine to show where I'd already walked, so as not to come back the same way again a few minutes later. So suddenly, all the little streets in the Trois-Cents *quartier*, in Savon and Comapon were marked with dozens and dozens of crosses of Lorraine. Whenever I saw one on the ground I'd exclaim: "Aha! There's a cross of Lorraine here! So I must have been past here already, I'd better go a different way where there aren't any crosses of Lorraine!" And off I'd go somewhere else, but then some young jokers started drawing crosses of Lorraine all over the place. I'd find them in places where I'd never set foot in my life. I got more and more lost, because it really wasn't easy to tell my crosses from those of the hoaxers, who had an undoubted gift for winding me up. So I stopped drawing crosses and spent my time instead rubbing them out, when I didn't just stay at home cultivating my garden. At that point people decided I really was crazy and I went along with it. I forgot I had a house, I was convinced that the streets and the bins of this town belonged to me, that they were in fact where I lived. And since they were where I lived, I made my home in the streets and in the bins... That's how I live now, outside, free, far from the wicked. What else can I do? Go round shouting that my last remaining shred of lucidity still outshines that of normal men? No, I've no time for that now, I'm exhausted, I've had it with all that. I like my life, I'm just going to sit and wait for my very last day, when I climb the stairway to heaven...'

He lifts his head and points up at the sky. I lift my head too, but I can't see the stairway up to heaven. He lowers his head and then hands me the old key. I'm so excited, I snatch it from his hands.

As I get up to go he says, 'Are you off for good then? Will I never see you again?'

I'm not listening though, I'm already running. I feel free, I can breathe deeply too. I feel like I can fly. I feel like I want to laugh like I've never laughed before. My feet hardly touch the ground. I think of Carl Lewis, and I run even faster.

I've already gone a long way, and I've even stopped thinking about the moment when I'll hand my mother the key, when I suddenly remember that I've forgotten to ask Little Pepper two important things. So I turn back and I find him still in the same spot, with his head still bowed. He lifts it and smiles, and it's as though he knew I would come back.

'Ah, you're back!'

'There are two things I forgot to ask you…'

'Then start with the first one.'

'Have you still got the little key you found when we were looking through the bin together?'

'Which little key?'

'The tiny one that opens the cans of headless sardines from Morocco.'

He fumbles in the pocket of his old coat and gives me the little key.

'What are you going to do with it, now I've given you a real one?'

Without thinking, I reply, 'Maybe the little one is the right one. I'm going to keep them both, just in case.'

'And what was the second thing you wanted to ask me?'

'Have you seen My Sister Star and My Sister No-name?'
He stopped laughing then.

'You didn't give me their real names! I meet so many people, and if I don't have their names I can't tell who's who, can I? Come back and see me any time, with your sisters' real names.'

I run off again, without saying goodbye. I'm scared the night will grab hold of me, just as each ghost is settling back in its grave for a rest, after a long walk through the town.

As I run I hear the two keys knocking together in my shorts pocket. The noise soothes me. I feel light, I still feel like laughing, like I did just now. But if I laugh, people will think that I'm a mad child. How else will they understand that I'm happy and I'm talking to myself because what I have in my pocket is the key to my mother's happiness, and my father's. And mine too?

I can see a fat woman talking to our neighbour, Yeza the joiner. I peer at them, and make out Maman Pauline with them too, and Papa Roger and Monsieur and Madame Mutombo. When people are talking to Yeza it's usually something to do with a coffin. Perhaps that's why the fat woman's crying and my mother and Madame Mutombo are comforting her.

As I'm now at our front door, I can't quite see what's going on. From this distance the faces seem blurred and when they talk it's as though there are no words coming out of their mouths. It's like those films in black and white that the priest sometimes shows us in the courtyard of the church of Saint-Jean-Bosco. There all you ever see is men, women and children on their knees praying.

I move forward into the middle of the lot and now I can see that the fat woman crying is the mother of Longombé, the apprentice. I recognise her, she's the one who always comes to ask her son for money outside Monsieur Mutombo's workshop. So I say to myself: 'That's it then, it must be Longombé the apprentice who's dead'. And I start thinking about how it always made him laugh when I came to the workshop. How he would take my father's trousers or my torn shirt and mend them. I'm not going to stay standing here in the middle of our lot. I want to know everything.

So here I am in front of Yeza's lot now. My mother's just

noticed me, and she shouts: 'Michel, don't just stand there, go on home!'

Longombé's mother disagrees. 'He can stay, Pauline, my son was fond of him.'

I go into the lot, and walk towards the sad little group. I discover that Longombé was hit by a car in the Block 55 *quartier*. The car had no brakes, and after knocking over the apprentice it crashed into an electric pylon. The driver ran off and they'll never find him if he goes to live in the bush, where most gangsters live, and where the police never go.

Longombé's mother yells that a young man like her son can't just die, the old should die before the young. 'Why didn't the car run me over, eh? It's witchcraft!'

According to her, Longombé had a spell put on him by someone, and it's not the driver's fault, they should let him be, because the accident happened in front of the shop that used to belong to the Senegali, Ousmane.

And she just goes on shouting: 'It's all Ousmane's fault, not the driver's! Ousmane used his magic mirror to make a sacrifice of my son and make lots of money for his shop!'

Now if I remember correctly, Ousmane doesn't own the shop in Block 55 any more. He's sold it, and opened another one in the Grand Marché. How can he still be doing his magic mirror when a Congolese has bought his shop?

It's as though Longombé's mother's read my mind. I hear her telling the others: 'Yes, and you'll tell me that Ousmane doesn't run the shop on Block 55 any more! He's sold it, you'll say! Oh yeah! You think I'll swallow that one? What am I, an idiot? My child's death makes nice business for him, because he was my only one. And only sons are the sacrifice the fetishers like best in this country. You think it was by chance he had this accident? No! No! No! That Senegali, Ousmane, he's the one behind all this. He sold his shop to that Congolese guy, and he sold him a piece of the magic mirror along with it! The two of them are in it together! And the mirror has to keep being fed with human blood, to create custom. The Congolese guy that runs that shop is his accomplice, they split the profits at night when everyone's asleep, and they decide which child around here's to be sacrificed next! You watch out, Pauline, you just be careful, one day they'll try to take your son too.'

She says Longombé was crossing the street in front of the Congolese bar, that he thought the car approaching from the right was a long way off, when in fact it was only a metre away. And bang! While she's talking I remember about the story of the magic mirror when I used to walk to school with Caroline and our parents would tell us not to go past Ousmane's shop. The cars would have run us over too, because of Ousmane's magic mirror.

Now they're discussing the price of the coffin.

Yeza wants far too much money. They're begging him to lower the price. They tell him that Longombé's mother is very poor, that she has no husband, that he ran off when Longombé was born. The joiner listens sympathetically. I get the feeling he's going to cry. He even takes out a handkerchief and wipes away a tear, then says: 'No, I'm sorry, I can't lower the price of a coffin. I've given you a good price, but wood's very expensive now. Go and ask the other joiners the price of a coffin and you'll see!'

Since Monsieur Mutombo and my father can't get him to change his mind, they get their money out and start counting. The joiner watches them, with the look of a greedy man with a tapeworm. His head bobs up and down each time a note comes out of the wallet and is laid on the bamboo table that stands in his yard. They hand over a lot of money, and he takes it and stuffs the whole lot in his pocket with a little smile that really irritates me. Then he gets the money out again, puts it back on the table and counts it as though he doesn't trust Monsieur Mutombo and my father.

The whole group leaves the lot. The joiner goes into his workshop and we can hear the noise of his saw cutting up the wood.

Maman Pauline comes over to me and leans forward slightly to talk to me without the others hearing: 'Michel, you must sleep on your own in the house tonight, your father and I are going to the wake. Don't forget to put up your mosquito net, and to switch out the lamp when you go to sleep.'

She hugs me tight and kisses me. It's the first time she's hugged me like that, and given me a kiss. My cheeks are wet with her tears. If Maman Pauline is crying, she must be really unhappy, it must all be too much for her. I don't want her to be unhappy. I know my mother isn't crying for the death of Longombé. She has often told me that when someone weeps for a death outside their own family it's because they're thinking about their own fears. But I'm not thinking about my own fears, I'm actually thinking about how Longombé used to laugh in the workshop, the way he used to look at the women getting undressed in front of him so he could take their measurements. And when all these thoughts come into my head then I do start to feel a bit of a bug in my eye.

I hold out my arms for my mother to kiss me again, because I don't know if she'll ever kiss me again one day, or if I'll have to wait for someone else round here to die first. She stoops down so she's at the same height as me. My voice won't come out, I don't know what to say to comfort her, to stop her crying over Longombé's corpse because she's thinking of her own fears. Since my mouth is pressed up against her ear, I whisper: 'Maman, I've got something for you...'

I take out the key and show it to her, she takes it quickly and starts crying really loud. When they hear her, the others think she's still crying about Longombé's death.

I see Monsieur Mutombo, Madame Mutombo, Maman Pauline and Papa Roger all walking away with Longombé's mother and several other people from the neighbourhood come to join them. My mother turns round every now and then to look at me. Papa Roger too. The two of them have just been talking, and I get the feeling my father has now put the key I gave Maman Pauline into his pocket. I can tell even from here, because he keeps touching his pocket, as though he's afraid the key might disappear. I do the same thing, touching the pocket of my shorts, and I can tell there's still a key there, the little key for opening tins of headless Moroccan sardines.

It's the first time I've been down to the river Tchinouka with Caroline. I asked her to come. I went past her house and whistled three times. I was worried it would be Lounès who came out, but I knew, too, that he wouldn't be there, that he'd gone into town with his father to buy fabric. So the day before, when he told me he was going out with Monsieur Mutombo, I said to myself: I have to meet Caroline, it's very important.

At the third whistle, Caroline came quickly out of their house. She stood barefoot outside their front door. She signalled to me to wait, then she went back inside. What was she going back to fetch?

She came back a few minutes later, nicely dressed, in a blue dress, white shoes, and a red scarf. I felt a bit scruffy in my blue trousers that were too short for me, and my brown shirt that her father made for me two years ago. I hadn't combed my hair and I looked like I'd just got out of bed.

Caroline looked at my feet: my plastic sandals were a bit worn looking.

'Where are we going then?'

'To the river.'

She wanted to go and walk about in town. I said no, because it's too far and you have to take the bus. Anyway, in the town centre we might run into Monsieur Mutombo and Lounès. Besides which, I'm scared of accidents now, with the buses going too fast, and not stopping at red lights.

We walked in silence. Caroline seemed to be walking slowly. So I slowed down too, to wait for her, and she gave me her hand, and I took it, and we went on our way like that, still not speaking, all the way to the river.

'Michel, what have we come down here for? I don't like this river, it smells, and the toads make such a noise! Did you know, toads are devils? They say they're bad people who've died and been turned into toads.'

I hear a plane. I can only make out its wing, the rest is hidden behind a big dark cloud. I don't want to try and guess which country it's going to, or the capital of the country. Instead I'm thinking about next year. Maybe I'll have my School Certificate in my pocket and I'll go to Trois-Glorieuses secondary school. I'll take the workers' train with my friends. I'll be in year 7, but Lounès will be in the big children's class, in year 9. I'll learn difficult things without worrying about becoming a madman like Little Pepper, Athena or Mango. I'll be a little chap with hair under my chin and down below, inside my pants. I'll walk faster than I do now because I'll have muscly legs. My voice will change too, it won't be high any more, and when I laugh people will say: 'Hey, that's a man laughing, not a little boy from Trois-Martyrs primary school, where water comes through the roof when it rains.'

Caroline gives me a shake, 'Michel, are you dreaming, or what?'

'I was thinking about next year when I go to big school.'

'Did you find your mother's key?'

I nod. Just now we were sitting down, but now she stands up suddenly and smiles at me.

'Where is the key? Can I see it too?'

'I gave it to my mother.'

I take out a little piece of paper from my pocket and hand it to her. She unfolds it to find the poem I wrote for her a long time back. Her lips move, her eyes fill up. But she doesn't tell me what she thinks. I know she likes the poem, even if it's not like the poem by Victor Hugo that her brother once recited.

She folds the piece of paper again, and hides it in her dress pocket. Just at that moment I take the key out of my pocket, the one that opens tins of headless sardines made in Morocco: 'Here, this is for you too. Look after it carefully. I know you'll need it one day to open your belly with.'

She has a bit of a bug in her eye and I can feel my heart dipping down into my stomach. I am so in love with her.

She tells me to get up and she takes me in her arms.

'Do you still want to have two children with me?'

'Of course.'

'I love you Michel.'

'I love you too and…'

'Tell me how you love me.'

'I love you like the red five-seater car we're going to have.'

'And the little white dog, don't forget!'

The wind blows and whips up the river. Perhaps it's going to rain. Caroline takes me by the hand and we leave the river. I'll walk her back to her house, then I'll go home, Maman Pauline will make me beef with beans this evening.

They buried poor Longombé a few weeks ago. I can't stop thinking about him. I can still see him, at the back of Monsieur Mutombo's workshop. He's a bit hazy now, because he's not of this world. I see him walking down a long road, with patches of grass here and there. It's the road that leads into our world and the one you walk back down the day you die. If you pass someone going the other way when you've just been born, that means they're already dead and it's their ghost returning to where they lived, first for the burial, then to go and collect their things before leaving this earth forever.

I'm looking for a different road, the road to happiness, to walk down in my bare feet in the heat of the sun, even if the tarmac burns my feet. I'll go far, far away, to where all roads meet, where you find all the people who've gone on ahead, and look different now, to how they did on earth. I have to keep the road fixed carefully in my head, I don't want to find when I'm older that it's vanished and I'm stuck with lots of bad people who don't love me, and want to hurt me.

I'll walk down this road the way the crabs walk on the sand on the Côte Sauvage: you think they're going left, then they turn back, they stop for no reason, they go round in circles, they set off fast to the right, then come back to the left again. But what I like about the crabs is, they always know where they want to go, and sooner or later they get there, even though they've lots of different feet that all want different things and quarrel along the way. When I'm on the road to happiness, then I'll know I've finally grown up, that I'm twenty at last. Maybe I'll have lots of brothers and sisters around me. And just for a moment I'll glance over at Maman Pauline, while Papa Roger's listening to Voice of America, or the singer with the moustache, weeping for his friend, the old oak, his *alter ego*, the one he should never have taken his eye off.

Afterword by J. M. G. Le Clézio

The publication of Alain Mabanckou's novel, *Broken Glass*, was an important landmark in francophone literature. With certain reservations one might compare its impact on francophone writing to that of *Sozaby*, by the Nigerian writer Ken Saro-Wiwa, on English literature – the reservations being partly that Mabanckou's novel was written in standard French, and partly that the relationship of the pidgin English used by Saro-Wiwa to the English language is more ongoing and symbiotic than that of Creole or any of the other hybrid African dialects to French. Like many novels inspired by the reality of the new Africa – *Waiting for Wild Beasts to Vote* by Ivory coast writer, Ahmadou Kourouma, or the famous *Palm-Wine Drinkard* by Nigerian, Amos Tutuola – Alain Mabanckou's novel derives its humour from the convention of the satirical tale, a genre in which the young generation, born during or immediately after Independence, revels. Critics and the general reading public alike gave a rapturous welcome to the oracular pronouncements of Broken Glass from the bar named – as though straight out of Céline – Credit Gone West. Bernard Pivot hailed the work as 'truculent, exuberant, garrulous, uproarious, no-holds-barred comedy'. The novel showed Mabanckou to be a true writer, with a story, a past, a literary context of his own, all of which were in fact already apparent in his early poetry and in his first published novel. As such it held out the promise of a great future.

Tomorrow I'll Be Twenty is the realisation of that promise.

The novel, or rather, first-person narrative, puts us inside the head of a young boy, Michel, born, raised and educated in an Africa which is his exact contemporary (as is the author himself), in which everything is in the throes of being invented, re-invented, reconstructed, amid the apparent chaos of a society caught between nostalgia for its colonial past, and the hope of freedom, or perhaps more accurately, between the illusion of ancestral wisdom and the reality of everyday life. Readers who are interested in this real Africa (worlds away from the exotic tales of twentieth-century explorers, as from the supposed philosophical profundities of the gurus of pan-Africanism), will be put in mind of other masterpieces of post-colonial literature in English, such as *Things Fall Apart* by Nigerian Chinua Achebe, or *Aké* by Wole Soyinka, another Nigerian, which also features a small boy, the same age as Michel.

Alain Mabanckou shows us his world through the naive, observant eyes of a child, and what is both captivating and moving is the child's take on the follies and contradictions of every aspect of post-colonial society, as seen through the prism of the immediate family circle: rampant capitalism dressed in the faded finery of the Marxist struggle, the greed of the moralising rich, absurd nostalgia for the myth of the Wretched of the Earth. And Congo-Brazzaville itself, which appears variously as Vietongo, with its capital Mapapouville, the Trois-Cents district in *Broken Glass*, Pointe-Noire, as described by the garrulous Moki, or even, in *Memoirs of a Porcupine*, as a well-watered land, home to the baobab trees so dear to Saint-Exupéry.

This country of domestic tyrants is also one of political tyrants, ministers, presidents, immortals, who for Michel are only slightly exaggerated versions of members of his own family. Everyday life, with its betrayals and vendettas, is the favourite arena of the comic writer. Mabanckou brilliantly conveys the tenor of this world, with all its derision and absurdity: the strength – physical and moral – of the women, the pain of a child betrayed by his mother, his longing for his two sisters who never lived, Sister Star and Sister No-name, his feelings for Caroline, the playmate who becomes his first love. In the hurly-burly of life on the street, every moment, every word spoken, has far-reaching consequences, even while nothing is truly serious – take, for example, the indignation of Uncle René, who removes a portrait of Victor Hugo from the living room on discovering that the illustrious writer once declared roundly: 'Oh what a land is Africa! Asia has its history, America has its history, even Australia has its history; Africa has no history.'

The story of Michel, the young hero of Mabanckou's novel, has nothing very unusual about it – just the discovery of life, the upsets and emotions, the tricks and traps which prepare a child to take its place in the adult word. His discoveries are not specifically Congolese, nor even African, though perhaps the hybrid nature of the society he lives in opens his eyes sooner rather than later. He discovers what adults are really like – often selfish and immature, unfailingly pathetic. Like children the world over – remember the fierce look of the small girl watching her parents rip each other apart in a novel by Colette – young Michel must find a place for himself, amid meanness, laughter and despair. Only youth can wipe away the hurt of the past and ward off future danger.

The odds seem very likely that Michel will take his place in the annals of the novel, alongside Holden Caulfield, of J.D. Salinger's *Catcher in the Rye*, and the unforgettable Miles Miles in *Miss Take* by Réjean Ducharme.